D0827703

Fire in the Firefly

DISCARDED

Bruce County Public Library
1243 Mackenzie Rd.
Port Elgin ON N0H 2C6

By the same author

The Dominion of Wyley McFadden
King John of Canada

Fire
in
the
Firefly

Scott Gardiner

TAP
BOOKS

Copyright © Scott Gardiner, 2016

All rights reserved. No part of this publication may be reproduced, stored in a retrieval system, or transmitted in any form or by any means, electronic, mechanical, photocopying, recording, or otherwise (except for brief passages for purpose of review) without the prior permission of TAP Books. Permission to photocopy should be requested from Access Copyright.

All characters in this work are fictitious. Any resemblance to real persons, living or dead, is purely coincidental.

Editor: Diane Young
Design: Laura Boyle
Cover Design: Laura Boyle
Printer: Webcom

The quotations on pages 9, 147, and 207 are from Sara M. Lewis and Christopher K. Crastley, "Flash Signal Evolution, Mate Choice, and Predation in Fireflies," in *The Annual Review of Entomology*, 2008. They are reprinted by permission.

The reprinting of the selected poem, "The Cremation of Sam McGee," on page 240 is used by the kind permission of M. William Krasilovsky, representing the Estate of Robert W. Service.

Library and Archives Canada Cataloguing in Publication

Gardiner, Scott, author
            Fire in the firefly / Scott Gardiner.

Issued in print and electronic formats.
ISBN 978-1-4597-3331-2 (paperback).--ISBN 978-1-4597-3332-9 (pdf).-- ISBN 978-1-4597-3333-6 (epub)

I. Title

PS8563.A6244F57 2016   C813'.6   C2015-904912-1
                                                   C2015-904913-X

1   2   3   4   5   20   19   18   17   16

We acknowledge the support of the **Canada Council for the Arts** and the **Ontario Arts Council** for our publishing program. We also acknowledge the financial support of the **Government of Canada** through the **Canada Book Fund** and **Livres Canada Books**, and the **Government of Ontario** through the **Ontario Book Publishing Tax Credit** and the **Ontario Media Development Corporation**.

Care has been taken to trace the ownership of copyright material used in this book. The author and the publisher welcome any information enabling them to rectify any references or credits in subsequent editions.

— *J. Kirk Howard, President*

The publisher is not responsible for websites or their content unless they are owned by the publisher.

Printed and bound in Canada.

VISIT US AT
www.dundurn.com/TAPbooks

TAP Books Ltd.
3 Church Street, Suite 500
Toronto, Ontario, Canada
M5E 1M2

This book is dedicated with love to my wife, Rennie Renelt, without whom, in so many ways, it would never have been possible.

Prologue

December 2010

It's snowing, and he's tired. It has been coming down like this for days. Cursing drivers rock their chassis deeper into drifts; spinning tires drone like brumal cicadas even through the walls of this café. There seems to be a business meeting underway two tables over—young men in goatees and horn-rims, who rammed to the door a few minutes ago in a tangerine Hummer. The management has strung up decorations, strings of winking bulbs, which only reinforce that jolly, festive atmosphere that happens every time the snow dumps down like this. Tiny lights sparkle and dance in the room. The guys with the show truck might as well have swapped their lattés for shots of tequila. They could be quieter.

He himself is not festive. His feet are soaked and frozen. He should have worn boots. He is an idiot for not having worn boots. But standing at the podium in snow boots would have looked even more ridiculous, apparently, than he sounded. Though no fault of his, half the audience stayed home. He should be grateful, realistically, that as many as did showed up. Even baby biz-heads love a snow day.

He is wondering if he should have hailed a cab. But of course the taxis today are buried like everyone else. Besides which, he can use the exercise.

On the way back from the counter, one of the young bucks leans back in his chair, the better to display whatever's dancing on his tablet, and nearly upends his cup. They have not even registered his passing.

He was expecting this. Fully. But even so, the change has rocked him. Monday night he nodded off again. No. Tuesday. Tuesday is taekwondo, so it had to be Tuesday. Story time, that much he remembers. And of course the reprimand. They haven't talked about it, naturally—any of it—and in the way of things he is fairly sure they never will. It works. It works for him, and it works for them, and with a little luck, it all will keep on working. Children grow older, timelines get shorter. Snow falls and smoothes away irregularities.

Part I

March–April 2008

Although mate choice in many animals favors the most conspicuous visual, acoustic, or olfactory signals, such signals may also attract attention from illegitimate eavesdropping predators.

Sara M. Lewis and Christopher K. Crastley,
"Flash Signal Evolution, Mate Choice, and Predation in Fireflies,"
The Annual Review of Entomology

1

Novelty is the ultimate cliché.
The Collected Sayings of Julius Roebuck

It's approaching midnight, and Roebuck is in his bedroom.
He'd been puttering in the kitchen earlier, getting started on tomorrow's lunches. But now he's done all that he can do in that regard.

The ritual of lunch-making is to Roebuck what yoga seems to be for Anne, at least according to his understanding—endless repetition of meaningless actions conceived to obliterate reason. Every morning he packs them and every evening they return to him, mostly uneaten. He'd be a rock star, he knows, if he sent his kids off with cookies and a can of Coke. But here at least Roebuck is old school, clinging to the antique notion that children's food is meant to be nutritious. Tomorrow it's chicken salad with chopped shallots and rosemary, sealed in the refrigerator overnight so the flavours will blend. Chicken is often acceptable to Morgan and sometimes to Zach, but will almost certainly go untouched by

Kate, his eldest. He has made enough for Anne as well, if she decides she wants some. Anne at least has the courtesy to pretend she's eaten hers.

Roebuck is also aware that his views on this topic are sometimes dangerously out of keeping with the professional side of his responsibilities. Just last month, he pitched a product that he would never, ever have fed to his own family. Participants in every focus group engulfed it like a pod of whales baleening plankton. So did their parents and so would *his* kids, for that matter, if he let them get their hands on the stuff.

Irresistibility. Is that a word? By design?

Stop that.

Most nights Roebuck will read for an hour before powering down, but tonight he thinks he'll attempt a frontal attack straight into sleep. He has opened up his laptop to check his email one last time.

"Oh," he says. "I didn't hear you coming in." Anne's room is on the other side of the adjoining bath. "How was dinner?"

But his wife first wants the fundamentals. "Kids in bed?" She is standing by the door, dug in.

Roebuck has tiptoed into each room on his way to the top floor. "Sound asleep, all three. Lunches in the fridge; chicken salad if you're interested." He tries again. "How was dinner?"

Anne has been out with Yasmin. He knows that after evenings like this, she likes to sit on his bed and debrief. Roebuck has put aside his laptop so as not to give the impression he is anything less than wholly attentive.

"She's *so* miserable."

"Ah."

He also knows that very little in the way of input will be required of him. A natural talker, Julius Roebuck is a formidable listener, too.

Anne removes her earrings and bracelet, returns to the bathroom where the two rooms meet. The renovation that permitted this arrangement was by far the most daunting to date. Brazilian cumaru floors, Afghan silk matting, Japanese soaker tub, Tuscan marble; the entire upper story ripped out and refitted. Most of that summer, Roebuck lived out of a hotel while Anne kept the kids at the cottage. But now that it's done, she loves the look. Anne sets her earrings on the vanity and walks back toward his bed, unbuttoning her blouse. "I think she's getting seriously depressed."

Anne and Yasmin operate an interior design studio that caters to up-market neighbourhoods like theirs. Several houses on this street, in fact, inhabit their portfolio. Anne drafts the architectural plans; Yasmin's talent is for sourcing the rare and exotic materials that concentrate their fees. It was Anne and Yasmin who planned and executed the most recent renovations to this house. Roebuck remembers it as a time of paint chips and fabric swatches held up against an endless stream of brushed metal light fixtures.

"How's Chalmers Crescent coming along?"

"Oh, you had to ask! The tile guy used quarter-inch spacers instead of eighth-inch and now the owner wants the whole wall replaced, so she's blaming herself for that too! She's in *such* a bad place."

Yasmin is that variety of woman that even Roebuck, whose profession is women, admits he can't decipher. She is beautiful. More than beautiful. The phrase *smoking hot* could have been coined with her in mind. As far as he can understand it, Yasmin's problem is that she's single. How a woman with her looks—one of their carpenters shot a nail through his hand when her blouse gaped over the blueprints—could fail to find a man remains beyond Roebuck's scope of understanding. Anne reminds him that the problem isn't that Yasmin can't find a man. It's that she can't find the *right* man. "You know, she's thinking about it more and more seriously."

"Thinking about what, more and more seriously?"

"Going it alone."

"Going what alone?"

Anne steps out of her skirt and regards him coolly. "We've talked about this before."

"I'm sorry." Roebuck should not have been joking. They have indeed talked about this before. It's just that he finds the subject too absurd to take seriously.

"She can't stop thinking about having a baby." Anne has tossed her skirt into a hamper in the bathroom, followed by her bra and panties. "She thinks that if she waits any longer, it will be too late."

"How old is she? She can't be old enough to worry."

"She's turning thirty-five."

"Oh, well. That's not old." His wife has disappeared into her room. She returns doing up her dressing gown. "If you remember, I had both Katie and Morgan before I was that age, and the doctor was worried about *me* while I was carrying Zach. All those ultra-sounds? Remember?"

"Yes, but ... "

"But what?"

Roebuck has realized, later than he should have, that his thoughts should remain unspoken on this subject too.

"Why don't we have her over for dinner?" he says. "She hasn't been here in ages. I'll make paella. That cheers everyone up."

"You just say that because *you* like paella."

"True. But so does everyone else."

"You make too much sangria whenever you cook Spanish. When people say they like it, it's the alcohol talking. But you're right. We haven't had her over for a while. I'll ask tomorrow." Roebuck wonders for a moment if she's about to kiss him, but she turns toward the door.

"Hey," he says. "Question?"

Anne stops and folds her arms. "What?"

"We're pitching tomorrow. I was wondering if I could, just ... run it by you. Briefly."

Anne sighs.

"This one's kind of fun." Roebuck is aware that possibly he's blushing. "Though we're up against some pretty big agencies."

His wife examines the ceiling. Taps a toe.

"What makes this one interesting is that they know already exactly who they're going after. That's why we're on the list, of course, but ..."

"So let me guess." She holds up a hand. "You're rolling out your usual—"

"Well, okay. But with *this* client ..."

"Know what I think?"

Roebuck has the feeling he wishes he didn't. "Please," he says politely. "Tell."

"I think that's just so *you*."

It takes him a minute to realize that's it.

"Good night," Anne says, closing the door behind her.

2

Only women count.
The Collected Sayings of Julius Roebuck

Roebuck savours the room, savours the phrase and repeats it. His words smoulder with certainty, crackle with conviction, indisputably—with passion. No one at the table can doubt for a moment that Roebuck is unshakably, omnifically, committed to the truth of his creation. But that's what they're looking for, passion un-zipped with conviction. "Look," he tells them, "you want to grow your brand, not shrink it, so why would you even think about mar-keting to men? Men don't make the decisions, they don't spend the money. They're just not *relevant*."

He'll pause here, most pitches, and smile at one of the women.

"Eighty percent of all consumer purchases," he says, "are made by women." He's ready to prove the point with a fat deck of refer-ences and tables, but clients know this part already. What they want from Roebuck is the understanding *behind* the understanding. If he thinks they can absorb it, he'll go so far as to tell them that this is the closest any of them will ever come to the ultimate creative brief, the Platonic ideal of a creative brief: the brief of which all other briefs are but dim and pale reflections. Packaged goods people tend to prepackaged thinking, though this account is definitely toward the outer edge. The girl in the white silk blouse holds his eye, unsmiling.

"Maleness," he says, spreading his arms like the marketing magus he makes it his business to be, "is, both literally and figuratively, petering out. We saw it on the news the other day: scientists are predicting that sometime up the road the Y chromosome itself will go extinct. Seriously folks, if you want to aim your brand toward the future, you want to aim it at women."

Now she's smiling. Almost. Not so much a smile as a twitch of lower lip, a crinkle at the eyes. Her blouse is opened perhaps a button more than is traditional for clients in this category. Roebuck glances at his notes which are not notes—when Roebuck speaks, he speaks from the heart—but a list of who's who in the room: Zhanna Lamb, product manager.

Everyone will be familiar with the Ripreeler story; it's passed into legend. But Roebuck is prepared to run through it anyway, because there's no better narrative to get to where he's driving. Also he thinks it fits with the girl in the blouse. So he smiles at the CEO, a middle-aged man with a shaven head who is already frowning at his Rolex, smiles at the VP of Brand Development whose shoes have been carved from the hide of some equatorial reptile, looks deep into each and every set of eyes around the table, and pictures Zhanna Lamb, product manager, naked with a Ripreeler Diving Minnow dangling from one pink and tender lobe, eagerly absorbing each and every word he is emitting.

"Only women count," he says again and launches his recital of how, ten years ago, he won that mighty piece of business.

But the CEO is having is having none of it.

Well before Roebuck gets to the part about the super-models, before he can invoke the famous Oprah segment and the fashion craze that started, before he even begins to outline the stratospheric shift in market share his client enjoys *to this very day*, Roebuck is asked to stop talking.

"Right," says the bullet-headed CEO, now distinctly pissed. "Skip the foreplay. We know all that ground-breaking work you've done for Ripreeler. That's why we're here. Tell us what you'll do for Artemis."

"Did I say how much I like that name?" Roebuck elects, just here, to stoke that other kind of branding. "Some of us wondered at the wisdom of naming your product after a goddess of virginity. Counterintuitive, if you don't mind me saying so. But she's also the goddess of the hunt. Which is *exactly* where we want to go. And such an elegant antithesis to all that other Greek material your competitors go out with. Artemis. Brilliant. Whoever came up with that was right on the money."

He knows, of course, that whoever came up with it is almost certainly here in this room. But little freebies never hurt, at least at the outset. Altogether there are eight of them; four men, four women; split right down the middle. Interesting too. The CEO is twirling his finger for Roebuck to move it along. All right then.

Roebuck spins his BlackBerry. "And you're quite correct, time ticks. Let's turn things over to Daniel. Daniel, as you know, has just joined the agency as art director. You are about to see why we're all so pleased to have him."

A younger man rises and takes over the floor. He's a little taller than Roebuck, though not quite so good looking—not, at least, as good looking as Roebuck was when he was that age. Daniel Greenwood nods politely, ambles to the front, and quietly begins placing foamboards on a shelf that runs along the wall. For the first few moments, his body blocks the view, but by the time he's got his third board set, the messages are visible to everyone.

The first one reads:

> When excuses Peter out.

The next says:

> For all those rinky-dink excuses.

Greenwood himself isn't talking. Good, thinks Roebuck. Okay.

> ~~Peter Paul~~ Mary.
> His bun. Your oven.
> Don't let the pricks get you down.

"That one," Roebuck says, "might step over the line. Still, worth a try."

> What's the difference between a sperm and a virus?
> Right.

> He says he wants to take the long view. But you know it's
> only Tunnel Vision.
> Tunnel Vision: His vision, your tunnel.

Someone snorts. Roebuck decides that now's the time to make the jump. "What you're seeing is the essence of a teaser campaign. Curious. Cryptic. Confrontational. Designed to pique interest. Think of this as the *anticipation* stage."

Greenwood has placed the last of his boards at the far end of the room:

> Like what socks are to your sock drawer.
> Yes, Virginia, there *is* a proper place for everything.

"They're transit ads," Roebuck tells them. "We'll show you dozens, but you get the picture. Snappy little one-liners. They're not just unbranded; they don't even name the product. People seeing them won't have a clue what it means. But they're curious. We'll blitz these above the seats in subway trains and buses. Then they'll disappear ..."

While Roebuck has been talking, Greenwood has worked his way back down the line, smoothly turning each board front to back. The reverse-sides show the same one-liners, but now the word *ARTEMIS* appears in eye-popping scarlet. Roebuck slows the pace. "These come next, right after the first collection vanishes. More mystery. Now our audience has the brand name, but they still don't know what Artemis *is*. Roebuck nods toward a board at Greenwood's left.

Long or short. Comic or Epic.
For whatever arc your story takes.
ARTEMIS

"Daniel thinks that one's too literary. We'll see."

The tricky thing, in a pitch, is deciding what to explain and what to let speak for itself. Roebuck is convinced, and in turn has convinced Greenwood—whose job it is to make Roebuck's convictions visible—that it's best to do as little talking here as possible.

Greenwood now silently displays a very different image.

It's a party scene, frozen in still life. A group of women stand in the foreground, drinks in hand, laughing and talking. They're obviously having a good time; relaxed; social. In the background, all the men are propped like mannequins against a wall. It takes a few seconds to realize that every man in the picture is encased in a giant see-through condom. Greenwood has drawn the reservoirs to look like silly hats perched above each dimly leering face. Some of the men are clean-cut, others bearded; some tall, others short; some fat, others thin. All are smiling idiotically. They look indescribably ridiculous. Below, the caption reads:

Too bad it won't fit over the rest of him. *ARTEMIS*

"Oh my God" says the girl in the white silk blouse. "I *love* the expressions!" She claps her hands with pleasure. "Such dorks!"

Roebuck has been reading the room. The women aren't his problem. "Daniel," he says, "why don't we go straight to the platform piece?" If Greenwood is startled, he doesn't show it. Greenwood crosses the floor and taps a keyboard. A giant screen lights up:

182 names ...

Adolf, Ankle Spanker, Baby-arm, Beaver Basher, Babymaker, Beef Whistle, Boomstick, Burrito, Bishop, Bratwurst, Braciole, Candle, Choad, Chopper, Cranny Axe, Cum Gun, Custard Launcher, Dagger, Deep-V-Diver, Dick, Dickie, **Ding Dong McDork,** Dirk, Dingus Disco Stick, Dog Head, Drum Stick, Dong, Donger, Dork, Dude Piston, Dragon, Eggroll, Easy Rider, Excalibur, Fang, Ferret, Flesh Flute, **Flesh Tower**, Foto, Fire Hose, Frodo, Fudgesicle, Fun Stick, Great Scott, Groin Ferret, Giggle Stick, Goofy Goober, Hairy the Hotdog, Heat-Seeking Moisture Missile, **Helmet Head,** Hose, Hog, Jackhammer, Jimmy, John, Johnson, John Thomas, Joystick, Kickstand, King Kong, King Sebastian, Knob, Lap Rocket, Lingam, Little Alex, Little Bob, Little Elvis, Lizard, Longfellow, Love Muscle, Love Rod, Love Stick, Love Whistle, Luigi, Manhood, Man Umbrella, Meat Popsicle, Meat Stick, Meat Sword, Meat Injection, Member,

Meter-Long-King-Kong-Dong, Microphone, Middle Stump, Mushroom Head, Mutton, Netherrod, Old Boy, Old Fellow, Old Man, Old Buddy, One-Eyed Anaconda, One-Eyed Trouser-Snake, One-Eyed Monster, **One-Eyed Wonder Weasel**, One-Eyed Yogurt Slinger, Pecker, Pedro, Percy, Peter, Pete, Pied Piper, Pigskin Bus, Pink Oboe, Pink Torpedo, Pink Weasel, Piston, Plug, Pinot, Poinswatter, Pork Sword, Prick, Prince, Price Hal, Prince Harry, Private Eye, Private Part, Purple-Helmeted Warrior of Love, Purple-Headed Yogurt Flinger, Quiver Bone, Rod, **Rod of Pleasure**, Rod of Doom, Roundhead, Sausage, Sebastianic Sword, Schlong, Schlong Dongadoodle, Schmuck, Shmuck, Schnitzel, Schwanz, Schwarz, Sea Monster, Shaft, Short Arm, Shotgun, Skin Flute, Soldier, **Spawn Hammer,** Stick Shift, Sub, Surfboard, Tallywhacker, Tan Bannana, Tassle, Third Leg, Thumper, Thunderbird, Thundersword, Tinker, Tod, Todger, Tonk, Tool, Trouser Snake, Tubesteak, Twig (& Berries), Twinkie, **Uncle Dick,** Vein, Wand, Wang, Wang Doodle, Wanger, Whoopie Stick, Wiener, Wiener Schnitzel, Wick, Willy, Wing Dang Doodle, Winkie, Yingyang, Yogurt Gun, Zorro.

... and every one accounted for. *ARTEMIS*

A longish silence.

"Adolf?" someone asks.

"Fudgesicle?"

Another snort. Roebuck wonders if it's the girl in the blouse, but he isn't looking. He's watching the CEO.

"Meter-Long-King-Kong-Dong?" A ripple passes through the room.

"Rod of Pleasure! Jesus, who came up with these? One-Eyed Wonder Weasel?"

Outright laughter now.

"I dated a guy who called his Clyde," remarks the VP Brand Development with the lizard-hide pumps. She looks over at Greenwood, arching eyebrows. I don't see *Clyde* on your list."

Greenwood doesn't miss a beat. "We'll add it. That'll make it one-eighty-three." The women titter. "Note, however, Pedro, Percy, Peter, and Pete ..."

"And Quiver Bone! God help us, Quiver Bone!"

Greenwood clears his throat. "This larger image is designed for bus shelters and subway platforms. It could go outdoors, of course, as well. Anywhere, really, that offers time and opportunity for our audience to take it in." The women seem to find this idea funny too. Roebuck is still concentrating on the CEO. The other three men present—brand stewards of various strains—have gone so quiet they're invisible. Roebuck gets out of his chair, leans in, and grips the CEO's shoulder. "You are not enjoying this, are you?"

"What the ...!" The man gapes and shakes him off. He is taken so off guard, he's speechless. But he recovers, furiously. "What are you running here, a fucking Tupperware party?" The women have stopped laughing.

Roebuck strolls back to his chair. "Come to think of it, that might be a strategy we can think about, in future. But for now I have to tell you how wonderfully you all have demonstrated the nature of this campaign." He clasps his hands behind his back and bows—to the women. "Thank you." The CEO begins to speak, but Roebuck cuts him off.

"Artemis is *female*. It's a *female* product. It's something used not so much *with* men as *despite* them. Your competitors have the *together* angle covered. There are lots of clever condom ads out there. It's a very creative field, if you'll forgive the levity. Artemis needs to differentiate. We know the standard condom ad is aimed at men. When they do target women, we also know they tend to take the rosy-pink approach. Artemis, therefore, is going bright blood red. Forget love. Forget closeness. Forget all that skin-to-skin togetherness crap. Artemis is a product women choose *apart* from men. *Despite* men. Daniel, show."

Greenwood touches the keyboard and a new frame appears. This time it's an image of a wood screw, jagged and rusty, crudely driven through a plank. The screw is *inside* a condom which has been drawn to cover it like a buffering sheath.

"Hard to miss the symbolism," Roebuck says. "But let's read the copy anyway."

ARTEMIS. A new twist on getting screwed.

He turns to face the CEO. "One of your people just hit the nail on the head. Dorks. That's what men are. And if they're not dorks, they're something worse. Artemis understands. From a cultural perspective, what we represent is one more element that has finally been pried away from men and placed with women, where it belongs."

Greenwood is quietly stacking his boards. "Five out of ten women with a college education or better," he says, "earn higher salaries than the man they live with. Men are falling behind, and women are picking up the slack …"

Roebuck waves him off. "Listen. A minute ago you asked why I was wasting your time with my canned history of the Ripreeler campaign. Point is, by doing things so differently, we caught a buzz. Whoever thought of using fashion models to promote fishing lures? Answer: The same folks advising you to run a condom campaign in which men are not relevant. You may not remember this as well as your female associates"—Roebuck is looking at the CEO, but talking to the women—"but because of that campaign, women actually started buying our merchandise as accessories. That was never part of the strategy, we just lucked out. *You* remember! How Oprah appeared on her show wearing a Yellow Dot Spinner, if memory serves. And suddenly women were wearing our lures out to the clubs on Saturday night!"

Roebuck draws a breath and appears to dial it down a notch. "The craze lasted all of five minutes, sure. That's the nature of buzz: it moves on. But meantime it moved, well, *lots* of units off the shelves and to this very day eight out of ten consumers will answer Ripreeler, if you ask them to name a brand of fishing lure. Happy to show you the data, if you're interested."

The CEO is not interested. "Are you trying to tell me you're expecting women to wear our condoms in their ears?"

Even as he says it, he realizes the extent of his misstep. Roebuck watches the man's mouth form a small, involuntary O, as if he hoped to suck the words back in. His female colleagues stiffen, some literally edging away.

"Here's what I *do* know." Roebuck is now back directly with the only audience that matters. "If there is one defining feature of our era, it's that this is a time when gender roles have never been so misaligned. There's a deck of research we're about to show you. But for now, I want to focus on its significance—significance for marketers, I mean. All the polling, all those satisfaction-surveys taken across the board by researchers of widely varying perspectives— all that sum of data informs us of a universal trend, and that's that women today are less happy than at any time since this kind of data started being gathered. That's my first observation. The second—and the more important corollary for our purposes—is that it's very, very easy nowadays to remind a woman how ..."

"*Pork sword!*" says the girl in the white silk blouse.

It's hard to tell which of them is more startled, Roebuck or the CEO.

"Uncle Dick," she chants. "Trouser Snake." She is pointing at the screen.

Greenwood has clicked back to his penis list. He looks around, reddening. "Notice how I've bolded the ones that seem a little more, um, egregious. I was thinking we could maybe even throw them out on Twitter ..."

"Clever," says the girl in the white silk blouse. "*So* clever." She is grinning as she says it, but it isn't Roebuck she is grinning at.

3

Philogyny means progeny.
The Collected Sayings of Julius Roebuck

Roebuck and Lily are having lunch. They have a lot of lunches; once or twice a week on average. Roebuck's favourites, Lily's too, are the ones they arrange to have at her place. But today's isn't one of those. Today they both have appointments: his with his chief financial officer, hers with the editor of a small-press literary magazine. Lily is nervous. It means a lot to her, this meeting. One of Roebuck's objectives is to put her mind at ease, to relax her, and send her off to this important interview confident and sure of her abilities. He tops her glass and recommends she take a little sip. They are sharing a bottle of her favourite Alsatian Riesling. Roebuck is not in the least concerned about his own engagement; he's sat through countless meetings with countless C-suite variations.

But he too is apprehensive. He has been apprehensive for quite some time and, right at this moment, his unease is notching sharply upward. A woman has entered the restaurant, backwards, in the way of women navigating baby strollers, pulling the rig in behind her. Lily has jumped to her feet to hold the door, but it's clear that mother and child will be through before she gets there. Lily settles back into her seat, sighing, staring, as Roebuck ponders his foreboding.

What matters is that he come to grips.

He spends the afternoon on Google. Results have not been reassuring. By now he's calmer and convinced himself Lily isn't pregnant—though this conviction arises more from intuition than any hard supporting evidence. But Roebuck has learned to trust his instinct, and Lily, somehow, doesn't *feel* pregnant. She's not behaving like she's pregnant, at least. He's been through three of them and, although he knows this doesn't guarantee him expertise, Roebuck believes he has developed a sense for how a pregnancy affects a woman's nature. It always did with Anne, certainly, and so far he hasn't picked up any similar indicators in Lily. What she *is* behaving like, though, is someone who *wishes* she were pregnant. Which is just about as bad.

He is acutely, agonizingly aware of his position.

Condoms.

Condoms or abstinence. That's it. One option so absurd it's farcical, like getting your lips sewn shut as a weight-gain prevention—only religious zealots or Austrian economists could come up with solutions so impossibly abstract. The other one vetoed by Lily herself. This was early on in their relationship. "I hate the feel of them," she'd said, gently taking the preventive from his hands into hers. "Plus, you know I'm on the pill. So why bother?"

And, to be fair, Roebuck has never put up much in the way of counterargument. But then again, how could he? "I don't sleep around," she told him, tossing his rubber like a Frisbee back into its shiny box. "And I assume the same of you." Part of him finds it almost comical. Roebuck has a native tolerance for comicality.

And he does trust Lily. Absolutely. It's just that professional experience has taught him how profoundly skilful people are at removing obstacles. Much as he adores her, much as he admires her integrity, much as he believes what she *herself* believes, Roebuck knows he would be foolish to overlook the fact that Lily belongs to precisely the demographic he has made his life's work studying. She is—according to *all* the literature—precisely the age when childless women start obsessing. Bang on. And she *has* been obsessing. Perhaps not consciously, but all the signs are there to see. Just this afternoon he found her gazing through the window of Baby Gap.

Roebuck knows he knows this. He, of all people. Reduced to its essentials, advertising is the business of encouraging the consumer to give herself permission to obtain the things she wants to obtain. Including things she thinks she shouldn't. Like, for example, his gametes. And he would be …

Although, not quite.

Not quite absolutely powerless. There is another option. *Plan V*, call it. It's been skulking in the undergrowth for quite some time now. Roebuck is not sure he likes it. In fact, he's certain he isn't going to like it. Gingerly, his fingers return to the keyboard and begin to type the word whose first three letters make his sphincter tighten. The door swings open, and Daniel Greenwood walks in.

"Got a minute?"

Roebuck almost answers no. It's on the tip of his tongue, just for an instant, to say the door was closed and what does that suggest? But his better nature reasserts itself. "What's up, Daniel?"

"Am I interrupting?"

Roebuck lets a little pause go by for Greenwood to absorb. "What can I do for you?" He nods toward an empty chair.

Greenwood replies with a calculated hesitation of his own, returns the nod, and then accepts the invitation. Once again, Roebuck finds himself expecting that he's going to like this guy.

"I've never seen a pitch go down quite like that."

"Pitch?" Roebuck has not yet returned to the present.

"The Artemis pitch. What other pitch was there?" Greenwood is puzzled. "I've never seen a creative director deliberately antagonize the head of a company he's courting. That, I have to admit, was a first."

Roebuck drags his eyes from his search engine. "That's because you haven't fully embraced the ethic here, Daniel. But you will." He removes his fingers from the keyboard. "When I say that only women count in this business, I mean it. Especially, especially with this account."

"You manhandled the CEO!"

"Manhandled." Roebuck rolls the word across his tongue. "Evocative. But sadly obsolete."

"The guy's the fucking *CEO*! If I were him, I'd just walk away. I think he's going to blow us off."

"You are not him. And he can't blow us off. That's what he's paying us to help him understand. That's the depth of insight we'll be billing him for. He's a man. It doesn't matter if he's CEO or the guy who mops the floors at 3:00 AM. If the women in that group have made up their minds they want this, there's no man going to contradict them. And don't worry, he gets that. He'd never have got this high up the ladder if he didn't. He's an MBA, for Christ's sake. He runs a condom company. That's the most important thing they teach them at biz school, the trick of taking pride in having no pride. He won't let *that* stand in the way."

"And I'm getting the impression you have an issue with MBAs?"

Roebuck considers. "My kid came home from school the other day, having learned that there are as many bacteria in our bodies as there are human cells."

"Yeah," says Greenwood. "I remember learning they play a cru-cial role and that we couldn't get along without them."

"So imagine you're a nascent batch of protoplasm, wondering what you're going to be when you grow up. Will you study hard and someday be a brain cell? Or maybe you'll stretch yourself until you get to be a neuron or a nice white corpuscle. Our MBA is the kid who decides he wants to be *E. coli* because there's double-digit growth-potential in the pathogen sector. I understand their func-tion. I just wouldn't want to be one."

"Right," says Greenwood. "Funny. Such a funny guy."

"Look. It's just good business. Artemis is a fempro. That's the brief—*internally*, with the client—not just the consumer. Think tampons. Think brassieres. Think IUDs. *Exclusively* female. That's our mindset. Something men have no business even *thinking* about. Never mind whose dick it ends up on, Daniel. Artemis is *female*."

"Then what are we for? If it's all about women, how do we fit in, guys like us? Wouldn't the client be smarter to go to an agency staffed exclusively by women and cut the dicks out altogether?"

Roebuck is certain, now, that this will be a fruitful relationship. He reaches across the desk and closes his laptop; Greenwood is humouring him and Roebuck has decided now will be as good a time as any.

"Because we're the experts, you and I," he says. "Because we've been programmed as advertisers—by virtue of our maleness—since the very first Y chromosomes mutated into being. We're the fiddle on the fiddler crab, Daniel. We're the lyre on the lyre bird. The antlers on the elk. The fire in the firefly. What we are, my friend, is billions and billions of years of evolutionary strategy aimed at one thing and one thing only: Getting Girls. We understand, you and I, as *advertisers*—above all else—that what life is all about is catching the female eye. That's it. Only women count. And by the way, you did great in there today. I had no idea."

Greenwood's iPhone has been pinging for the latter part of Roebuck's spiel. He fishes it out. "It's Artemis," he says, scanning. "Product manager. She wants to book a lunch."

Roebuck takes his time. "Who?" He's reaching for his laptop.

"Lamb." Greenwood thumbs the text. "Zhanna Lamb."

Roebuck spreads his arms, exultant. "See!"

4

Nouns have gender. People have sex.
The Collected Sayings of Julius Roebuck

It's 4:23 AM, and Roebuck is wide, wide awake.

This happens. More often than before; he has a feeling he should brace himself for more of it to come. Insomnia, for Roebuck, tends to be coordinated chiefly with his wife. Back when they were lovers, he would press against her during nights like this, artfully moulding his shape into hers. The key was to go slowly, to listen, feeling for that catch of breath, that bend of knee, those early, drowsy stirrings of gravitational pull. A gamble, of course, like everything else. If she stayed asleep, it only made the wait for morning that much longer. But often as not the risk paid out: a shift of hip, that flutter of pulse, the soft return of pelvic pressure and finally, irreversibly, those moving, rousing hands. He always thought how wonderful it must have been, to come awake like that into the full flush of arousal, carnality unconstrained by consciousness. *In medias res.*

A rationalization?

Sure.

But every absolution wears its flip side. Anne, for her part, never seemed to mind. Much the reverse in those days. And she had that awesome knack for falling back to sleep barely minutes after, arms and legs woven like a basket all around him, snoring in his ear. He'd be wanting sleep himself by then, tapped out. But the intertwine was sometimes so complex he couldn't move without displacing her, and he was loath to wake her twice. So he would close his eyes and wait it out, trussed, wrapped into his sleeping wife until her own dreams took her back to her side of the bed. Roebuck is practised in the art of wakeful reflection.

Love?

A word so freighted with commercial application its value is persuasion only.

Love is sugar. Love is salt. It's the sum of those trans-fats we're advised to do without. In his youth he once believed the same applied to writing: that love is a device employed to cheat the reader into reading on. One day he will have the nerve to make that argument with Lily. But not yet.

That always cheers him up.

Oh Lord, not yet.

Roebuck clamps shut his eyes, conscious of his wife asleep in the next room. He is still awake when the alarm goes off.

It's 9:01 AM, and Roebuck's turn to burst into his art director's office, slapping down the morning paper. "There!" he says.

Greenwood is surprised—not by Roebuck's appearance at this hour, he's done this before and everyone knows it's his way of ensuring people make it in to work on time. Roebuck is a morning person; he resents the tendency of his fellow creatives to slouch in after ten. What surprises Greenwood is the broadsheet.

"You still read *paper*?"

"Print goes better with coffee. Have a look."

Greenwood scans the headline. "President Bush Eyes Legacy? Interesting. I would not have thought you leaned Republican."

"Not the front! Back page." Roebuck snatches the paper and reads aloud.

" 'A recent study asked 1,000 women if they could remember the first shoes they bought with their own money. Ninety-two percent reported that they could. The same survey found that only 67 percent of the women questioned remembered the name of the first boy they kissed ...' Now what does that tell you?"

"That the survey was commissioned by a shoe company?"

"Excellent! Bonus marks. But the sample set was over 1,000 so statically it's valid."

"I admit it's surprising."

"No! It's not! You say that because you're a man and therefore a romantic. You want to believe that you are significant to women in the same way they are significant to you. Serious error. Who was the first girl you kissed?"

"Brenda Levi, Grade Six."

"Theresa Anderson, Grade Eight. Things took longer in my day. What about the shoes?"

"Greenwood laughs. "Okay. Point taken." He shoots a leg out from under the chair and studies his foot. "I'd be hard pressed to recall the brand name of the *last* pair I bought ...""

"That's because it was probably purchased for you by a woman."

The reaction is almost entertaining. Greenwood actually covers his mouth with his hands, staring wide-eyed at Roebuck across the table. "Holy shit! I think you're right! I think my mom got me these last Christmas."

"Think of it like a coin toss," Roebuck says. "If you know that eight out of ten times it's going to land on heads, you're pretty comfortable knowing where to place your bet. The vast majority of consumer purchases are made by women. Imagine zither music when you sing that phrase. Hum it like a mantra ..."

As Roebuck rises to leave, he feels his cellphone purr. He removes it from his pocket, checks the number, then slips it back in again where it goes on vibrating privately against his chest.

"Hey!" says Greenwood, stopping him. He has his device out too. "I just got a message from that product manager at Artemis ... She says she wants to book a lunch for one o'clock this aft." He minimizes and consults his calendar. "Yeah, I can make that. You?" Greenwood drums his fingers. "Strange, though, that a product manager is initiating this, not someone higher up. You find that strange?"

"One way to find out."

"I guess," says Greenwood. "Coming?"

"Regrettably, I have another appointment. But I know you'll do us proud."

When Roebuck is in the office, the policy is open door, a must for a creative shop. But it's closed today for this call.

"It's me."

"Julius! Hi. I'm sorry for calling at work."

"Don't worry. It's fine. You okay? "

"I just wanted to try to explain. I don't know what's wrong with me lately. But listen, can I call you right back?"

"Um, sure."

Julius Roebuck is a student of creative irony. He has to be. He accepts the premise that opposing principles can be simultaneously true. He is at peace with his conviction that having Lily in his life has made his marriage sounder. His wife is hard. Roebuck understands the many ways that he deserves this. It is also true that he could not imagine life without her. Is that what love means? Without his kids, life itself would not be worth the effort. So that's love. That one's easy. Anne is hard, though. Lily isn't hard at all.

Lily is a poet; a real one. She is often in the literary magazines and has published two volumes of verse; *slim* volumes, she calls them. Lily herself is slim and packed with meaning. Roebuck has calculated that the sum total of her earnings from all her published works amounts to less than he makes in any average week; in a good week, like this one is shaping up to be, quite a lot less. She is also a graphic designer of notable worth. Lily does freelance work for Roebuck's agency. It's a point of pride for both of them that all her contracts are arranged through his account people, not him.

One of the suits had brought her in to introduce around the office. It was a Friday afternoon in summer; Lily joined them after work at the pub downstairs. Anne had departed already with the kids for the cottage. He and Lily found themselves sitting with their chairs together as his colleagues drifted home, three or four pints down by then, arguing definitions of *creative*. She called him a purveyor of cliché. As far as Roebuck was concerned, no one could have said a better thing. Roebuck did what he is very good at doing. He told a story.

"When I was younger, I thought I wanted to be a novelist. I got myself accepted into the Writers' Workshop at the University of Iowa"—maybe she had heard of it?—"tracking for an MFA. They kept telling me that fine writing, above all else, must avoid cliché."

He remembers swallowing his drink to stretch the point, touching his glass deliberately to hers. "I held out for a full semester, mostly because the place was stuffed so full of women. But eventually, I couldn't stand it any longer. So I quit, came home, and enrolled in Women's Studies, which, may I tell you, provides an even better ratio."

"*You* took Women's Studies?"

"The only straight guy in my class."

"What was the problem, at Iowa?"

"It's the business of writers to create clichés, not to avoid them. Their operating philosophy was completely backward."

"Mmm, now there's a perspective."

"Pick a great writer, start with Shakespeare. Open your search engine and type, 'Shakespeare, clichés.' You'll get a list of hundreds, *hundreds* of phrases we use every day: a fool's paradise; a foregone conclusion; a sea change; a rose by any other name; all's well that ends well; as pure as driven snow; as dead as a doornail. I could go on—those are just a handful of the ones that start with *A*. It's the same with every major writer—Dickens, Homer, the funhouse boys who built the Bible. Take your pick." He set his glass down on the table. Despite his intentions, Roebuck that day was taking himself seriously too. "A cliché is just a phrase so closely associated with a certain thing that it pops into your head whenever you think about that thing."

"You've given this speech before, I take it?"

"What I know is that our job is to create clichés, not combat them. Sometimes, clients don't understand that."

"But you persuade them?"

"That is one of my functions, yes."

Lily took a sip, regarding. "They wouldn't have admitted you into the program," she said, touching her tongue to the foam on her lip, "unless you'd shown them some very strong samples. I'm guessing a collection of short stories, maybe the sketch of a novel. Where is it now?"

He unbuttoned her shirt and unzipped her jeans for the first time that night. Roebuck loves sleeping with Lily. Every bit as much as he loves talking with her. Cliché has always been his strong suit.

When the phone rings again he's there and is waiting.

"Hi."

"Hi."

"I'm here."

"Can you talk?"

"The door is closed; I'm in conference.

"I'm sorry."

"You keep saying that."

"I know. I know. It's just that something is eating at me lately. We've been through this before; it's not your fault. There's nothing you can do about it."

He doesn't know what to say to this so he says nothing.

"Please don't be mad."

"I'm not mad. I'm just … apprehensive."

"Well, that makes two of us." She laughs. "It's no excuse, I know, but I got my period this morning. I'm vindictive."

His relief is so intense he worries for a moment that she will hear it in his voice.

"Julius? Are you there?"

"You know …" he says, "I almost wish I knew what that felt like. So I could know what to say …"

"No, you don't! But you're probably the only man I'd believe when you make a claim like that. You are entertaining, I'll give you that."

"And that, I keep telling you, is my job."

"Well, *I'm* not entertaining for the next few days. Call me next week, and we'll see if the bloom is back on the rose."

"O Lily thou art sick. The invisible worm that flies in the night …"

"*Enough* with the Blake! I hate that one especially. That guy was such a fraud."

He has steered them both to solider ground. This is an old, familiar theme.

"Anyhow," she says, "I have work to do even if you don't. Call next week."

Roebuck disconnects and sits for a moment, attempting breathing exercises learned and forgotten long ago on an aromatic yoga mat. His door is still closed. He can dispute with himself if he wants to. Roebuck pulls the laptop front and centre, opens up the Google page, draws another breath deep into his diaphragm, clicks to Wikipedia and types the necessary letters.

Vasectomy

Vasectomy is a minor surgical procedure wherein the *vasa deferentia* of a man are severed and then tied or sealed in a manner to prevent sperm from entering the seminal stream (ejaculate).

The procedure is usually done in an outpatient setting. A traditional vasectomy involves numbing of the scrotum, using a local anesthetic, after which one (or two) small incisions are made, allowing a surgeon to gain access to the vas deferens. The "tubes" are cut and sealed by tying, stitching, cauterization (burning), or otherwise clamped to prevent sperm from entering the seminal stream. When the vasectomy is complete, sperm cannot exit the body through the penis.

After vasectomy, the testes remain in the scrotum where they continue to produce testosterone and other male hormones that continue to be secreted into the blood stream. Sperm are still produced by the testicles, but they are broken down and absorbed by the body.

It is generally accepted that the failure rate of this procedure is in line with that of other contraceptives.

Worldwide, approximately 6 percent of married women using contraception rely on vasectomy.

He has crossed his legs then consciously uncrossed them. The words *scrotum* and *incision* should not be placed together in a single sentence—and *cauterizing*? Worse than he imagined. Roebuck fights the urge to get up and walk around. He's fairly certain he's been squirming. He reminds himself that he survived three years of Women's Studies; he can manage a minor procedure performed in an outpatient setting.

And he does admire the phrasing of that last bit: that 6 percent of married *women* rely on vasectomy as their choice of contraceptive. The only point of view that counts is female, even here. He is surprised that this surprises him, and this too is consoling.

Roebuck is further encouraged by the discovery of a product interestingly marketed as "The No-Scalpel Vasectomy." His professional interest is aroused. Here is the case of a service being advertised not for what it is, but for what it's not. Experience has taught him the many drawbacks of this approach. On the other hand, *no scalpel* has an undeniably affirming ring. And there are definite, marketable, claims. "The No-Scalpel method reduces healing time and lowers the chance of infection." That's the kind of powerful statement consumers want to hear. Roebuck correctly guesses there has to be a downside buried somewhere. Clearly, the copywriter would not be using this technique if not to minimize some drawback. If not scalpel, then what?

A haemostat, that's what.

He has done an image search and wishes he had not. A haemostat turns out to be a kind of long, sharp needle with jaws used to puncture the scrotum. Various similes enter his mind involving burst balloons and ruptured dirigibles; the Hindenburg aflame and peeling. Roebuck beats them back. He sifts through the material, but he's fairly certain by now that he has identified the central claim: "Following the procedure, men with non-physical employment like office jobs can usually return to work the next day."

So it's not about the instrument. It's about recovery time.

That is good. If the day after you're back in the saddle, then it can't be all that bad. He wonders if the promoters gave any thought to calling it "The Next Day Vasectomy"? But no, that phrasing might suggest postponement. It's a unique selling point, regardless—and in Roebuck's case resoundingly decisive.

He refines his search geographically and almost immediately turns up a website posted by an outfit called "The No Fuss Vasectomy Clinic," located at an address not twenty minutes from his office. Roebuck himself is a no fuss kind of guy. The colour scheme's a little much—he could live without the baby-blue—but otherwise the site is well laid out. Lots of facts, though not enough to overwhelm. He also admires the frequent repetition of the word *gentle*. Roebuck has not the slightest objection to gentle.

There's an FAQ that reiterates much of what he's read already: Q: When can I get back to work? A: Next day, unless your job involves heavy lifting. Q: Will it hurt? A: No, at least not very much. Q: Will it affect my sex life? A: Yes. You will never have to worry about unwanted pregnancy again. Q: How soon will I be able to resume having sex? A: You are advised to avoid intercourse for the week following the procedure. Q: How soon after can I stop worrying about causing a pregnancy? A: Eight weeks and twenty ejaculations …

Eight weeks?

… Patients are also advised to undergo sperm-tests twice following the vasectomy: after twenty ejaculations and then again at the end of eight weeks.

Eight weeks?

Roebuck mulls the implications. With Anne, eight weeks is not significant. Months go by sometimes with Anne. Years. After Zach was born, Anne pretty much lost interest. But Lily? Lily takes that part of their relationship seriously. Putting Lily off for two full months will strain Roebuck's creativity to the limit. Perhaps a little health issue? A hernia? How exactly do you get a hernia? He'll need to do better than that.

He's stalling. He knows he's stalling. There's a button in the centre of the page:

CLICK HERE

Roebuck clicks. Precisely as he does, his phone rings. It's Daniel Greenwood on his mobile, six blocks south, walking back from lunch. "I'm in the middle of something, Daniel. Can this wait until this afternoon?" Greenwood, oddly reluctant, agrees to meet later and disconnects.

The page shows a stilted photograph of a doctor standing at the doors of a clinic: a securely middle-aged man in a lab coat. Roebuck admits to himself that he is relieved it's not a woman— then wonders why. Again, the stalling …

More bumf about a consultation that will take place prior to the procedure followed by some information about costs and then, below that, the form itself. Roebuck elects to provide his private cellphone number only and decides against submitting an email address. He is given pause, too, over what to divulge about his marital status. If he ticks "Married," it asks for the name of his spouse. Roebuck is definitely not about to open any lines of communication running in that direction. It's bad luck to say "Divorced," so he ticks "Separated" as a kind of compromise, though he doesn't like this option either. It's a relief to find that the rest of the form is the usual list of questions about pre-existing medical conditions and health insurance. Before he knows it, he is contemplating the "Send" button at the bottom of the page. Roebuck allows himself a little ceremony: one finger, one crook of one finger, one last moment of teetering anxiety, then he presses the button.

He is working through a backlog of email when Greenwood sticks his head around the door. It's immediately clear that Daniel would rather be elsewhere; he's agitated, nervous in a way that Roebuck hasn't seen before.

"I can come back if this isn't a good time?"

Roebuck draws the inescapable conclusion. "*Really?*" he says, slamming his fist on the table. "Damn. Damn. *Damn!*"

Greenwood shuffles the rest of the way in. He seems not to want to sit. Or know where to begin. "Umm …"

"Bastard! I have to say I'm extremely surprised."

"Honestly, I thought it was going to be just an ordinary, get-acquainted lunch."

"So *she* does the dirty work? I would never have thought …"

"How did you know? Really, I had no idea until … How did …? "

"Look at you! It's all over your face."

Greenwood passes a hand over his chin. "They had towels and everything," he says, examining his palm. "And very deep sinks, come to think of it."

"Towels?"

"A big pile of them, just for that. And a hamper to throw them in when you're done. There was even a copy of the *Kama Sutra.*"

"Daniel, what are you talking about?"

"Wait a minute. What are *you* talking about?"

They eye each other quietly. Roebuck is first to break the impasse. "All right, let's back this up. You phoned an hour ago on the way back from your lunch …"

"Yes."

"And that lunch was with Artemis?"

"Well, umm, yes. Correct. But only Zhanna ..."

"So I'm assuming you were calling to tell me where things stand with our pitch?"

"Well, yes, sort of. I mean, I was ... mostly just calling to see whether you wanted me to pick you up a sandwich or something."

"A sandwich?"

"Or maybe a falafel."

"Out with it."

"Like I said, honestly, it was the last thing I expected."

"Daniel, did we win the account or no?"

"Well, as a matter of fact ... That subject never really came up."

"*What!* How can ...?" But Roebuck has finally assembled the pieces. "Did you say *Kama Sutra*—at the restaurant?"

Greenwood is backing out the door. "Listen, I think this conversation is based on a complete misunderstanding."

"You took her to *Alison's*?"

Greenwood stops dead. "How did you know? And anyway it was *her* idea."

"Never mind." A welter of thoughts and emotions are surfacing in Roebuck's brain, but the one that bubbles up above the rest startles them both. He can't help it. He'll sort out the elements later, but for now Roebuck is overwhelmed, utterly, helplessly overwhelmed with choking, wheezing, rib-racking mirth. "Sit down," he says when he is able, rubbing a tear from his eye. He is surprised at himself.

"You find this funny?"

Roebuck waves a hand toward the chair, wheezing still. "Daniel, sit down. Please." He thumps himself on the sternum. "I don't think I've laughed like that since ... Alison's! She chose Alison's. A client!"

"That's what I wanted to tell you when I called. She's not a client. Not anymore. Well, she's almost not a client." Greenwood seems eager to transition over into indignation.

"Clearly …" says Roebuck, reining it in. "Clearly there's a story here. Daniel, honestly, sit down. You know the old song, 'Alison's Restaurant?'" Roebuck clears his throat and tries to sing: "… you can get anything you want, at Alison's Restaurant …"

"It's Alice's Restaurant," says Greenwood primly, "not Alison's. We learned it at camp."

"You know, I think you're right. Maybe there was a copyright issue. Anyhow, Alison's is known—or should I say the restrooms at Alison's are known—among certain clientele as being deliberately conducive to … ah … well, what I gather you've experienced during your lunch … with a prospective *client*."

"She's not a prospective client! That's what I've been trying to say!"

"Let's begin there. How is a client not a client, prospective or otherwise?"

"When she submits her resignation. Or at least, when she submits the resignation she has written and is ready to print and hand in this afternoon."

"An employee in body, as it were, but not in spirit …" Greenwood is up on his feet again before Roebuck can prevent him. "Oh, lighten up, Daniel! I'm just jealous. So you're telling me Zhanna Lamb is no longer product manager at Artemis?"

"She told me she intended to deliver her letter of resignation immediately following our lunch."

This last statement, delivered deadpan, almost does Roebuck in again. "Some people call their attorneys before making big career moves. Others need a drink. Our Zhanna Lamb bonks clients in the john." Greenwood glowers, and Roebuck makes a show of studying his watch. "Speaking of drinks," he says, "this is not the kind of conversation properly suited to the workplace. Let's take it downstairs." He aims an accusative finger. "You didn't have too much to drink, did you? How many martinis? That *would* be serious. Lechers I can live with, but drunks I won't tolerate. I'm joking, Daniel, relax. Oysters, though," he says after a pause, "generally do require something to wash them down."

"You seem to know an awful lot about this place."

"Today, Daniel, you are the storyteller. I am the audience."

A pint of Guinness in him and halfway down his second, Greenwood is warming to his narrative. Their twelfth-floor suite of offices contains two boardrooms. Roebuck has named them, somewhat facetiously and somewhat not, Matrix One and Matrix Two. A fair amount of business, though, takes place at the brewpub on the ground floor below, which his people have taken to calling Matrix Three. The barmen know to begin pulling a pint of lager when they spot Roebuck coming through the door. Every so often he'll order an ale instead to keep them on their toes. The bartender is obliged to drink the lager, Roebuck nurses his ale, pays for both, and maintains key friendships in important places. He wouldn't have put Greenwood down as a Guinness man, but today is a day of surprises.

"Before I forget," he says, "don't even think about expensing that. That one's on you. Virtue has to be its own reward. How did you say she was dressed?"

"Black, soft, clingy ..."

"And no underwear?"

"But that wasn't until ..."

"Sorry. I'm interrupting." Greenwood has reached the interesting part, but he seems to be turning shy again. "Right." Roebuck summarizes. "So she meets you at the table in a little black dress. What's she drinking?"

"Gin."

"God, I love this girl! Pretty soon she's touching your hand, then your arm, then resting her hand on your knee. Once the plates are cleared, she excuses herself to powder her nose. That, I'm assuming, is when she peels off the thong and stashes it in her purse. And all the while you're manfully trying to keep the conversation professional ..."

"Okay I'll admit that by this time I'd pretty much given up on shop talk."

"But at some point she must have told you she was leaving Artemis?"

"That was early on, before the food came. And by the way it wasn't oysters. Or martinis either. At least for me." There's a faintly ridiculous smugness in Greenwood's tone that has Roebuck struggling to hide his smile. "She said she had better things to do in life than help a bunch of dinks sell rubbers, however creatively promoted."

Roebuck whistles. "I really do admire this girl. But she couldn't tell you which way they were leaning?"

"All she could say was that there had been no hints so far from management. But she also said she'd pretty much checked out by then, so she wasn't really paying attention."

He considers implications and decides there are none. "Okay, so now you've paid the bill, you're getting up to leave. She takes your arm and the two of you stroll to the coat check."

"The restrooms in this place are unisex," says Greenwood.

Roebuck nods. "Plush, if I recall. Roomy."

"The coats are hanging in the same alcove as the bathrooms. She's still hugging my arm. Before I know it, we've carried on past the coat rack and straight through one of the doors."

"Aha!" says Roebuck. "This is where the conversation gets interesting. Damn. Hang on a sec." His cellphone is going off. Roebuck carries a BlackBerry for business purposes plus an old-fashioned clam-phone he reserves for personal use. Only his wife, his kids,

Lily, and a handful of his most important clients have access to this private number.

"Hello."

"Julius Roebuck?"

"Yes."

"This is the No Fuss Vasectomy Clinic calling."

"Oh."

"We have an appointment available for you."

"I see. Um." Roebuck stares wide-eyed at Greenwood, who politely looks elsewhere.

"We can schedule you for next Thursday at 10:00 AM."

"Next week? Next week! But that's ... soon!"

"I understand. You'll need to make arrangements with your place of employment. Would the following Thursday be preferable, same time?"

"That is also ... very soon."

"When would be a good time for you, Mr. Roebuck?"

He's aware of Greenwood picking up a menu, furrowing his brow in manifest preoccupation. "Look, can I call you back?"

"Often, we find that clients' first impulse is to delay the procedure. But that of course just lengthens your worrying time. And I assure you, Mr. Roebuck, there's absolutely nothing to be anxious about. Have you visited our website?"

"I have. Yes. Absolutely."

"I'm happy to answer any questions. Some clients are concerned ..."

"Can I call you back?

"Of course, Mr. Roebuck. Take your time."

"What was that all about?" asks Greenwood, waving at the waiter for another pint.

5

Advertising is psychology monetized.
The Collected Sayings of Julius Roebuck

Over the years, Roebuck has developed a reliable sense of how things are moving along. When he weighs the pros and cons objectively, he has to conclude that the odds are in favour of landing the Artemis account. He has carefully evaluated the merits of each agency on the short list. Young & Rubicam will give him a run for his money, so will Chiat Day. But Y & R have just lost their creative director and the new guy they've moved in from Hong Kong isn't meshing. Chiat has failed to win three pitches in a row; something there is misfiring. There's a hot new digital agency that had him worried, but by good fortune they were hacked last week and are now fending off a data-leak investigation. All things considered, especially in light of that remarkable pitch—and it was remarkable, no matter how Greenwood sees it—he figures they're the top contender.

The call comes in as expected, ten days after expiration of the deadline. The CEO wastes no time in small talk. Roebuck knows what will be said before it is spoken.

"Congratulations, I am pleased to be informing you ..." There's a case of Dom he keeps in the storeroom for occasions like these. It's good for staff morale to pop some corks and pass around the flutes. Many of his competitors are cutting back on the perks, clients have been slashing advertising budgets, and agencies are feeling the squeeze, but Roebuck considers moxie-boosters an essential cost of doing business. In a minute, he'll see about sending someone out for a side of smoked salmon and some canapés. He will also need to issue an All Staff announcement. It's Friday, a perfect note to end the week. Matrix Three will be humming tonight. But somehow Roebuck can't work himself into the mood. It's his own morale he knows is suspect.

He's jealous. He would never admit it, even to himself. But he knows it. Greenwood has let on, a little casually, a little understatedly, that he and Zhanna are now going out on regular dates: dinners and movies and such. Roebuck is happy for him. He harbours no ill will—of this he *is* certain. But he wishes it were him, not Greenwood, grazing Zhanna's ankle in the unlit zone beneath the table. On the call with Artemis he had made a point, just to hear it spoken, of mentioning how much he's looking forward to working with that insightful marketing team, particularly that bright young product manager. "Regrettably, Zhanna Lamb has left the company ..." Foolish, asking openly like that. Slap-to-the-side-of-the-head stupid.

Even so, he can't seem to shake it, so when an email from Lily appears with "A Proposition" blinking in the subject line, Roebuck pounces on the keyboard. He hasn't heard from Lily all week.

"Darling ..."

When did she start saying *darling*? He never calls her darling. Maybe time to start.

Congratulate me! I've just won a juicy little contract at McCann. The specs won't be ready until next week so I'm thinking … why don't you come over for lunch Wednesday? After Wednesday I'm slammed, but before … Can you free yourself up? I'll cook.
I know your preferences.

Roebuck hits "Reply." He doesn't even bother looking at his calendar. He's in the middle of composing a gleeful response, when his fingers halt and retreat from the keyboard. When Lily takes a contract, she goes at it full tilt. After Wednesday, she'll be beyond reach for a week at least. Roebuck drums his fingers; then opens up the No Fuss Vasectomy Clinic's website. Yes, he has remembered correctly: Eight weeks.

In all fairness he deserves a last hurrah. Roebuck picks up the phone.

"This is Julius Roebuck. You contacted me earlier about an appointment. Is that slot still available?"

"What was the date you wanted, Mr. Roebuck?"

"I believe it was next Thursday, 10:00 AM."

A pause. "I'm sorry. That appointment is booked."

"Damn. What about the next day, Friday?"

"The clinic is closed Mondays and Fridays."

"I see."

"We do have a cancellation. Let me check. How is Wednesday afternoon, same week?"

"*Wednesday?* No, definitely not Wednesday. Wait! Did you say *afternoon?* How late in the afternoon?"

"It's the last appointment. Four o'clock."

Roebuck excels at rapid calculation. "Fine," he says. "Book me in."

Darling,

    You're just what the doctor ordered. But can we make it early?

    I have a 4 PM I can't afford to miss.

6

Civilization sacrifices parents for children.
Barbarism, the other way around.
The Collected Sayings of Julius Roebuck

There's a level of synchronicity they have managed to achieve, he and Anne, which Roebuck has for many years admired, an interdisciplining of agendas. It is one thing they've agreed on since the start, since before their first pregnancy, even: that they will make a habit of sitting down together as a family to eat. Admittedly this is not always feasible. Roebuck has his business meetings, and Anne, too, her own affairs. But more often than not, the dinner hour will find the five of them at the table all together, passing the salad and news of whatever has been happening since breakfast.

When he contemplates old age, there isn't much hilarity in view. But the prospect of talking politics and abstract religion with his adult children is a pleasure Roebuck anticipates with what for him are the very highest of his hopes.

For now, though, they are still in the stage when no line of reasoning survives for more than three minutes before complete annihilation by some unrelated train of thought. It's a challenge when company comes, but a rule is a rule and the kids eat with them even when guests are being entertained. Yasmin is holding up her end of things quite well. But then again, she's practising.

Morgan has been at pains to tell them how she's doing *all* the work on her science project, while the other girls aren't doing anything, *anything*, especially Ginny Moragani, that bitch. Anne and Roebuck spin heads in parallel reproach while Zach keeps cutting in asking if he—Dad—would rather fight a grizzly bear or an adult Siberian tiger? Also he wants to know what Yasmin would do if an Albertosaurus poked its head through the window. Forsaking the last of her manners, Morgan hurls a mussel shell, aiming at Zach but missing on account of aerodynamics and nearly grazing Yasmin, who bats it down with catlike reflex. Roebuck has been given to understand that the topic for later is likely going to be the lonely womb. He admits a certain level of curiosity.

After the usual string of arguments and obfuscations, the kids troop upstairs to brush their teeth. Anne goes along for good-night kisses and soon is back down, escorted by a sulking Zach in his Sponge Bob pyjamas. Zach thinks it's totally unfair he isn't getting any bedtime story. Roebuck excuses himself. Story time has always been a favourite. With a little luck, they'll have the dishes cleared before he's back.

He is good at this, more so now the older girls are not as interested. Back when they were younger, they were always, always, wanting princesses and mermaids. Roebuck—like his wife a product of more hopeful times—disapproves of princesses and finds it challenging to make them sympathetic, at least the versions Katie and Morgan demanded. His son prefers zombies and hammerhead sharks. For a year or more the two streams could sometimes be merged, and Roebuck struck narrative gold with hybrid creations involving both royal daughters *and* interesting carnivores, a far more satisfying arc. But now the girls have mostly opted out. Kate has her own Facebook account; already she has taken to closing her door. It won't be long before they're fretting in the dark about what kind of photographs she's posting.

Tonight, though, Zach says he doesn't want a made-up story. He wants a real one, from a book. The one about the farting dog. Roebuck hates that farting dog and lobbies for Kipling. What about "The Elephant's Child," which he knows Zach doesn't mind and which he really does enjoy because of all the different voices he gets to put on? Zach wants nothing to do with his father's attempts at zoomorphic accents. It ruins the story. Then how about "The Cremation of Sam McGee?" Roebuck has this one down by heart. Some mornings, for drill, he runs through the whole of it on his drive into work.

"Sam McGee sucks."

"Zachary!"

They settle for a Dr. Seuss, which has the advantage of being short. Roebuck is getting curious about how the conversation downstairs has been moving along.

Anne and Yasmin are head to head when he switches off the light and tiptoes back downstairs. The dishes are still heaped in the middle of the table. Yasmin glances up and smiles, though his wife seems oblivious to his return. Roebuck gathers plates and fades back into the kitchen.

When he thinks about Yasmin—which happens far, far more often than he knows it should—he reminds himself that in fairness he must always factor in the liabilities of beauty. Women who are constantly watched fall into the habit of watching themselves. And certainly, Roebuck watches Yasmin. A phrase from somewhere nudges in; he pauses, tracking it. "When contemplating her, the mind leaps instantly to bed." He can't recall the source, much less the author, but his own mind, undeniably, has jumped into bed with Yasmin so often it's worn out the springs. No fault of hers either; he concedes this point as well. There's just something about his wife's partner that sets his nostrils flaring and his hooves pounding whenever he inhales in her vicinity, or on the brink of flaring and pounding before he reins it in and locks it back inside the stable and bolts the door. No one, not Yasmin (or Anne either, more succinctly), no one at all but Roebuck himself is aware of the physical effect she has on him.

The irony's so blatant he almost enjoys it. He doesn't even *like* Yasmin. In fact, truth be told, his feelings probably shade closer to active dislike. She is, as far as he can tell, a truly one-dimensional being; the kind of person who values only what reflects her own self back. Still, he's hardly one to talk. Where Yasmin is concerned, Roebuck's own reactions are as basic as a bulb of mercury in heat. If he were a less forgiving soul, he'd be ashamed of himself.

He has kept up with the research on pheromones: those intriguing chemicals that geneticists know stimulate sexual attraction. Marketers have been trying for years to replicate them in the lab and infuse them into products. The romantic side of Roebuck hopes they never do; his business is art, as he understands it, not science. But he sympathizes. Chemistry's a wonderful explainer of the inexplicable.

It's a blessing, all in all, that she is so unappealing in so many other respects. Though here again, he needs to watch himself. Anne's attachment puzzles. He knows from long experience that his wife is never one to suffer fools gladly. So there has to be something there Anne sees and he doesn't. The two of them, somehow, complement each other at some level he is unable to access. The topic hasn't shifted when he steps back into the dining room.

"Maybe it just isn't meant to be ..."

"Oh, Yasmin, don't even *say* that!" Anne's face wears the same earnest, loving look that comes over it whenever one of the kids arrives home with bad news from school. "You *know*! You know you know."

Yasmin needs persuading. "God, I hope you're right! Maybe you are …"

"Of course I am. Of *course* I am." Anne reaches across the table and takes Yasmin's hand. Roebuck gathers cutlery.

All this while they've been working through the question of Yasmin's fitness for parenthood. After much reflection, much self-doubt, many conscious and unconscious allusions to a higher destiny, they have together arrived at the conclusion that it is a positive thing, on balance, the fact that Yasmin is tearing herself apart over this. That she has invested so much in contemplation of her own suitability speaks favourably for how genuinely she approaches the subject. He can hear them from the kitchen. Yasmin's voice rising and falling; Anne's steady, calm, encouraging …

One of the things they do particularly well together, he and Anne, is parenting. They are firmly together on that plank at least. Still are. He can't help thinking that, deep down, Anne must share his opinion that Yasmin is definitely *not* cut out for motherhood, especially the single-parent variation. He wishes he could ask.

His wife is constantly perplexed by her friend's inability to land a mate. Roebuck's own theory—far from bullet-proof—is that Yasmin is intelligent enough to want a thinker, but not enough of a thinker to keep one. He was foolish enough to suggest this once and watched the subject take an instant and dramatic shift into a detailed and much more clearly articulated assessment of his own shortcomings—and who the fuck was he to think he was so smart? Since then, whenever Anne talks about Yasmin, Roebuck sighs and shakes his head and says it's a puzzler all right: so smart, so beautiful, such a lovely personality: it just doesn't add up. But he can't help believing that, at heart, her truer feelings are probably in line with his.

Roebuck refills glasses. "That's the last of it," he says, setting down the empty jug. Yasmin has clasped her hands together like an ornament between her breasts. Anne nods and passes him the pitcher. "Why don't you make us up a fresh batch?"

Last summer, with Anne away at the cottage during so much of the renovations, they spent a fair amount of time together, he and Yasmin. All major decisions were made without reference to him, naturally. Anne and Yasmin spoke each day by phone and kept in constant touch by email. They'd decided it had to be *his* project too. So once or twice a week throughout that August, he would climb the stairs behind the mesmerizing spheres of Yasmin's rump to the top floor of his empty house, where she would lead him, room to room, navigating scaffolds, stirring motes of drywall dust into the musk of her perfume, while he assumed the role of doubtful, cautious client—questioning the colour of this finish or the placement of that vent—whose reservations she was on the ground to manage and subdue. If the work crews had left for the day they would drink a glass of wine afterward, in the shade of the backyard, certifying progress to date. Yasmin would talk about Yasmin. Roebuck would contemplate same.

He discovered then that with a little tinkering, she could be made to stimulate two very distinct regions of his brain. His primitive, limbic system reacted on its own. No need for analysis there. But as the summer passed and exposure lengthened, Roebuck learned the trick of inducting Yasmin to the abstract, more complicated regions of his thinking. It was—and still is, as he perceives it—a form of compensation; something useful in exchange for something not. By now it's settled into a conceptual exercise, a kind of thought-experiment. He imagines Yasmin as a sort of meta-Yasmin: The Ideal Customer; the sum of all women. The challenge is then to figure how to pitch her. Recently, he's been adding Greenwood to the mental mix as collaborator on a common cause. "Look," he tells his phantom art director. "Study. This is your model. This is who we're talking to ..."

"More brandy, less sugar." Yasmin is standing at his elbow, holding out the bottle of Courvoisier.

"Don't listen to her," Anne calls through the door. "That last batch was plenty strong enough."

Roebuck smiles, takes the bottle from her hands, and pours as she watches. "More," says Yasmin, watching still.

Roebuck pours again.

"We have a question for you when you come back out," Yasmin says as she wanders back to the dining room.

He crushes some ice, slices an orange, splashes the wine, and then, because curiosity is driving him again, adds another slug of brandy. *Sangria* comes from the Spanish word for *blood*. They are waiting for him at the table.

"So," he says, prevaricating. "Will there be a black president?" This shot is aimed at his wife, whose feminist sensibilities are rooting for Hillary Clinton. Roebuck is defensively inserting mischief.

"Who cares!" Yasmin has been primed for this all night. "This is serious!"

"We want your opinion," says Anne, "as a man."

"Ah," he says. "Not my field ..."

"Yes, yes ..." His wife cuts across the caveat. "Your expertise is women, blah, blah, et cetera, et cetera. We know all that. Still, we would like you to give this one a shot."

But it's true. Roebuck *is* far more confident of his understanding of women than of men. He seldom gives much thought to other men except from time to time to wonder if he himself is fairly representative. Research suggests that probably he is. But it's also true he really doesn't care. Men are not significant.

Yasmin drives straight to the point. "Why would a man donate sperm?"

"She means to a sperm bank." Anne is a great one for clarification. "What would be his *motivation*?"

"Ah."

So the topic has matured. Roebuck fills their glasses and settles into his chair. The expression on both women's faces might be well described as *avid*. He takes a sip, considering. How can he not be enjoying this? "Off the top of my head, two possibilities, starting with money …"

"Nope."

"Guess how much sperm donors get paid?" Anne asks. Clearly, they have looked into this together. Roebuck hasn't a clue what sperm donors get paid.

"Fifty bucks. *Fifty!*"

Yasmin draws a look of irritation from his wife, who really had intended him to guess. "There's new legislation," Anne explains, "prohibiting payment for reproductive cells. It's not like in the old days when a guy with a strong wrist and a high sperm count could put himself through med school. Nowadays, donors only receive a token reimbursement to cover out-of-pocket expenses."

"Out of pocket, my ass!" Yasmin's tone makes it obvious there is something here she finds offensive. "Fifty hardly even covers lunch!"

Roebuck considers mentioning that there are a lot of things a lot of people will do for a lot less than that, but takes her point. For Yasmin, anyone who'd consider fifty dollars real money ought to be forbidden from producing sperm, let alone providing it for public consumption.

"All right," he says. "Then it has to be frogs."

Anne sighs. She is acquainted with her husband's stagecraft. Yasmin offers better satisfaction. "What's that supposed to mean?"

"If we take it as a given," says Roebuck, grinning at his wife, "that the ultimate goal of all living things is reproduction—and by the way that's at the core of understanding branding, too, in my business—then the question is: How to maximize achievement of that goal? Different organisms use different strategies. Frogs, for example, take what you might call the scattergun approach. Frogs release huge numbers of eggs—flooding the market, if you like. Once the eggs are fertilized, that's the end of their involvement. Frogs place their faith in quantity. Other animals take a more qualitative approach. Elephants, if I'm not mistaken, produce only one offspring every three or four years but dedicate enormous energy to guarding and protecting that investment. On the surface, you'd think that humans are more like elephants, because we devote even more time and energy toward raising our young. But if you look at the differences between men and women, in terms of reproductive capacity, you'll see it's more complicated ..."

Anne is gazing at the ceiling again, all but rolling her eyes, though at least she isn't cutting in. Yasmin, on the other hand, is leaning forward, wholly receptive. Roebuck reminds himself to keep his gaze eye-level or above. He's enjoying this a little more than he acknowledges is wise.

"Human females produce a very limited number of eggs over their lifetimes, released only one at a time. When one gets fertilized, it can be months, years before the next one come along. Men, on the other hand, pump out enough sperm on any given Saturday night to knock up every female in the county, if only we could nail down the logistics."

"So men are frogs and women are elephants," Anne says. "You should write a sex-ed guide."

"All I'm saying, and only because you asked, is that maybe your donor is practising the frog's strategy: availing himself of the sperm banks in order to broadcast his DNA as widely as possible, under-standing that his involvement ends right there, but hoping that the sheer number of opportunities will increase the likelihood of spreading his genes."

"I think he's right!" Yasmin's look gives his own testicles a jolt. "I never thought of it that way. But it makes sense." She turns to Anne. "He's not stupid, sometimes, your husband."

"You don't have to live with him. And I'm not convinced. If it's such a good strategy, why don't all men use it? Why don't all men donate to sperm banks? Most don't, I think. Why not? Would you?"

It has all the hallmarks of a trap, but it doesn't matter because the answer—the true and shining answer—is right there in front of him and absolutely danger free.

"No," he says. He doesn't even have to think about it. "No, I would not."

"Why?"

"Because my strategy is the elephant's." He has realized, quite suddenly, how profoundly true this is. "I've chosen a wife—in bio-logical terms, I've selected a mate, who to my extreme good for-tune has likewise selected me, and together we have produced our children. That's *my* genetic investment. That's the sum, the *full sum* of my genetic investment. That's all I want. That's all I planned for. My reproductive strategy is, and always will be, to devote all I have to protecting that investment, not diluting it."

It's a pretty good answer; the kind of statement you'd think any wife would want to hear, and all the better because it's absolutely, unequivocally honest. But Anne is glaring at him, furious, because something in what he's said has tripped a switch in Yasmin.

She's still staring. She's still examining him. But now her expres-sion is transforming. Yasmin's eyes are misting over. She sniffles. "You're so *lucky!*" she moans to Anne who—to his astonishment—isn't disagreeing, but instead has stomped his foot under the table.

Yasmin has begun to cry. Her shoulders tremble. "Frogs or failures!" she sobs, "Those are my choices. I'll never be a mother!" A single tear, plump and glistening, rolls past her cheek and lips and begins to trickle down her neck.

"Oh, honey, but you will, *you will!*" Anne gestures angrily at Roebuck to pass a napkin from the stack on the buffet.

"No, no! Julius has said it. If I can't find a good man willing to make a baby with me—and I can't!—my only other option is the sperm banks. But Julius has made all that so clear, too. The only sperm there comes from welfare bums or sneaky frogs ... and I can't let the father of my baby be that!" Yasmin's chest is rising and falling; she has thrown herself back into the dining room chair. She's sobbing now so hard the straps of her dress have slipped below her shoulders. He looks over at Anne, but Anne is dabbing Yasmin with a napkin. "You're so lucky!" she moans.

"I know, I know ..."

Roebuck is transfixed. He doesn't know which image is the most astounding: his wife *agreeing* with Yasmin's that she's lucky to have him or Yasmin herself, whose sudden grief is so ... spectacular. He watches, mesmerized. A tear pauses in the hollow of her throat then trickles down to vanish in the mist between her breasts. Roebuck tastes salt.

"Why can't ordinary guys like Julius donate sperm?"

"Maybe they do ..."

"No. He's right! They don't." Yasmin has settled into a rhythmical, hiccupping pant.

"He doesn't know what he's talking about!" says Anne. "He never does!"

"No. He's right."

"Julius! I'm sure in your usual way you were just talking to hear yourself speak. I'm sure men like you would be willing to donate to a sperm bank."

"But I was only saying ..."

"Haven't you said enough?" Anne hisses, still fussing with the straps of Yasmin's dress. Roebuck attempts to pass another napkin.

"Well, all right," he says. "Sure, I guess, given ..."

You would?

"Yes, well, I mean ..."

"Oh, thank you!"

Yasmin has thrown her arms around Anne's neck. "Thank you! Thank you! Oh, you've saved my life! I can tell you now ..." She's still hiccupping, bubbling, panting her breath. Glistening. "Lately, you know, every time I cross the Leaside Bridge, I think to myself: Just climb over the rail, a few seconds ... But all that's over now! Oh Anne, I just can't thank you enough!"

"What?" Anne says.

Roebuck's tongue is stuck inside his mouth.

"I must have been somebody really, really good, in my last life, to deserve a friend like you!"

"Yasmin ..."

"It'll be just as if you were a normal donor!" Yasmin has aimed her attention back at Roebuck. "Except you're you. You donate it, I use it, and now I have a baby whose genes I know I can trust! It's so simple! Why didn't we think of this sooner?"

"Um, I don't think it's quite that ..."

Yasmin is staring at him hungrily. Anne has shifted her focus to stare at him too. Roebuck tries to articulate what he means to say, but his wife's look tells him to keep his mouth completely shut, so that's what he does. He clears his throat, picks up a salad bowl, and carries it into the kitchen.

Behind him, he hears the women talking.

7

Men are sperm, women are egg.
One is the wager, the other the stake.
The Collected Sayings of Julius Roebuck

Sun pours into his bedroom and Roebuck returns to consciousness, slowly, to the sound of Anne in the shower. He blinks, rubs his eyes, and checks the bedside clock. He's slept in. He draws a breath, puts both hands behind his head beneath the pillow, and feels the pressure of his back against the mattress. There was a time—not so long ago—when he woke aroused like this each and every morning. Not so often now, but still … He hears the water stop and in a little while the door to Anne's bedroom closing. Roebuck and his tumescence take their turn in the shower. It's Monday morning.

His car is in the centre lane, moving well for once at a steady 120 klicks. Roebuck knows it's dangerous fool around with buttons while he's driving so he activates the hands-free and tells it to connect to his number at the office. He is not what some would call an early adopter, but he appreciates this particular technology. He has just remembered that he wants to make a note; something that came out the other night, just before events began their tilt. Even as he was saying it, he recognized it as the kind of thought he should be writing down. He didn't, though he can hardly blame himself. Truth be told, in light of everything that happened after, he's more than a little proud of himself for recalling it or anything at all beyond ...

How did it go?

Reproduction. Yes. Roebuck clears his throat as the phone on the desk at his office begins to ring. He waits until he hears his own voice through the earpiece. "This is Julius Roebuck. Please leave a message ..."

"Branding," Roebuck says after the beep, "is not about moving the product on the shelf. It's about selling the product that isn't there." He is being careful to enunciate clearly, leaving space around each word. "Wait. No. Scratch that." There's a knot of traffic bunching up ahead; he eases off the gas. "Branding is about selling the product that replaces the product that's on the shelf today. Good. The focus of branding, like the focus of reproduction, is aimed wholly at the future. That'll do."

He disconnects. Not bad. So-so, anyway. He can tighten it later. Roebuck drums his fingers on the steering wheel.

His mind keeps sneaking back, though it knows it's not supposed to. His intention today is to focus on the intake meeting at Artemis, twenty minutes up the highway if the traffic keeps moving as nicely, as it has until now. Conscientiously, he checks the rearview mirror. There is Greenwood, five or six lengths behind, keeping pace. Roebuck is planning an early departure.

He has loaded all the account folks into Greenwood's car. That way they can get to know each other; nothing like a long commute for team building. Clients are always located in the suburbs, though Artemis, by a stretch, is farther out than most. For his part, Roebuck aims to avoid as much of this stage as possible, starting with ducking out this morning ahead of schedule. He needs some time alone. He's not supposed to be thinking about Yasmin; he is meant to be laser-focused on the brand. But his head keeps cycling back.

He has validated his conclusions over days and hours of critical assessment—every conscious moment, basically, between now and that astonishing dinner—sorting through the possibilities; linking up the dots. Roebuck is happy with the soundness of his reasoning. Though he still can't quite believe where it has led him: Yasmin wants his sperm. Which means, by logical extension, that Yasmin wants *him*.

It's the ironies surrounding this conclusion that give him qualms. He just wasn't thinking. It's that he finds it hardest to look back on: that his own stupidity could not have been more brilliant. The ringtone startles him. "You just missed the exit," says Greenwood's voice in his ear.

"Damn." Roebuck scans the GPS. "No." he says. "Next one's better." He really *had* intended them to take the exit they've just passed, but the screen is telling him the one ahead is four minutes faster. Everything, lately, is turning out for the better.

Roebuck examines his eyes in the rearview mirror. "Fool," he says and watches himself smile back.

The morning's first surprise is Zhanna Lamb, seated primly at the conference table in a pencil skirt and three-inch heels, not a flicker of anything passing between her and Greenwood, who must have known that she'd be there. "Well, now," Roebuck says shaking hands. "I was under the impression you had left the company."

"Zhanna has graciously agreed to stay with us a little longer to ensure a smooth transition," explains the CEO, shepherding him on to the next introduction. Several times throughout the meeting Roebuck tries catching Greenwood's eye, but Greenwood isn't playing.

It's not until noon that he manages his getaway. He has said everything he needs to say; there's a mountain of material still to go through, but for now the group is scheduled to break for lunch. Roebuck scrambles to his feet, BlackBerry in hand. "Unfortunately, something has come up. But I know that, with Daniel, I am leaving you in capable hands." He can't help sneaking a final peek at Zhanna, who gazes back with equal innocence, then delivers the morning's second surprise. "Would you mind if I asked for a lift? I'm taking the afternoon off too."

"I'm not taking the afternoon off!"

"Of course you're not. You have an agency to run. But I am. Can I hitch a ride?"

Generally speaking, these kick-off meetings are where the partnership between agency and client finally gets rolling. The analogy, for Roebuck, is like what happens once you've gone to bed together for the first time with a new lover. All that best behaviour leading up to consummation is behind you now—the deed is done—and true personalities are free to emerge. He tells the juniors that from this point forward it's all about the pulse of the relationship itself. It's now that clients reveal their business plans; this is when you see each other truly naked; when budgets are tabled and conflicts start to show. Maybe it's more like a marriage, he says. You've solemnized your vows; the ceremony's over. Now it's time to sort out who pays which bills.

He has also reminded the creative team that they'll need to brace themselves because, odds are, all that lovely work they've done so far is headed for the toilet. "In the courting stages, clients love you when you're bold and daring. But once the contract is signed, they'll expect you to settle down and see things exactly the way they do."

He and Greenwood have been planning for eventualities. Daniel's been in the business long enough to know the drill, still Roebuck has been surprised—pleasantly surprised—to see how firmly Greenwood is standing up, how determined he's become to make this campaign fly. Fire in the belly and all. That's the other reason he's decided to take an early leave and let this afternoon be the Greenwood Show. Later, if necessary, he can play the seasoned veteran, reigning in that youthful energy. But for now his gut is telling him that it's Greenwood who should be pushing things along.

"Any chance they'll keep the creative?" he asks, buckling up.

Zhanna all but snorts. "Are you kidding? It's a *condom* company. Daniel's in for major disappointment."

Roebuck sighs. They've left the parking lot and turned on to the service road that links Artemis to the highway, where they are waiting for the light.

"*You* really believe that stuff, though, don't you?"

"Sorry?"

"Your trademark shtick: 'Only women count.' Daniel thinks you really do believe it. He says that with you it's more than just a posture."

"As postures go, it's one you can take to the bank."

"He says he's never known anyone who tries so hard to think like a woman."

The light turns green; Roebuck accelerates toward the ramp. He doesn't know quite how to answer this. He's not sure, either, if he's enjoying having Greenwood's pillow talk served up secondhand. "I don't know if it's so much thinking *like* women as it is thinking *about* them. But now it's my turn. I have a question for you."

"All right." Her knees are pressed against the gearshift. She has turned as much as possible to face him. "Ask."

"How would you describe the sound of your shoes?"

"My *shoes* …?"

"When we took our break this morning and everyone went off to get coffee, I could *hear* you walking back. Before I could see you, I knew it was you. Everyone did. It was a clear, acoustical signature. There's a certain sound that high heels make that says 'beautiful woman approaching.' What I'm wondering is how to describe that sound."

She doesn't answer, though her body language tells him that she is not displeased. Roebuck refines the probe. "We all know what high heels do for a woman: Your legs get longer and your hips move forward and your butt pushes back and everything wonderful moves in all that mesmerizing magic. Everybody gets the visual. But there's an *auditory* appeal that might possibly be more interesting still. I've never had a shoe account, but if I were representing Christian Louboutin, say, or Manolo Blahnik, or Drogonie Claude, I think I'd seriously consider branding my client by sound."

"Clever."

He's not sure if she is commenting on the subtleness of his compliment or the concept itself. In either case, Roebuck agrees. "You haven't answered my question."

"You know there are classes you can take. Loads of websites, too, all about walking in heels. There are actual courses with practical lessons."

"Interesting. That *is* interesting … I wonder if they'd accept applications from men." Again he drums his fingers on the steering wheel. "Just between you and me," he says—because this last bit *has* startled her—"there *is* a high-end shoe company that is rumoured to be unhappy with its present agency. If the account comes up, I'm considering a pitch."

"So learning how to walk in high heel shoes would be …?"

"A glittering example of resumé-building. Clients eat up that kind of initiative. And by the way, I'm trusting you not to pass any of this on to your old friends at Artemis. They prefer to think our hearts belongs to them and no one else."

"Okay. I get how important it is for you to make your clients think that you believe it. That only women matter. But, really, do you?"

"Yes."

"In what way?"

"In every way."

This disappoints. "Nevertheless," he says, "it's true."

"We both know that claiming something is true is just a way of neutralizing counter-truths. That's another of those things they teach in biz school."

So the exchange of information goes two ways between Greenwood and Zhanna. "Hmm," he says. "Remind me to write that one down." He thinks about it seriously for a second, but doesn't want to break the flow. "So what's the truth I'm neutralizing?"

"That only you count."

"Men, you mean?" Roebuck laughs. "That's so last-century. Three-quarters of the people losing their jobs in this recession are male. We're in a post-industrial economy, and those jobs aren't coming back. For the first time ever, women outnumber men in the workforce. Way, way more women graduate from college than men, and every year the discrepancy gets bigger. Men are falling behind. Did you know that parents who choose the sex of their children are choosing to have girls more often than boys now? That's another first in human history. The new economy is female."

Zhanna waits him out. "I read your deck, remember? It's not men, plural, I'm asking about. I'm asking about one who's doing all the talking."

"Me? Me in particular? Well, of course it's true in *my* case!"

"And don't you think the same applies to other men?"

"Funny, my wife just asked the same question."

"What did you tell her?"

"That I don't speak for other men. Men are not my interest. My sole preoccupation is with women."

Zhanna brings her hands together in picturesque applause. "I'm sure that went over well."

"It's my job."

"And you think she believed *that*?"

"But it's true!"

"We were just talking about how conveniently one truth disguises another ..."

"Fair enough. So what am I disguising?"

"That your interest in women is not a function of your job. It's the other way around."

There's a snarl of traffic up ahead, and Roebuck is glad of it. "Here's what I think." They've come to a full stop, bumper to bumper; he powers down the window. "You're right. Absolutely. But I believe the same is true for all men. I think the grand truth we're disguising is that *everything* men do, we do for women. I think we're hard-wired to value nothing on earth more than we value women. All of us. I also think we spend enormous social energy trying to convince ourselves this isn't true, which is bullshit, in my opinion, and why I don't like to think about men. I prefer to do what I'm programmed to do, which is focus on women."

"Intently, by all accounts."

"Listen, you and I know as marketers that we're living in a culture that sanctifies everything female. Little girls go to school dressed in outfits hookers wouldn't have dared wear in their mothers' time. The rules for male comportment, meanwhile, have never been tighter. The only thing absolutely guaranteed to end a politician's career is to be caught cheating on his wife. They can embezzle, they can steal, they can lie; they can go to prison and still get themselves re-elected. But God help them if they're ever caught unzipped with an admin assistant."

"I'm guessing that's why you decided not to go into politics."

"It's not just politics! It's religious leaders, marquee athletes, movie stars; never mind the Bill Clintons, it's any guy at the top of his game. The interesting thing about them is all the editorializing that goes out afterwards. 'He worked so hard, he sacrificed so much to get to the top, and then he threw it all away!' It all so misses the point. The point of being an alpha male is that alpha males get females. There *is* no other point. We don't gather riches and power and fame in order to gather riches and power and fame. Only psychopaths are into power for power's sake. We work our asses off to get all that stuff because that stuff gets us women. The prize is always women. There's no game worth playing if the prize isn't women. That's why politicians are always so pathetic—the male ones, I mean—they have to be geldings to do their job, but politics is no game for geldings."

"Then why are most of them still men?"

"Ah. Now we're back to my area of expertise. Good. I'll tell you why. Because politics—contemporary politics, at least—doesn't give women what they want. So most women sensibly avoid it."

"I'm afraid to ask. What do women want?"

Roebuck hesitates and then ploughs ahead. "Stuff. Goods. Hard assets. Securities. That, and the validation that they *deserve* the things they get. Which is, by the way, the central premise of the advertising industry. But you know that part already."

"For a second, there, I was thinking you had a romantic streak."

"I'm in advertising. Of course I'm a romantic. It's you guys on the client side who take the darker view." He falters, but rallies again. "Want to know the real deal between the sexes? It's this. Throughout human history men have used stuff to get women, and women have used men to get stuff. That's the deal. That's the human equation. That's what's been the basis of our relationship since we climbed down from the trees. Since before we climbed down from the trees.

What's new, though—and for the first time in history—is that human females don't need males to get stuff anymore. Now they can get it all on their own and—more importantly—spend it, which is where my professional interest comes into play. Yours too."

The brake lights on the car in front blink off, and traffic starts to move. Roebuck veers into the other lane to get a better view, but there is nothing to be seen. A little while goes by in silence. Too bad.

She reaches into her handbag, opens up her phone, stares, and puts it back. "I was class president, you know, in high school."

"Doesn't surprise me. Funny, my wife ran the council at her school too. She's a great debater."

"Also at university, I was into student politics. In those days I gave some serious thought to a career in politics. Tell me then, why didn't I?"

"Because your beauty and intelligence combined to inform you that you could do better. Please don't take that as a compliment." He wants to reach up and tilt the rearview mirror so he can meet her, eye to eye. "It's a statement of pure objective truth," he says. "Men go into politics because they're hard-wired to believe that power and authority will also bring them women. That's why their careers flame out so often once they get what they want. Women are motivated differently. Power and celebrity—without the *stuff* that supposed to come with it—doesn't cut it. Believe me when I tell that the world would be a better place if women ran it. Honestly. But there are just too many better ways for a woman to get what she wants than through politics. Most women aren't interested. They're far better off as MBAs like you."

"Or ad execs, like you?"

"Except that we males are programmed by a billion years of evolution to do whatever it takes to attract the attention of women. We have a natural advantage in the field of advertising."

"So Daniel's been telling me. Antlers on the elk, fire in the firefly, et cetera."

"Full marks to Greenwood."

She is quiet for a spell. "I'll concede some truth is possible in what you say, but you're wrong about the bigger picture. Maybe someday I *will* run for office."

"When I was a kid, I wanted to be a novelist. Maybe someday I'll go back to unpaid scribbling. Meantime, what do you plan to do with yourself, now you've given up peddling safes?"

"Peddle something else, I guess. That's what I do. But first I think I'll travel for a while. I've never seen India. Maybe Nepal ..."

"Food for the soul."

"You know I can't decide if you're a genuine cynic or just another asshole romantic in hiding."

"All cynics are romantics at heart, so either way you've nailed me."

"You see yourself as a romantic?"

"I spent *my* university years trying to define that term. Never did. Closest I can come, I think, is to say that a romantic is someone who understands the value of beauty. There are stricter definitions, sure. But that one works for me."

"This should be interesting. How does Julius Roebuck define beauty?"

He turns his head and holds her eyes for as long as the road permits. "You," he says. "That really should be obvious."

They pass a police car parked on the shoulder, lights flashing. A man in a turban sits in the cab of a dump truck, massaging his dastar. "You wouldn't think," says Roebuck, "that that would be enough to stop traffic." The towers of the city rise and shimmer in the heat ahead. They've worked back up to speed again.

"Don't take it personally. I mean that. It's not you individually. It's just that there's nothing in the world more beautiful than a beautiful woman. I'll tell you a story."

"I'm told you have a story for everything."

"There *is* a story for everything. But this one's about me so it's especially apt."

They have reached the outskirts of the city proper, entering the canyon of new condominiums. Construction cranes are working everywhere, pulling towers of glass up through the rubble of yesterday's mortar and brick. Every surface here is clad in mirror. She has told him that she's planning to go shopping. Roebuck has agreed to drop her at an intersection not far from his office.

"When I was young and travelling," he says, "the focus was still Europe. Nowadays people head to the East, but in my day it was Paris and London and Rome. So picture me in the Vatican, Sistine Chapel, to be precise, taking in the splendours. Except there's this girl …" Their exit is coming up; Roebuck interrupts himself to execute a lane change. "She's Scandinavian, I think, though she could have been from Winnipeg, for all I know. I never heard her speak. The key was that she's beautiful. Not one-in-a-million beautiful, just ordinary everyday beautiful. Beautiful enough, though, to be more interesting than anything painted on plaster or carved into marble. So there's our twenty-something Julius, telling himself to pay attention to *The Creation of Adam* and *The Last Judgement*, and all those amazing Botticellis, but who keeps looking at this girl—this ordinary girl—who is still more beautiful and fascinating that anything Michelangelo ever made, or could, or anybody else. That was my lesson, that day, that there is nothing on earth more beautiful than women."

"You never outgrew it?"

He barks a laugh. "Fact is, everything I've learned since then has reinforced it. I *have* seen the Himalayas. I've watched the sun go down over the Serengeti, and the moon on the canals of Venice, et cetera, et cetera. All that good stuff. All those things that are supposed to be beautiful. They *are* beautiful. They are. But there's no painting, no sculpture, no glorious sunset or pristine mountain that's as beautiful as a beautiful woman."

"And you can't fuck a mountain, after all."

For the second time that day, Roebuck misses his exit. It takes him several moments to come to terms with the depth of his appreciation. "That," he says, reorienting, "was the best thing … that was … perfect." He cranes his neck, changes lanes, and shoots down the next ramp. They will have to work their way back now from the opposite direction. He's still chuckling, still shaking his head when they reach their intersection. Roebuck pulls the car into an empty taxi stand. "If I ever write my memoir," he says, "that'll be the title. *You Can't Fuck a Mountain.* Zhanna, you're amazing."

"Thanks." She pulls her cellphone from her bag and checks the time. "Plans for lunch?"

For a moment, for a nanosecond there, he thinks about proposing *Alison's*. But Roebuck is a man of principle. "Regrettably," he says, "I have another appointment."

"Daniel! Daniel! Dan?"

Roebuck is striding down the hall toward his office, calling as he goes, then remembers that Greenwood is still at the intake meeting out at Artemis. He goes back to his desk, opens up the intranet and checks relevant schedules. There's an hour block that works tomorrow afternoon. Roebuck books Greenwood and his creative team for a meeting in his office. "SHOE ACCOUNT???" he taps into the subject line. "IDEATION …"

When he looks at his inbox, he finds a note from Zhanna Lamb.

DRAG AND CLOP

That's the sound a heel makes on pavement. A dragging
sound, followed by a clop. Problem with your marketing
concept: How to make drag and clop sexy? Know you'll
think of something. Thx for the ride. Z

Roebuck re-opens the intranet, erases what he's written, and
types DRAG AND CLOP?

Daniel Greenwood is a lucky man. He is fond of Daniel
Greenwood.

Roebuck opens the door that night to a house full of balloons. All
red; all wearing happy faces above the lettering in brazen pink:
"THANKS!!!" Anne is limp in the centre of the room, wordless.
There are dozens, no, hundreds, nudging at the ceiling, trailing
ribbons like the tails of jostling sperm. Is the imagery deliberate
or is this just his own interpretation? He is learning not to underestimate Yasmin's natural talents. Roebuck herds them together
and pushes them in bunches out the door. Threads of carmine
tadpoles stream toward the setting sun.

They had decided—he and Anne together—that their first, best
hope was Yasmin's waking up with sober second thoughts. "I'm
sure that once she understands how uncomfortable this is," Anne
said, "she'll just drop the whole idea."

"*I* was the one uncomfortable. You were the one making it
worse!"

"Please don't start that again."

That was Saturday night, the acrid end of long deliberations in
the wake of Yasmin's raptures. Sunday: silence. Monday: a house-
ful of balloons.

He has seldom seen Anne so utterly speechless, though she wasn't that night. But this is no time for pity. "It's all your doing," he says, standing in the doorway.

"Oh, God! Please don't keep saying that. What are we going to do?"

"I don't see what else we *can* do. I don't see what other choice you've left us."

He still can't quite believe it. He still can't believe how this has come together. "No," he'd blurted in blind refusal. "Yasmin, get that idea right out of your head." She had stared at him, trembling, then collapsed into another spasm of tears. And then Anne, his own wife, Anne, who even then—even in circumstances as unequivocal as these—could not resist her role as spousal opposition. "Julius, please!"

What he recalls is the cramp of betrayal, the feeling of connectedness spinning apart. Yasmin had recommenced her rhythmic moan, face down on the tablecloth. How could she? How could Anne fail to take his side, even in a thing like this? Dumbstruck, Roebuck retreated to the bathroom.

It was then as he remembers it, just then, seated numbly on the john, that he recollected his appointment at the No Fuss Vasectomy Clinic at four o'clock this Wednesday afternoon. The spinning stopped, turned, and began to rotate in the opposite direction. Roebuck sat on a little longer, weighing probability.

"All right," he said, rejoining the women. "If that's what you both want, I'm prepared to do it."

"Julius!" cried Yasmin, surging to her feet.

"*Julius?*" said Anne.

"Oh, Julius!" purred Yasmin, arms now clasped around his neck.

Later that night, much later, they had faced the situation objectively, he and Anne, and decided that for now there was nothing they could do. It was wait and see, at this stage. The rest of the weekend came and went: Morgan had a soccer match; Katie a friend's birthday party; Anne, as usual, arranged the buying and wrapping of an age-appropriate gift. Roebuck mowed the lawn and washed the car and drove out to the soccer pitch. On Sunday afternoon he put in two good hours at the gym; Anne managed a few sets of tennis.

Monday afternoon: clarity.

"This is all your doing," says Roebuck, standing in the doorway, spilling red balloons into the willing sky.

8

A novel is a month with a woman you love.
A short story is a weekend with a woman you like.
A newspaper is an hour with a call girl.
A blog is four minutes with a heroin hooker.
Copywriting is the same again, except you're the one
giving the blow job.
The Collected Sayings of Julius Roebuck

Greenwood likes the idea from the start, or almost the start, a fortunate thing for them both because the meeting at Artemis has returned him to work flatter than spilt beer. Roebuck has occupied his art director's office bright and early Tuesday morning with a pot of coffee and two cups on a platter. It's obvious, glancing around, that Daniel's being kept too busy to have achieved much in the way of workspace decor. ADs, in Roebuck's experience, tend to cover every surface with gaudy prints and blocks of edgy, out-of-focus close-ups. All that Greenwood has got up so far is his picture of the condom and the screw—the same board he showed the client—and a framed poster Roebuck recognizes, but hasn't seen in decades. He stands with his coffee mug, studying it. It's a dappled photo of a spotted fawn, sleeping peacefully on a forest floor above the text: "If you love something, set it free. If it comes back to you, it's yours. If it doesn't, it never was." The image sends Roebuck straight back to his student days.

"Five minutes after you left," says Greenwood, tossing his jacket on a chair and accepting a mug from Roebuck's tray, "they sat me down with the VP, Brand Engagement." Greenwood drops into the seat behind his desk. "She just couldn't wait to tell me how much she loved the campaign. *Loved it! Loved* our ideas. Loved, loved, *loved* all the original thinking, and all that bold imagination! Thought it was just so awesome …"

Roebuck is still gazing at the poster. He sets down the empty tray. "But now," he says, "they were very pleased to take this opportunity to provide you with some insight on how your boards could be improved."

"You got it." Greenwood is rubbing his face, eyes squeezed shut. "Starting with the teasers. *Such a terrific idea!* So cool. So totally out-of-the-box. *Wow!* They just loved the concept. She went on and on about how everyone thought it was *so creative* …"

"But they think it might be just a tad offensive."

Greenwood is speaking from behind his fingers. He opens his eyes, one at a time and retrieves his cup. "She said they worry how something that aggressive can ever earn consumers' trust."

"Valid point."

"But that *was* the point, leveraging mistrust! Losing that will gut the whole campaign."

"It's okay, Dan. We'll push back. This always happens, you know that. Clients need to see that you can think outside the box so that when they stuff you back inside it, you'll still come up with something worth their money. That's how it works."

"Yeah but ..."

"Don't worry about that right now. There's something else I want to talk about. Have you checked your calendar?"

"I just walked in."

Roebuck looks at his watch.

"They kept me out there last night till way past dinner time!"

"When you do get around to starting your day ..."

"I'd have started by now if you ..."

"You'll note that you are booked for a two o'clock meeting."

Greenwood has booted up and is peering at his screen. "Drag and Clop. What the hell?"

"You can thank your friend Zhanna for that."

"Zhanna?"

"I gave her a lift from Artemis. It was only yesterday."

"Right. So much went on after you guys left. What does Zhanna have to do with ..." He stares at the screen "Drag and Clop?"

"That's the sound of high heels."

"Can I ask what is it with you and women's shoes?"

"No names mentioned, strictly between you and me for the time being, but a certain producer of high-end women's footwear may be unhappy with its present image in the marketplace."

"You're looking to pitch a shoe account?"

"I congratulate myself daily for the wisdom of your hire."

"I repeat, what is it with you and women's shoes?"

"Listen, nobody has ever marketed shoes by *sound*. I'm thinking it's a whole new model of branding."

"Drag and clop?" Are you kidding me?"

"Think of it like a mating call."

"And there you go again with the mating calls ..."

"Zhanna pointed out the problem. How do you make drag and clop sexy?"

"What *is* drag and clop?"

"You're not listening. It's the sound of high heel shoes. A *drag* sound, followed by a *clop* sound. That's the first order of business, to run some acoustics. But I think she's pretty much nailed it. You haven't talked to her since yesterday?"

"No."

"Clever girl. Incredibly insightful. She should run for office."

"Zhanna? In politics? There's a thought." Greenwood squints again. "But I think I'm beginning to hear what you're saying. The sound of high heel shoes, in action …"

"Picture a woman walking in heels," says Roebuck. "Got it? What we're looking for is the sound she's creating. Now imagine her walking toward you down a sidewalk, say, or the terrazzo floor of a shopping mall."

"All right." Greenwood's eyes snap open. "Interesting. Automatically, *automatically*, I'm seeing her as attractive."

"Is it the heels or the way she's walking?"

"For the purpose of this exercise I would say there's no distinction."

Roebuck nods and scribbles a note. Greenwood has settled back into his chair. "Okay. I do hear a kind of a dragging sound—as the hard part of the heel scrapes along the ground. Then the rest of the foot comes down. That would be your *clop*, I guess." His face has softened and the corners of his lips turn up.

"Look at you" Roebuck says. "You're smiling!"

"It *is* pleasurable, that sound."

"I bet if we put a monitor on you, it'd show your heart rate spiking. Your frontal cortex is getting a major hit of oxytocin."

"Worth running some tests. Client pay?"

"There is no client, Daniel. Not at present. But I admire your instinct. For the sake of argument, let's say there is a client, and the client has money for a television campaign."

"Drag and clop … Not the most lyrical of phrases."

"But maybe we don't have to use it as a phrase. Maybe we rely on the sound itself? Do we need to say it in words? Make a high-fidelity recording of a model walking down a runway, enhance the acoustics, and play with that?"

"Like the background beat in the soundtrack? I get it. Sure, it's definitely percussive. Sort of like the drum track in a piece of music. There's a rhythm."

"Good! I like that." Roebuck swirls the coffee in his mug like wine. "Though there's something about drag and clop I also like. It's so clunky, so ugly. The client would hate it. Guaranteed to get attention."

"That's your technique, isn't it? Piss them off then talk them around."

"Seems to work."

But Greenwood isn't listening. "I'm thinking about your mating calls." He sits up straighter, hands on his knees, fingers tapping. "What if we use animals?"

"Animals? What, wearing stilettos?"

"It's *your* idea! Antlers on the moose, mane on the lion; all that crap you're always on about. They're all some form of mating call. You said so yourself!"

Greenwood is on his feet. "Here's what I'm seeing." He comes to a stop in the centre of the room, hands poised mid-air like a conductor stretching the hold between notes. "Opening frame is your classic nature-shot: A moose, say, standing in a pool of lily pads, water streaming off his head as he lifts it up out of the water. *Natural Geographic* stuff. We hear the sound of a moose call. Moose make mating calls, don't they?"

Roebuck has to think. "Yes. Hunters use moose calls, so moose must too. Yes, definitely. Moose make mating calls."

"Then they're likely to be loud. Perfect. When he hears the call, our moose turns his massive head, immediately searching for the source of the sound. Then the image changes. To what? To a lion! Do lions call?"

"I don't know …"

"What animals call?"

"Well, birds. Lots of birds … Wolves. Wolves howl."

"Wolves! Wolves are good! Yeah. Wolves are perfect. So now we see a wolf, gliding through his forest. Suddenly we hear a howl, off screen—everybody recognizes a wolf howl—and instantly our wolf stops dead and turns to look. What other animals? We need a few. What other animals make good mating howls?"

"What am I, Marlin Perkins?"

"Who's Marlin Perkins?"

"Never mind. How about loons? Loons make excellent calls."

"Not sure. Loons have a bit of an image, but maybe that's good. Whatever. Let's go with loons for now. Same style of shot, then, but this time it's a loon, paddling around on some glittering lake. He hears that famous call and frantically points his bill, searching … searching … Maybe he fluffs his feathers, looking eager. Or maybe there's a group of loons, suddenly all getting worked up. With me? It's a sequence of shorts, all animals—four or five different kinds, if we can squeeze them in—all responding to mating calls, all of them hard-wired by instinct to follow that sound."

"I see what you're saying. But where is it taking me?"

"So here comes the finale. Underneath it all we lay down your drag and clop soundtrack; running right through the whole segment. Very faint at the beginning; so soft you can hardly hear it in the moose sequence. But getting louder as the spot goes on. By the last vignette—the loon or the wolf or whatever—it's definitely audible, but it's still a mystery to the audience because it doesn't fit, this weird sound threading through the background of all these Nature Channel images. The last one's the reveal. Suddenly there's a woman on-screen. Or maybe we never even see the woman herself, just her feet—that might be effective—she's wearing the brand of shoe we're marketing, walking, walking … Drag and clop, drag and clop goes the soundtrack, and now we've identified the source of that incongruous sound. With me so far?"

Roebuck spins a finger.

"Okay, so the very last sequence—the scene that everything else that's happened so far has been teeing-up—is a man ... or possibly a group of men ... sitting in a café, let's say. They're minding their own business, intent on whatever they're doing, talking, laughing—until they hear that sound: that mesmerizing sound of a woman walking by in heels. The instant they hear it, the very second, they stop, they freeze, all of them stare in the same direction—just like all the other animals we've been watching—because nothing else matters now, but locating the source of that sound. Then we run the tag. Call of the Wild or something like that, alongside the logo. What do you think?"

"Call of the Wild ... That's good! You could build a whole campaign around a theme like that. I definitely like Call of the Wild. Wonder if the copyright's expired? Jack London's been dead at least a century. Funny, Zach and I read it just last week."

Greenwood isn't listening. "The premise is that the sound our product makes appeals straight to men's animal instincts. The reptilian brain, and all. There's a lot you can play with. And you're right; it would be fun to pitch. It'd be one for the history books, for sure, if we could get away with it. It could do well on the Net."

"Agreed!" Roebuck is up on his feet now, too. "But I'm a little worried about all that nature footage. Not exactly up our alley. Where'd we get the video? It would cost a fortune to commission."

"You'd be surprised how much of that stuff is out there in stock. Some of these wildlife guys spend weeks in the woods, filming, hiding in the bushes, and what not. For them that's the money shot. That's how they make their living."

"How do you know all this?"

"It's my job."

"So it is." Roebuck returns his mug to the tray and does the same with Greenwood's. "Where did you find that poster?"

Greenwood follows Roebuck's eyes to the image of the sleeping fawn. "Isn't it great! I picked it up in one of those secondhand shops down in the Junction. It's from sometime in the eighties, I think. So retro. Clients will appreciate the irony."

They intended something quite apart from irony, in Roebuck's memory, those girls who taped that poster to the dorm walls of his youth. "So we're set then. Good. I'll be curious to hear what the rest of the group thinks."

"See you at two!" says Greenwood, smirking at his fawn.

⟲⟳

At 1:45 PM Anne walks past the receptionist and straight into Roebuck's office. "News." She seats herself in the chair on the near side of his desk.

Roebuck pushes away his work. "I'm guessing it starts with a Y?" They study one another carefully.

"She's been in touch with several clinics. Apparently, if you want to be a donor ..."

"Which I absolutely don't."

"...there's a protocol. The clinic has to run a background check, test your blood, analyze your sperm, and so on. Then there's a waiver and a bunch of legal disclaimers you'll have to sign."

"You know as well as I do ..."

"Yes! *Exactly!*"

But what, exactly, she means to say is postponed for the moment by the appearance of Daniel Greenwood, striding through the door of Roebuck's office. "The meeting's here, I take it. Oh, sorry!" Greenwood has skidded to a halt on Roebuck's Tibetan rug. "I didn't know you were with someone."

"Daniel, you haven't met my wife. Anne, meet Daniel Greenwood. Daniel is shaping up to be a major acquisition."

"Hello, Daniel."

"A pleasure to meet you, Anne."

Roebuck has risen to his feet and come around his desk. "Daniel," he says, "I'm sorry to say that something has come up. I'm going to ask you to flesh out your ideas with the team. By all means use this office, but Matrix Two is also available if you would be more comfortable there. You've floated some interesting concepts. Listen to what the juniors have to say and, remember, this is only ideation. There's no actual client for the present."

Anne, too, has risen to her feet and is standing beside her husband by the door. Roebuck takes her elbow and steers them through.

"Nice to meet you, Daniel," she says over her shoulder.

Roebuck leads his wife to a bistro down the block. "I didn't ask you if you've eaten."

"I have," she says. "Yasmin needed lunch. But I could use a glass of wine."

"I didn't want to have this conversation in the office. Daniel can handle things for an hour or so. Besides, we haven't been to lunch in months, just the two of us."

"He's so young!"

"Daniel? Older than he looks. He's been around. More and more, I'm thinking he's an ideal fit."

A server comes to take their order. Roebuck has already had a sandwich at his desk. They settle on a bottle of house white and a bowl of frites to share.

He's had the time to think things over and has decided that from here on in, it's equilibrium. He will be content, from this point forward, to leave matters in the hands of fate. "I'll tell you one thing," he says, pouring for them both. "There's no way I'm adding myself to the roster of a ..." even the words feel uncomfortable, "... sperm bank. I just don't have time for that. To say nothing of inclination."

"That's exactly what I told her! Julius, don't you see? This is our out!" Anne is looking happier than he's seen her in ages. "She can't expect you to put yourself at the service of some ..."

"You think?"

"Yes! Yes, absolutely!"

"Well, it's true. I *don't* have time to take off work and sit around ..." Roebuck lets the sentence finish itself. "I'm just not prepared to get into all that."

"And I don't see why you should! That's exactly what I said to Yasmin. I said, Yasmin, Julius has an advertising agency to run. You can't expect him to go through all that ... performance."

"What did she say?"

"Well, she was disappointed, of course. But she agreed that you're a busy man. I think it's finally sunk in, how completely unreasonable she's being."

"What else?"

"What do you mean what else?"

"What else did she say?"

"That's it. That she knows you're very busy and that she understands that you want nothing to do with being a supplier, or donor, or whatever they call it."

"It seems a little inconclusive ..."

"Not at all. If we stand firm on this, Julius, that's that. This is our solution."

"Well, you know better."

"I do. And I think that we can finally put all this behind us."

"I'll drink to that."

Anne raises her glass. They touch rims across the table.

"God, it's such a relief!"

9

Women recognize. Men discover.
The Collected Sayings of Julius Roebuck

Wednesday morning is a restful one in light of what's ahead. Roebuck spends it on the telephone, reassuring clients that he thinks about them night and day. It's religion with him, keeping up connections. Come a weekday morning, and Julius Roebuck is likely to call out of the blue, just to say hello. Mostly it's the upper levels—Presidents, VPs, CEOs—though he always keeps a bright light burning for the good folks in the dimmer echelons as well. And it's true that he genuinely understands their business: Roebuck really does think about his clients every waking hour. He is almost always ready with some useful piece of information he's picked up to pass along.

All morning, he's been monitoring email. Nothing so far from Lily, which means by now the light must be green. It's not uncommon for one of them to have to cancel last minute. But if something had come up, she'd have let him know by now. Roebuck has ensured that his own afternoon is in no way double-booked. He is contemplating whether to use the flower shop just down the street or a better one he knows on the far side of the viaduct when the phone on his desk lights up. For a moment he's afraid it's Lily calling to cancel, but this is the internal line.

"I have someone here to see you," the receptionist says.

"I'm just heading into a meeting." Roebuck makes a mental note to have another chat about the functions of front desk personnel. "Who is it?"

"She says she's your designer. She says to say it's Yasmin."

It strikes Roebuck with an almost physical shock that the woman who walks into his office is the same one he was conjuring with Greenwood only yesterday. Exactly what his mind's eye was presenting.

"Hello, Julius. What are you mumbling?"

"Yasmin. Hello." Roebuck hurries to the door to head her off before she gets too far inside. "Only that I'm just on my way out." He stops, steps back, and offers up a formal handshake.

Yasmin takes his hand and slips behind him and into his chair, crossing an eternity of naked leg. "Then I won't keep you." One shoe dangles in the way of women who loll their pumps so perfectly. Roebuck breathes her scent. He perches on the edge of his desk and looks pointedly at the clock, certain that his pupils are dilating and his nostrils commencing to flutter. "Allergies," he says, fishing out a Kleenex. It's unlikely she dressed like this for lunch with Anne. Then again, she might have. Yasmin is more and more an unknown quality.

"I know you're busy, so I'll come straight to the point."

"Honestly, Yasmin. Really, it's ..."

"We don't have to use a clinic."

"Sorry?"

He watches her rise from the chair and step in close, just short of touching. "If you have a problem with a clinic," she says, "we don't have to use one. In fact, it's easier this way." She has positioned herself with her feet between his legs. There's nowhere for Roebuck to retreat. Yasmin takes his hand in both of hers.

"Yasmin. I …"

"Next week," she says, lowering her voice—Roebuck feels something warm pressed against his palm—"next week is when it happens."

"Next week?" His voice has died away from want of oxygen.

"Next week," she whispers, "I'm *ovulating*."

It takes him several heartbeats to understand that the thing in his hand is a plastic receptacle. Roebuck gazes at it mutely. Yasmin strokes the inside of his wrist. What he's holding is a squat transparent jar like the one his doctor provides when he needs a sample for Roebuck's yearly physical. There's a paper seal with a label and an orange lid. He can feel her breath against his ear. "I'm *regular*," she murmurs, "so I *know* it's going to be next week. I'll monitor my temperature, and when I'm certain, I'll call. You just …" she walks her fingers up the jar; Roebuck feels it rocking in his palm, "…then I'll wrap it up and take it home."

She steps away and smooths her dress. "I know you're in a hurry, so I'll be on my way. But the thing is, Julius, if you want …" Yasmin has paused in the doorway. "If you want, we don't have to tell Anne. We can do this any way you want to do it."

They have never been the kind of couple who fall instantly to bed. They'll talk before, during, and afterwards, too, time permitting. The relationship is highly verbal. But today he is hardly through the door before he has his hand beneath her skirt and her panties pushed below her knees. "Julius!" she says, hands against his shoulders. He has lifted her against the wooden casement of the fireplace, the fabric of her skirt caught up around her waist. "My goodness!" says Lily. Roebuck groans.

"Only you ..." But the act of considering how this sentence ought to end calms him so that he is able to withdraw and begin again more carefully and so acquit himself over the next few minutes—very few minutes, still—without too much cause for self-recrimination.

"Okay," he says, recovering his breath and kicking off his shoes. "I owe you one."

"How long have you got?"

Roebuck lifts her arm and looks at Lily's watch. "I absolutely need to be out the door by three-fifteen. Latest."

"Then I absolutely intend to collect. But first," she says, pulling him by the hand, "I've made some lunch."

He has always loved her kitchen—pumpkin pine, raw ceramics, pots of basil in the windows facing south—her whole house, for that matter, a tiny east-end semi so different from his own. She has left her skirt and panties in the crumpled heap where he dropped them by the hearth and stands in the sunlight by the counter cutting bread, the tails of her long, loose cotton shirt trailing down her thighs. She's humming.

Weighing his timing, Roebuck clears his throat, clasps his hands behind his back, and like a schoolboy from another era solemnly declaims a verse he has been saving for a time just like today.

> The modest Rose puts forth a thorn,
> The Humble Sheep a threat'ning horn:
> While the Lilly white shall in Love delight,
> Nor a thorn, nor a threat, stain her beauty bright.

"Delight? Did you say *delight*? You fuck me on the woodstove, come before I even know you're there, and now you're at me with William Blake? You're too much," she says, popping a heart of artichoke into his mouth and licking the oil she has spilled beneath his lip.

Roebuck, chewing, marshals his reply. " 'He who desires but acts not, breeds pestilence.' Besides," he says, reflecting, "that's not a woodstove. I would describe it as a traditional brick fireplace."

"A *scratchy* brick fireplace. And don't get me started on pestilence."

" 'The Eternal Female Groan'd! / It was heard all over the Earth.' That one," he says, "I admire in particular."

"Enough! Seriously! Enough with the Blake. Everything that guy ever wrote was rant. The only interest Blake ever had in any ideas outside his own was to refute them."

"I like rant."

"Well, at least that's vaguely original."

What he adores about Lily is that she loves this pointless, lowbrow banter every bit as much as he does. Arguing for them is like sex: pleasure for pleasure's sake alone, or so he's always thought.

"What are you working on?"

Always, always he is flattered when she offers him her pages, tracing with a finger over passages she feels are not quite right, sounding out her cadence like a brush against his ear. Roebuck listens with his own eyes closed, sublimating syntax. On a good day he will offer a word she hadn't yet considered and marvel at the jolt of pleasure if she pauses, tries it on her tongue, then nods, and writes it in. Roebuck keeps copies of every magazine and journal Lily's verses have appeared in—tucked into careful nooks and crannies at his office or mixed discreetly with the books and periodicals that line his bedroom shelves—though he does not share her admiration for most of her contemporaries. Interchangeable, he tells her, as the voices of the boy bands his daughter makes him listen to on their morning drive to school. But he loves what Lily writes, and quotes it back to her by heart.

She sighs, and he hears suppressed regret. "That's on the back burner for now. It's strictly meat and potatoes this week. The McCann gig ramped up sooner than expected. They wanted me in today, but I told them I had a doctor's appointment."

He is startled by the overlapping fictions and very nearly blurts out where he's going, once he leaves this house. "What's the job?" he asks instead.

"Boring. I'll show you after we eat. Pays the bills. Which reminds me, I haven't asked about your onboarding session at Artemis. How'd that go?"

"They're throwing out the creative."

She pauses, a tactful pause, and stirs her soup. "That might not be such a bad thing."

It cuts both ways with Lily. If she values his input, his esteem for hers is even higher. Roebuck waits a little longer while she fishes out a sprig of thyme, balanced on a wooden spoon, considering her words. Lily has a way with tone. He sent her jpegs of the presentation, asking for her thoughts.

"The execution's very sharp. Your new guy definitely has an eye. I just wonder where the concept is taking you."

"Meaning?"

"I think you are shading a little too far into the exploitive."

He knows there's more she means to say. Lily places the spoon on a dish beside the pot, then puts her arm around his waist, and leans against him. "Don't you think," she asks, "that there's enough acrimony out there already without you creating more?"

"It's only branding."

He has chosen his reply as deliberately as she has phrased her question. They have ploughed this ground before, the two of them. Branding—as she has more than once reminded him—is what cowpokes do to cattle to establish ownership of meat. "In this context," Roebuck counters, "all it means is getting people attached to something through emotion. That's all it is, Lily. And anger is as valid an emotion as any."

"Valid," she says. "Tried and true. Hitler got people attached to his ideas by getting them to hate the Jews. You're motivating women to buy your product by setting them against their boy-friends, even husbands ..."

This makes him smile. "Since when are you a defender of husbands?"

When it is clear there will be no reply, he tries another tack. "There's a rule in debating, you know, that says if you bring Nazis into it, you lose automatically."

"So I lose automatically?"

He wants to take the ladle and stir the soup himself, but Roebuck holds his ground. "I'll waive it for today because you make a useful point. Sure, Goebbels tapped into a pre-existing well of anti-Semitism and malignantly pumped it for all it was worth. Am I doing the same with women and men? All right. Yes. Women have always been pissed off with men; that's the historical truth I'm exploiting. But consider it from our perspective. Or mine, at least."

"Give me a sec to brace myself this time."

"Men of my generation have made enormous efforts to make the world a better place for women. We've gone so far as to become like women ourselves, the better to level the field. So what hap-pens? Exactly what was supposed to happen. Women have caught up. Or if they haven't yet, they soon will. But somehow they're more pissed off than ever. The difference now is that they also have the economic power to express their anger. And boy, do they ever. But it's kind of a drag for the guys of my era who really thought that what they were doing was a good thing. So you can't really blame us for making the best of a bad situation by using it to sell you stuff. There's got to be a silver lining somewhere."

"Fuck, do you spin."

"Self-depreciating, is all. You women have been self-depreciating from the get-go. We're just catching up. Know what I adore about you?" he asks, watching as she rolls up the sleeves of her shirt, one and then the other.

"Uh-oh."

"That you don't argue first-person. Nine out of ten women would have shot back that *they* weren't angry with men, meaning to say that they'd just blown my argument out of the water."

"That's because I'm not angry with men in general. Only with you, in particular. Which, by the way, invalidates your previous statements."

"See what I mean? Is that soup ready?"

"In a rush?"

"Anyhow, they're throwing out the creative. So we're back to rewriting the brief."

She hands him the bottle of Riesling he'd brought along with the flowers and hunts for a corkscrew. It occurs to him to wonder if he's meant to be abstaining. Or not eating, either, come to think of it, before the procedure. He can't recall seeing anything about this on the clinic's website. Roebuck checks the clock on Lily's stove.

"Cheers," he says, handing her a glass. She is busy with the bowls and ladle so he sets it out of harm's way on the counter. Sunlight pours through the window while tendrils of steam weave around Lily's naked arms, beading on the inside of her wrist. She is humming again.

"God," he says, "you can be beautiful."

"And you could sell Christmas trees on Boxing Day."

The bowls are placed, steaming, on the table. Lily lifts her chin, deliberately, meets his eyes, and holds them. "After we eat," she says, "I have something else in mind for that nimble tongue of yours."

Roebuck clasps his hands above his heart and bows. "*Salute*," he says, savouring the diction of this narrative, too.

10

Intelligence begins with doubt and ends with certainty.
The Collected Sayings of Julius Roebuck

He awakes with blood in his jockstrap. Roebuck listens for the sound of Anne in the shower and, wincing, pulls on a pair of pants and a shirt—then remembers to check the sheets. No blood. He did indeed take sleeping pills last night. No mistruth on that account. But the Ambien on top of all the Ibuprofen has left his stomach lurching up toward his throat. The throb in Roebuck's head is almost as unnerving as the pounding in his scrotum.

He cups his balls and presses his face against the doorjamb. There are several issues—unanticipated issues—he needs to contend with. Starting with the fact that he's been shaved. He should have asked how long pubic hair takes to regrow. But things, by that stage, were already heading south. More immediately, there's the question of what to do about the peas.

The nurse had made it clear upfront that she was not an ally.

"You were supposed to do this yourself," she'd said, rasping his groin like a motorist scraping ice from a windshield.

"That hurts!" Roebuck said. A little shaving cream might have been a good idea. "I was?"

"Didn't you read the instructions? It also says you should show up for your appointment fifteen minutes early. Most people shower beforehand too."

It was clear by her expression she was finding evidence of Lily's recent presence. Here again a healthy lathering of mentholated foam might have done a world of good. But yes, he should have showered. No argument there. Their legs had barely given over twitching before Roebuck was racing through the kitchen, peering under the table, hunting for his shirt. "Your pants are by the fireplace," she called down to him, nestled in the pillows of her big white bed upstairs. "Christ!" said Roebuck. "Have you seen my socks?" She was asleep, he's fairly certain, before he'd locked the door behind him.

"Put this on," the nurse commanded, pocketing her razor, and handing him a shiny metal disk like the lid from a soup can. Roebuck's testicles had started aching in the taxi, miles before they reached their destination.

"What's this?"

"Anesthetic. Apply it to your scrotum. Did you bring your jockstrap?"

He vaguely recollected some instructions about jockstraps. "Sorry, no."

"In that case, you're lucky we stock them for patients like you."

"Yes."

"Not here!" Roebuck had tentatively pressed the tin-can lid against the area she'd exfoliated. "In the men's room! Now put your pants on." When he'd zipped and buckled up, she handed him a paper bag. "Once you're finished, go to the waiting room. I'll come and get you when the doctor's ready."

The paper bag was folded shut. Roebuck open it. "The men's room!" barked the nurse, jabbing a finger at the door behind him.

The stall was like an ordinary public washroom: tile floor, metallic walls in glossy finish, except that these were done in baby blue. For a second he was tempted to take out a pen and write "NO FUSS???" on the spotless paint above the latch—he had formed a very pleasant image of the nurse in rubber gloves and disinfectant, cursing as she scrubbed—but Roebuck didn't want to jinx himself. He peered into the paper bag: a pill bottle with half-a-dozen painkillers; an empty shrink-wrap the size and shape of his medicated disk (the nurse must have unpackaged it then stuffed the plastic wrapper back inside); instructions on how to apply it: "position at the base of the penis above the scrotum, secure in place"; a plastic sample bottle with an orange lid exactly like the one Yasmin had given him earlier that day; and a quantity of cheerful pamphlets. Roebuck curled his fingers to hold the anesthetic disk in position. He couldn't tell if anything was feeling any different. After a while he returned to the bag, fishing for reading material. The instant he relaxed his grip, the disk slipped out, and dropped into the toilet. Roebuck stood. There it lay, shining at the bottom of the bowl. He unspooled lengths of toilet paper until it settled on the surface in an opaque mass.

On the way out, he swallowed half the pills.

There were three other men in the waiting room, all accompanied by wives who held their hands and patted their knees and murmured soothingly in soft and gentling tones. "Six percent of married women," he remembered, "rely on vasectomy as their choice of contraceptive." Why did that fact stay with him and not the part about the shaving? The nurse emerged and smiled at the one of the couples. "Your husband is next, Mrs. Felstead."

She turned to Roebuck, holding out one hand. "The bag!" she said, snapping her fingers. "The bag! The bag!"

Roebuck gave her his paper bag. She opened it and tucked what he assumed to be his new athletic support in among the other items, then closed it, folded it, and let it drop into his lap. "For the recovery phase," she said with evident regret. All the other husbands were sitting quietly, hands folded in their laps, staring at the carpet. Their wives had followed the exchange closely. Roebuck met the eye of one and winked. She was a robust blonde who, in other circumstances, he might have entertained himself with chatting up. She caught her breath and looked away.

Half an hour later, he was brought to the procedure room.

He wasn't sure what he'd been expecting; maybe something in the order of an operating theatre. This place felt more like an office with a hospital bed. "Make yourself comfortable," said the nurse. There was a single chair in the corner. Roebuck sat there. He noticed, now that he could see it, that the bed was equipped with stirrups at one end.

"Mr. Roebuck?"

"That's me."

"Oh?" The doctor stopped mid-stride at the door. "You're not on the table."

"I was supposed to be on the table?"

"But you *have* had your consultation?"

"Consultation?"

"Helen! Has this man had his consultation?"

The nurse reappeared. There was discussion. Roebuck could not make out the words—they'd moved back out into the hall—but it was her voice he heard the most of, rising. In a few moments the nurse reappeared, alone.

"Hello, Helen!" said Roebuck. "Great to see you again."

"Take off your pants and lower your undershorts. Then get on the table."

"So it is a table!" Roebuck was doing his best to keep the mood upbeat. "I was wondering if it was called a table or a bed."

The nurse, expressionless, consulted her clipboard while he removed his shoes and his pants. Roebuck climbed up.

"Undershorts." She had moved to the foot of the contraption. "Feet in the stirrups."

Roebuck removed his underwear. He was immediately conscious that his penis was shrunken to a tiny fraction of its former self. His testicles, too, seemed to have burrowed somewhere deep inside his body. Nurse Helen wet her lips and clicked her pen.

"Do you have a heart condition?"

"No."

"Do you have high blood pressure?"

"No."

"Hypertension?"

"No."

"Diabetes?"

"No."

When she got to the bottom of the page, she flipped the sheet. "Syphilis?"

"No."

"Gonorrhea?"

"No."

"Chlamydia?"

"No."

She leaned over to see for herself. "Genital warts?"

"No."

"Scabies?"

"No."

"Do you understand the nature of this procedure?"

"Yes."

Reaching between the stirrups, absent-mindedly knocking the retracted essence of Julius Roebuck with the corner of her clipboard, Nurse Helen passed him a consent form. "Read this carefully and sign at the bottom. The doctor will be with you in due course."

Roebuck was left alone again, underwear around his ankles.

He read through the disclaimer and signed the form. Then, because there was nothing else to do, he read it again. After twenty minutes he started to feel himself becoming uncomfortably cool. By the thirty-minute mark he was weighing the pros and cons of pulling up his undershorts when the nurse reappeared, smiling.

"Because you arrived late and because you are here unprepared, the doctor is now with another patient. He will fit you in as soon as possible."

He had barely got his shorts pulled up when the doctor strolled in. "Oh," he said. "Your shorts are still on."

Roebuck removed his shorts and placed his feet back in the stirrups.

"Did you use the medicated patch?"

It took him a moment to remember the tin-can lid on the bottom of the toilet bowl.

"Yes," said Roebuck for simplicity's sake.

"Then this should hardly hurt at all." The doctor was humming. "Is it cold in here," he asked, plunging a needle into Roebuck's scrotum, "or is it just me?"

Roebuck did his best to remain on the table, but what he really wanted at that moment was to shoot to the ceiling and cling by his claws, shuddering, like the cat in the Warner Brothers cartoons. He willed himself to stillness, sucking in his lower lip between his teeth and biting.

"There," said the doctor, withdrawing the syringe. "Now the incision. There's only one, you know, with the no-scalpel method ..."

Roebuck had the impression he was meant to reply, here, with something gratefully affirmative. Words failed.

"Now then," said the doctor. "We'll start with the one on the right."

He had read somewhere that physicians are trained to begin from the right. Roebuck tried to focus on why this might be. The doctor reached into a tray and picked out an elongated pair of pliers with a vicious point.

"Haemostat!" Roebuck croaked, attempting to keep up his part of the conversation.

"Yes! So you *have* been doing your reading? Yes. This is what we use to puncture the scrotum."

Roebuck closed his eyes and willed his heart to stay inside his chest. Maybe it was the anesthetic kicking in, but this part was not as bad as he'd imagined.

"So," said the doctor, chloroforming him with small talk, "what do you do for a living?"

Roebuck had decided it was better to avoid eye contact.

"Advertising," he said, staring at the ceiling. "I'm in advertising." He tried to clear his throat.

"Advertising! How about that! Is it true you guys deliberately annoy people to get them to remember your product?"

"No."

The doctor paused, perhaps waiting for him to expand the point. But Roebuck had nothing further to say on this matter. "What makes a person decide on a career in advertising?" asked the doctor, plugging on.

"What makes a person take up scrotum-stabbing?"

That's what Roebuck almost said, but didn't because a) this man had a pair of pliers in one hand and his balls in the other and b) the answer to both questions was the same.

"Money," he said.

"Of course." The doctor sighed. "Good money, I imagine?"

"Yes."

"You may feel a slight tug."

Tug was not the appropriate word. Far less *slight*. Again Roebuck bit down and again tasted his own blood. "I'm clamping the right vas," said the doctor. The room went white with pain. "Good. Now we'll cauterize." There was a smell of burning, a distressing quantity of smoke, and a sudden, vivid memory of Zach incinerating ants on the driveway with a magnifying glass. "Now the clip." Roebuck felt more than heard the tiny metal widget snapping into place. "There. I use clips *and* cauterizing, you know. Just to be sure." The doctor paused and wiped his brow with satisfaction. "That wasn't so bad? Now, to the left ..."

But the left was not so obliging. Perhaps, apprehending what had happened to its brother, it had tried a final, reckless flight into the citadel of Roebuck's abdomen. Or maybe it was just constriction. Whatever the cause, the doctor was having trouble locating his other vas deferens, probing, frowning, and pursing his lips. Even the needle didn't seem to go where it was aimed. Roebuck's testicles, perceiving the renewed attack, sent a desperate stream of maydays to their allies in his brain. Flee! Fight! Fight! Flee! He forced himself to breathe. "We can get through this," he said.

"What?"

The doctor was looking up at him, his brow beading with perspiration.

"Nothing."

Roebuck closed his eyes and told his heart to beat more slowly. He watched despite his best intentions as the doctor altered his position, readjusting the light, changed the angle of his chair, muttering to himself. "I'm going to have to widen the opening," he said after a while, reaching for a scalpel. Roebuck focused on the pattern of the ceiling tiles. "There's more tissue here than ..." He was probing, now, with another, larger, sharper instrument. Roebuck gripped his left hand with his right and squeezed until he heard the knuckles pop.

"Aha!" said the doctor. "There it is!"

"I just wanted to remind you that your court is booked for six-fifteen," said Nurse Helen from the doorway.

"What? Dammit, I lost it. *Damn!*"

"What?"

"It's all right." The doctor was not speaking to Roebuck. "Call Jerry and tell him I'll be late. No, tell him we'll book again next week. Then put on a gown and get back in here."

"What's going on?"

But the doctor never said.

◉◉

The peas, now fully thawed, present the more immediate concern. Wincing, Roebuck draws the sheets to cover them. There's a lump visible in the middle of his bed, but he'll have to risk it. Anne is knocking at his bedroom door.

"Julius? Julius? Are you all right?"

He coughs, staggers, and undoes the lock.

"I think I have a touch of flu," he says.

Anne is wrapped up in the housecoat she bought last year in Dallas. She smells of lavender and soap. "You look awful!"

Roebuck steadies himself against the jamb. He feels awful; his groin has gone the colour of Indian ink. But at least there's no bleeding. The jockstrap! Where's the jockstrap? Still on him, yes; safely out of sight beneath his pants.

"You need to see a doctor!" says his wife.

"No!" He can tell his vehemence surprises her. "Sorry," he says. "I only need a bit of rest."

"Look at you! You shouldn't be going to work!"

He fends off a fresh wave of nausea. "Maybe you're right." Roebuck wants the bathroom, but suspects she'll follow him in.

"Are you all right?"

"No. Yes, I mean." He has spotted the plastic sample bottle with its bright orange lid in Anne's left hand. "What I need is a cup of coffee! Is there coffee?"

"Coffee? I don't think you should be having coffee. What about some mild tea with honey?"

"Chamomile. Do we have chamomile?"

"Of course we have chamomile. Are you feverish?" Anne puts her hand up to his forehead; he steadies himself to submit without flinching. "I think you have a fever."

He puts his own hand up. "Yes," he says. "I think I have a fever."

"I'll make a nice sweet cup of chamomile." It's the same voice she uses when the kids are sick. "I don't think you should be going in to work today."

"You're right. I'll call as soon as I've had a little rest."

The minute Anne is out of sight, he staggers to the bathroom and locks both doors. Then, remembering the peas, unbolts his side again, grabs the bag from underneath the sheets, and scuttles back into the bathroom. It's a small bag, fortunately, a ten-ouncer. He rips it open with his teeth and dumps the sodden mass into the toilet. Most of the peas flush down. The rest float back up and bob around the surface.

While he's waiting for the tank to refill, Roebuck examines his testicles, which are swollen to the size of tennis balls. "Keep them iced," the doctor warned. "The edema should reduce in a week or so." Roebuck saw him in the parking lot, tossing his racquet into the back of his Range Rover. He should have asked then how long it takes for pubic hair to regrow. Maybe this is something he can Google. The dried blood on the jockstrap is crusty; he'll have to change the dressing soon, but that can wait. The bandages! Where are the bandages? In his briefcase; yes, out of sight in his briefcase. When the coast is clear, he'll replace the gauze and flush that down the toilet too. It looks as if the bleeding has stopped. He cracks the door an inch and listens, then makes another painful dash for his pyjamas.

Safely back behind the bathroom door, Roebuck drops his pants into the hamper, then scoops them out again to check for stains. Satisfied, he puts on his pyjamas, gingerly, and flushes again: half a dozen peas still cycle round the bowl.

"Julius?" says Anne, tapping at the other side. "Are you in there?"

"Just a sec!" His stomach is heaving. Roebuck does his toilet paper trick again—imagine a world without TP?—and flushes a third time.

There, all gone.

"Julius?"

He folds the plastic pea bag and stuffs it in his jock strap. Sweating, Roebuck knots the string of his pyjama bottoms. "You're an angel," he says, hands shaking as he accepts his mug of tea.

Anne's lips are pursed with worry. This is the look she wears during any kind of family emergency. It's her mother's face. No sign now of the sample jar. "You need to get back into bed," she says.

"Yes," he answers gratefully. His teeth are chattering. She tucks him in, mounds the pillows, draws the comforter to his chin, and carefully sits on a corner of his bed. Roebuck sips his honeyed tea.

"I'm calling Yasmin." Anne has lifted the phone from its cradle on his nightstand. "We have a builder coming in this morning, but she can handle that. I'm taking you to the doctor."

Roebuck lets the sweet tea trickle down his throat. "Speaking of Yasmin …"

Anne puts down the phone. She reaches into the pocket of her housecoat. "Yes." She is gazing at the sample bottle. "What does this mean?"

"Yasmin's reply." Roebuck's hands have stopped shaking. The tea is actually helping.

"I read that part." She has taken out his yellow post-it note, stuck like a butterfly to the pad of one finger.

"But what does it mean?"

Two things Roebuck did last night before dragging himself to his bed. Three, if you count stopping at the corner store to buy the frozen peas. The first was to place an order with the florist for the delivery of a dozen roses to Nurse Helen at the clinic. The other, and far more significant, was the sample jar. He's actually rather proud of himself for the flowers.

"How was yoga?"

"What?"

Anne was at yoga last night. She'd arranged for the sitter to stay late and put the kids to bed. That's how he succeeded in getting himself into his room unobserved. Before he'd locked the door, Roebuck had placed the jar and note where she would find it on her pillow.

"Yoga was fine." Anne tells him. "What does this mean?"

Back before his testicles were lanced, he'd done some careful thinking and decided that Anne would have to be told.

"Yasmin wants to bypass the clinic."

"What! What does *that* mean?"

She came to see me in my office. Yesterday. She said that if I was uncomfortable with using a fertility clinic we could, well, skip the middleman I guess is how you'd describe it. Then she gave me that sample jar. She said she'd call when she was ovulating. All I have to do ..." He gestures to the plastic jar. "Then afterwards she'll come and take it home with her."

"You're fucking joking?"

"I wish I was."

"That *bitch!*"

"Now, now. You said it yourself. Yasmin's going through a rough patch …"

"But … Oh, God. That must have been so *uncomfortable!*"

"Well, I admit, it was not the most relaxing meeting I had that day."

"Look at you! You're so upset you're sick!"

"No. Don't think that. I'm sure this has nothing to do with Yasmin."

"Well, *I* know it hasn't helped."

"Listen," he says, "Yasmin is your friend. I know the two of you will see your way through all this."

"Oh, Julius! What are we going to do?"

Roebuck yawns. The tea has definitely helped. "I don't know. But right now I'm not going to think about it."

Anne scrambles to her feet. "I'm sorry! You shouldn't be worrying about this now."

"Maybe I should try to get some sleep."

"Yes. That's the best thing. Oh Julius, I'm so sorry! This is all my fault."

"No." he says. "Don't worry. In sickness and in health." He yawns, a real yawn. "We'll sort this out."

She leans across the bed and kisses him. He can't remember the last time that happened.

"You're sure you shouldn't see a doctor?"

"I'm sure."

"Then I'm going straight to the studio to have a little chat with Yasmin."

"Mmm," he says. Roebuck wishes he could be the fly on the wall for that one.

Anne has tiptoed out and closed the door; he can hear her steps receding down the stairs. There are several things he knows that *won't* be said. Yasmin will not mention anything about her scheme to go behind Anne's back because she will know—three minutes into the conversation, she'll be certain—that *he* hasn't said a word about that either. He feels the beginning of arousal, and the answering stab of scrotal anguish.

But it's good to know that everything still appears to be in working order.

11

Near is for ants, far is for eagles.
The Collected Sayings of Julius Roebuck

By Friday, Roebuck's condition has improved. Appropriately hoarse, he has left a voicemail informing his receptionist that he is staying home in bed today, running a fever, and that he would appreciate not being bothered with anything that wasn't an emergency. She, in turn, had sent out an All Staff Notice, advising everyone that the boss was down with the flu. Roebuck is very seldom sick; when he is, it's taken seriously. His people circled the wagons. All day Thursday, his phone did not ring once. He kept his laptop and BlackBerry handy on the bed beside him and caught up on his reading. A little past noon he heard the front door opening. Roebuck settled back beneath the covers, switched off the light, and closed his eyes. Finding her ailing husband breathing evenly in restful sleep, Anne left a tray of chicken soup and flatbread on his bedside table and silently crept out again. This was repeated—poached salmon on white rice—several hours later at dinner. He is still extremely curious to learn the outcome of her conversation with Yasmin. All in good time.

Earlier this morning, unshaven, pale in his pyjamas, Roebuck had teetered through the bathroom and carefully positioned himself on the edge of Anne's bed. Getting up and sitting down still hurts; anything that bumps induces sparks of pain. Roebuck's infirmity convinces. Anne's alarm has just gone off; she is barely awake.

"I've been so worried. Julius, you never sleep this much!"

"I think I'm feeling better."

She sits up and puts her hand against his forehead. "You're still running a fever."

This surprises him. "I am?"

"And Julius, you smell."

He hasn't bathed since early Wednesday morning. Quite a lot has happened between now and then. "I'll try later," he tells her, shivering. The doctor warned him not to shower for 48 hours, so he's right on schedule. He has also been advised to avoid all stretching of the abdomen: "No heavy lifting, no straining, nothing than makes you grunt."

"Is it okay if the kids come in to see you?" Anne asks. "They've been so worried."

"It's just the flu," says Roebuck. "It's not as if I've lost a lung. Just tell them not to jump on me."

"Of course they won't jump on you!"

"My stomach's still a little woozy."

"I think you should stay home again today."

"I hate to do that. People depend on me. But maybe you're right. Can you take the kids to school again this morning, do you mind?" Getting the kids to school is one of Roebuck's normal functions.

"Of course I can! Don't be silly."

"I'll be fine by Monday."

"That's the spirit."

"Then, I guess I'll stay home."

"What about a bit of breakfast?" Anne has gotten out of bed and slipped into her housecoat; she's moving toward the door. "A little toast? Could you hold down a soft boiled egg?"

"Don't worry." Roebuck's mind has turned to other matters. "I'll make something later. So …" he says, casually reaching for a tissue from the box beside by her bed. "Yasmin?"

Anne turns. It's a look he can't interpret because he's making such a point of blowing his nose.

"I talked to her."

At that moment the children burst in. "Dad!" shouts Zach. "Dad! You're still alive!"

"Don't jump!" his father shouts back.

12

The steer will always hate the bull.
The Collected Sayings of Julius Roebuck

By Saturday morning Roebuck has showered and shaved and assured himself he's healing. Even his lacerated testicles look and feel more wholesome. He has—as per instructions—blocked the hole at the base of his penis with the medicated goop prescribed to keep the moisture out. By appearance, at least, it's improving. He has changed his dressing and flushed the wad of crusty gauze down the toilet. It still hurts, though: a dull, pulsing, background throb. Several years ago while penalty-killing late in the third of a beer-league playoff game, Roebuck took a deflection to the groin that dropped him to the ice like a dying millipede. It feels like that now, say thirty minutes after. That's improvement.

He has switched from the jockstrap (now wrapped neatly in a plastic bag, tucked into his briefcase for disposal at a later date) to a much more comfortable set of snug-fitting boxer shorts. He has made himself a plate of scrambled eggs with minced shallots and dabs of runny cheddar and drunk a pot of coffee. All in all, definitely improvement. He has caught up on his email—still in PJs, working at the kitchen table—and booked a conference call with a group of clients based in Framingham, Massachusetts, who see a budget squeeze ahead and want more campaign, thanks, for less money. He has left a voice mail with Finance, requesting the job sum, and got a head start on the plasticine brain.

Lately it seems that every piece of homework is an art project in disguise. Last week it was Morgan's collage of restaurant items, all labelled in French. Today it's an anatomical model of the human brain required for Zach's Science class. Google Translator provided the spellings and appropriate accents for every word on Morgan's list; the hard part was sourcing and printing the accompanying pictures and neatly laying out the project on a sheet of foamboard. That took up most of the evening. Both Morgan and Katie are pulling off As in French, though Roebuck doubts that either one of them would get much past *bonjour* if ever required to actually speak it. Zach, on the other hand, who has not yet come to terms with the imperative of cut-and-paste, hovers in the middle Cs. Roebuck is kneading a mass of grey material they will use to represent the cerebellum and has set aside a lump of pink stuff for the hypothalamus, when he hears the doorbells chime.

Daniel Greenwood is standing in the portico, a leather courier bag slung across his chest.

Roebuck opens the door and coughs.

He doesn't really need to cough; there's nothing wrong with his lungs. But he's been keeping up appearances so effectively these last two days that now his chest behaves as if it really is congested. "Ugly time of year for flu," says Greenwood, staring up into the thin March sun. "That so sucks."

"Come in, Daniel."

"Wow!" Greenwood has stepped into the foyer, whistling.

"Beautiful."

"My wife is an interior designer."

"Is she really? I didn't know!"

Roebuck coughs again and taps his chest. Greenwood angles his neck to peer into his face. He's a little taller than Roebuck; Roebuck has never noticed this. "You look bagged," he says. "But I brought something to cheer you up." Greenwood snaps the strap of his courier bag. All creative types below a certain age have taken to these floppy, purse-like items. "Maybe I should have waited?"

"Come in, Daniel. I have a pot of coffee going."

They walk together through the house and into the kitchen at the back. When the main floor was expanded, Anne and Yasmin sourced a slab of Indonesian teak that now runs, carved and polished, like a backbone down the centre of the room. "Sit there," says Roebuck.

"That's one hunk of timber."

"Three and a half feet wide by twenty long, if memory serves. My wife, or I should say her partner, arranged to have it freighted out through Burma."

"Beautiful. The whole house is beautiful."

"She has an eye."

"You can say that again."

"But now she thinks the kitchen's getting tired." Roebuck himself is feeling tired. He pours the coffee. There's an espresso machine from Italy, but he seldom bothers. "So ...?"

Greenwood has unslung his pouch and removed a laptop. "It's just a seventeen-inch screen," he says apologetically, "but it'll give you a rough idea."

"Of what, roughly speaking?" Roebuck watches Greenwood's fingers dance across the keyboard. When did it happen, that people emerged from the womb, typing eighty words a minute?

"I've been working on some concepts for Drag and Clop," Greenwood says a little shyly. "It's just a ripomatic, but I thought you'd better have a look before I take it any further."

"But, Daniel ..."

"There!" Greenwood spins the monitor so that Roebuck can observe it, free of glare.

For a second, he thinks he's watching a clip from a David Attenborough wildlife special. He looks up at Greenwood—who nods—then back at the laptop. A bull elk occupies the screen, standing in a clearing, snow-capped mountains marching off into the background. The animal's magnificence alone is arresting. Roebuck reaches for his coffee as the elk lowers its enormous head, tears a hunk of grass, then raises it again, jaws grinding. A forest of antlers sweeps the autumn air; muscle undulates beneath the surface of its skin; velvet ears twitch placidly. Vaguely, almost inaudibly, Roebuck discerns the sound of chewing and the muffled stamp of hoof. Then, piercingly, the calm is shattered by a bugling shriek. Instantly, the elk is transformed. The tendons of its neck inflate, its chest expands, everything about it seems suddenly intensified. Stamping, it swings its massive rack and stares hungrily toward the camera. Twin plumes of steam jet from flaring nostrils. Greenwood freezes the screen.

"Isn't that a crazy sound!" he says. "It blew me away."

"Where did you get this?"

"Wait!" Greenwood touches a key. "Listen."

The elk snorts. And there it is ... faintly in the background: a different sound. A new sound, so low you wouldn't hear if you weren't already straining your ears.

"But that's ..."

"Look!"

The elk has arched its swollen neck. It's scanning the horizon, then it vanishes.

A lion takes its place: a huge male lion, sleeping in the swaying grass of an African savanna. Its jaw rests on a forepaw, a slight breeze ruffles the strands of its enormous mane. There's the soft, low buzz of insects; a fly lands on its golden flank, pauses, flits away. Haunches shimmer in the heat, but the lion does not stir. And then the roar. Roebuck is expecting it, but still the volume startles him. One moment the animal is asleep, inert, at peace, the next it's standing on its tiptoes, quivering as its eyes rake the grasslands, searching, searching …

"Where did …?"

"Wait!"

The lion's tongue snakes across its muzzle. And there is again … that sound—so anomalous—rhythmic like a drumbeat, but not … something else … Roebuck feels a shiver, literally, running up his own spine.

"Amazing," he says.

"I'm thinking we can start to jack the volume here." Greenwood kills the picture.

"There's more?"

"Not yet."

"Where did all this come from?"

"Well, you know, it's all out there on YouTube. Though so far no usable moose, which surprised me. You'd think moose videos would be a dime a dozen, but not compared to elk."

"This is very effective, Daniel. The elk is perfect."

"Thanks. I'm pretty sure we'll be able to buy that clip. Fairly cheap too, if you want it."

"Want it? Those vapour trails out the nostrils … Fantastic!"

"What I couldn't believe was the sound those guys make! They call it bugling."

"Reminds me more of a string section, fortissimo, all sawing at once."

"You like it ... so far?

"Like is not the word!" To his surprise, Roebuck is standing, pacing up and down Anne's span of bootlegged hardwood. He doesn't remember getting to his feet. "This is far beyond the concept stage ..."

"It's not like in the old days, pencil and paper and all that crap. Everybody and his mother puts stuff up on the web. You can cherry pick what you want. This didn't take me long at all."

"Can we use it?"

"Most of it. If not, I'll download something else. Of course for the last scene we talked about—the guys at the café—that'll need to be original footage. We'll have to shoot that segment ourselves."

"And the soundtrack? That background, your drag and clop rendition? I can't believe how *exactly* it matches the sound I had in mind."

"That was Zhanna."

"Our Zhanna?" Roebuck self-corrects. "Zhanna Lamb, I mean?"

"Walking up and down the foyer of her condo. Nice marble floor, ridiculously good acoustics. She brought six different pairs of shoes to try. The track you're listening to are the ones that sounded best."

"But ..."

"I recorded it myself, then took it over to the sound engineer. We enhanced it here and there, cleaned it up a bit ..."

But Roebuck's concentration has suddenly faded. Something like this always seems to happen when Greenwood and Zhanna Lamb are brought together in his mind. "Amazing ..." he says, still adjusting.

The enthusiasm seems to have leaked out of Greenwood too.

"She's leaving, you know."

"Leaving?"

"India, Nepal, those kind of places. Backpacking!" Greenwood is shaking his head. "A year. Maybe two she says. By herself! I just can't imagine Zhanna with a backpack."

Roebuck can. He can imagine Zhanna in anything. "The world is that girl's oyster," he says softly. For reasons that he can't quite come to terms with, this piece of news has revived his spirits.

Not Greenwood's. "That's such a stupid expression."

"Sorry?"

"The world is your oyster. It's disgusting."

"That's only because you don't like oysters."

"What makes you think I don't like oysters?"

Roebuck pulls a stool out from under Anne's teak tabletop. "I don't know," he says. It's just that Greenwood strikes him as the kind of person who would not like oysters.

"I love oysters. And you're wrong about women, too."

"Wrong?"

"About what women really want."

"Oh," says Roebuck, sighing. "Please. What do women really want?"

"What they want is to be truly *seen*. To be understood for what they really *are* ... "

"Right. Sure. Beautiful and good and smart ... "

"No! That's the part you're wrong about. That's what *needs* to be said! That she's beautiful and smart and good. That she's totally unique. You can't repeat that too often. It's what every woman *needs* to hear."

"And you don't think she'll pick up the irony?"

"Irony? What are you talking about?"

"That every woman is unique? *Every* woman."

"Women don't like irony."

"Well, you're on to something there. Also I'll agree it's standard practice. Tell her she's beautiful and smart and good. Then say it again. Then say it again and again and again and again and then, when you think she can't possibly fail to see where you're going, say it again a half a dozen more times because you're absolutely right, most women can never hear it enough. But it gets tedious, doesn't it? I mean from our perspective? The messenger's?"

"What *are you* saying?"

"It's like a form of sexual patriotism. Like America. You tell Americans they're exceptional. You tell them they're brave and true and good. You keep on saying it. You're the best. You're the best. You're the best. Because they never get tired of it. Never. Sure, you can attach that message to your brand, and they'll wear it as proudly as they do their flag. But doesn't it get boring? Doesn't it get just, so ... easy?"

"But that's our job! That's ... Jesus, Julius."

"Please don't get me wrong. I love women. Truly. But at least we can add a little nuance. If not for their sake, then for ours."

"You are making me worried."

"Remember that lesson you learned, back when you started, that it really *does* work? Flattery. That she really *will* believe it? It's a hard lesson—that you honestly *can* shoot fish in a barrel. I remember it with sadness." Roebuck stoops and leans against the table. "But maybe you haven't got there yet ..." he's searching Greenwood's face. "No," he says, deciding. "Not possible. But it was depressing, wasn't it? When you realized the truth of it. That if you tell a woman what she wants to hear, she really will buy into whatever you're selling." He draws a breath. "It's demotivating."

Greenwood is staring as if Roebuck has admitted some communicable disease.

"Anyway," Roebuck says—he is fading—"there are other ways of saying the same thing, but at least more indirectly. Ways that involve at least a little more ... complexity. A little more interesting, maybe, somehow. A little more ... fair." Still leaning on the table, a bit light-headed, now, Roebuck throws a leg over the stool, drops into the seat and then, too late—far, far too late—recalls the terrible unwisdom of this act. A white-hot blast has detonated upward from his groin and echoes through the sudden vacuum in his chest. It takes all of his willpower not to reach between his legs and cradle the shriek in his scrotum. He stops the hand—barely— and presses it instead into his abdomen.

"Are you all right?" Greenwood has jumped to his feet.

Roebuck can't speak. He nods, sucks air.

"Jesus, that's one bad case of stomach flu!"

"It'll pass." Roebuck's lungs are beginning to function.

Greenwood is folding up his laptop. "Have you seen a doctor?"

"Oh yes ..." The worst of it is nearly over. Roebuck draws a ragged breath. "This is terrific work, Daniel. I'm extremely impressed ..."

Greenwood has stuffed the laptop back inside his bag and drawn the leather strap across his chest. He looks like some kind of Mexican bandit about to saddle up and vamoose across the border. "I hope you're not contagious."

He is out the door and gone before Roebuck can remind either one of them that they don't even have this hypothetical account; still don't even know if it's available. But on the other hand, that's how you pursue things in life—isn't it?—in the hope of expectation. Roebuck pours himself a cup of coffee and seats himself more carefully this time, testicles thrumming like a hive of frightened bees.

13

Art for art's sake is like cooking for cooking's sake.
We don't cook for the sake of cooking; we cook for the
sake of eating.
The Collected Sayings of Julius Roebuck

The rest of the weekend flows by almost pleasantly. He could get used to this, if he isn't careful, life in his pyjamas. In the eyes of his household Roebuck remains an invalid, though convalescing well. He is excused from most domestic chores. Anne even drives Zach to his Sunday morning baseball practice. Roebuck feels genuinely guilty, though it's only just this once. She's back now, making lunch; another task that most weekends would fall to him. All three kids are partial to grilled cheese with a side of dilly gherkin, thinly sliced.

Working upstairs where things are quiet, he has just discovered a new email from Lily. "Hear you're down with a bug. Worn out?" He is formulating his reply when the doorbell chimes. Lily, too, will need some careful managing, which in turn reminds him that above all he must come to terms with the challenge of his new Brazilian. Roebuck understands that there are men in this new era who shave their bodies like women. But he also knows that Lily knows he is definitely not a member of that demographic. The only safe solution is to avoid her altogether until everything has grown back. Besides, the No Fuss Clinic website reminds him that he's still fertile, technically, for a minimum of eight weeks and twenty ejaculations until the last of the swimmers are safely cleansed from his system. Roebuck has promised himself that Lily's eggs and his departing sperm will, from this point forward, have zero opportunity to meet and greet. He foresees a lot of unexpected business travel in the weeks ahead and a wealth of headaches. This will take some honest creativity.

"If I'm not mistaken," he writes, "*you* were the one unconscious before I even left the house ..."

Anne and Yasmin walk into his room together.

"Look," Anne says brightly. "You have a visitor!"

Yasmin is carrying a bouquet of flowers. They are exactly the variety of roses he sent to Helen at the clinic. Roebuck hits "Save" and closes down his mail. To give himself more time, he coughs, then coughs again. He will have to work around that Karma at some time in the future.

"Poor sick man!" Yasmin shapes her lips into a sympathetic pout.

"Just between the two of us, I think he's starting to enjoy it."

Roebuck coughs a third time, more forcefully, and reaches for his Kleenex.

"Well, I'm sure he deserves it."

Anne shoots Yasmin a look. Roebuck's senses go on high alert. "Are those for me?" he asks, swallowing.

"You see! His voice is so crackly!"

"Actually," says Yasmin, "they're for both of you: Yellow roses ... for friendship, a precious thing I almost threw away." She extends the bouquet—after a moment it becomes clear that Yasmin is asking for someone to take the flowers off her hands. Roebuck draws the sheets more tightly to his body; he is feeling seriously chilled.

"I'll get a vase," Anne says, though it's also clear that she is hesitant to leave the room.

"Don't worry," Yasmin tells her, "I promise to wait until you're back."

The two women smile. Anne takes the flowers in her arms, "I won't be a moment."

Roebuck feels a dampness spreading in his armpits, a quivering of nerves between his shoulders.

Yasmin stands in the middle of his room; Roebuck lies with his back against a mound of pillows piled against the headboard. The two of them listen to the sound of Anne receding down the stairs. Yasmin takes a quick step back, quietly, and then another, leaning out the door to scan the hall. Her skirt rides high and stretches taut.

An instant later, she's on top of him.

"It's *now*!" she says kneading the back of Roebuck's neck.

Yasmin's hair falls against his cheek; he feels the swelter of her breath against his skin. "Now!" Her hands go sliding up and down his arms like she's squeezing something out of him, silk blouse gaping open. Roebuck breathes the waves of puckered heat. "Wouldn't you know! It's *right* fucking now!" Yasmin's bra is yellow, too, like the roses but with leopard spots. She straightens abruptly, listens— nods—then twitches something from her purse. "Look!" A pink thermometer gleams between her fingers then slides into her mouth. Roebuck watches, blood-hot, as Yasmin's lips close then part again as it emerges, dewy and glistening. "See! A full degree above my basal body temperature!" She groans and drops it back into the purse. "Do you think …? No, too late!" Her hand slips back into the bag and emerges with something else. "Yes" she says, deciding. "No. Not this time." There is now an orange-lidded sample jar clasped against

her breast. Yasmin's eyes have closed; she's counting days. "And anyway, you might still be contagious." He can feel the mattress vibrate
as she slithers off the bed. "We'll just have to wait another month."

Her hearing must be sharper than his because a few seconds
later Anne comes through the door with his roses arranged in a
vase. Yasmin has already smoothed her skirt and returned to the
spot where she was standing. "There!" says Anne, setting the flowers
where he can see them on his nightstand. "Aren't they beautiful?"
She is looking at Yasmin, who returns the warmth.

Roebuck's knees are drawn up almost to his chin in order to
conceal the enormity of his arousal.

"Well, then," says Yasmin, rubbing a dab of sanitizing gel between her palms. "I'll say what I came to say and leave you two to
enjoy the rest of your weekend in peace and harmony." Roebuck
looks at Anne, who is watching her friend as if she's part of an
audience awaiting its cue to applaud.

Yasmin clears her throat.

"I just wanted to say how sorry I am ... Anne, Julius ... I've
been so selfish. I know how uncomfortable this has made you.
Anne, both of you ..." She turns, here, and looks soulfully at
Roebuck whose erection oscillates like a sentient metronome with
each contraction of his heart. "I promise you," Yasmin has locked
eyes again with Anne, "I promise you that you won't have to worry
about this anymore! Can you forgive me?" Roebuck slides a pillow
from behind his back, drops it in his lap, and rests his elbows on
the hump. Anne's eyes are gleaming. "Oh, honey, of course I do!"

The women embrace.

Thank God he's on his sickbed, because for a second Anne looks
like she wants him to get up and join the hug. Roebuck thunks
another pillow on the heap. It takes a while, but in due course
Yasmin dabs the corner of her eye with a tissue winkled from the
box beside his bed and announces it's time she's on her way.

"I'll see you out," Anne tells her fondly.

"Thank you for the flowers," murmurs Roebuck.

"Oh, listen to that voice! He's still so hoarse."

"Make him take his vitamins." Yasmin wets her lips again and Roebuck has to look away.

He listens to them chatting as they make their way downstairs. "While you're here," Anne says, "I should show you the engineer's report for Russell Hill ..."

"It's back already?"

"Last week."

"Oh God, Anne! I'm *so* sorry! I haven't been paying attention. It's like I've been insane."

"Don't worry. We'll put all that behind us now ..."

It's the last thing he hears before they've moved on out of earshot. Cautiously, Roebuck makes his way into the bathroom. Although the clinic website has advised that sexual intercourse, per se, ought to be avoided, it also says that "gentle sex" (defined as "getting an erection and ejaculating") should be safe to undertake at any time. He locks both bathroom doors and turns on all the faucets.

"If I'm not mistaken," Roebuck continues, much relieved though still extremely tender, "*you* were the one unconscious before I even left the house. But be that as it may ..."

There's an empty, tingling kind of soreness, a vacant after-throb—but now at least his mind is clear, and it's a great relief to know for certain; he was genuinely anxious that he'd blown some kind of valve. There must still be water in his ear, because he hasn't heard Anne at all until he glances up and sees her standing by the corner of his bed. Roebuck closes down his laptop.

"You had a shower?"

"I did."

"Feeling better?"

"Much."

She pushes the computer off his lap and sits beside him. "You *are* feeling better. I can tell."

"True. I am."

"Isn't it such a relief?"

"I can't begin to express ... How'd you do it?"

"I just sat her down and told her in no uncertain terms that it wasn't going to happen. Period. Then I showed her some articles I printed off the Internet that talked about how common it is, that kind of obsession, when a woman her age wants a child so desperately ..."

"And she said ...?"

"You heard."

"I did. Yes."

"She promised me she's never going to bring this up again. I think that Yasmin understands herself much better now."

"Well. That's that, then."

Anne has reached across his lap and taken his hand. It's the kind of thing she might have done in former times to signal something else. He is not sure what to say.

"I have a question," Roebuck asks into the pause. "Why me?"

Anne releases his hand. "Because you're so successful as a father." The way she's circled round the emphasis makes very clear that, as a husband, his qualities are far less evident, but that she does agree with Yasmin on this quintessential point. "She sees how wonderful you are with our kids. It shows you're prime material." Anne folds her hands together in her lap. "It's what every woman's looking for, really, when it comes right down to it."

"Yes, but ..."

"I know. I know. But like I said before, she hasn't been thinking straight."

They sit for a moment together in silence.

"Right." Anne says, rising. "You're still not feeling well."

> If I'm not mistaken, you were the one unconscious before I even left the house. But be that as it may (and leaving aside the insignificance of origin), yes, I've caught a bug. Had to take a few days off. Weird time of year, as everyone keeps saying, but I'm mostly better now. The plan is to be up and back at work tomorrow morning. It's looking like the next few weeks are shaping up as challenging. How are you, Slumber Queen? Did I mention you snore?

Roebuck pushes "Send."

She must be at her desk because, moments later, her reply comes pinging back:

> I do not. But speaking of chamber music: you should hear yourself (once you've stopped talking). I'll remind you next time. Which by the sound of it may not happen for a bit. But catch-up works for me too. McCann wants me working out of their office for the rest of this month, maybe longer. So don't upset your diligence on my account. At least I'll have the pleasure of your company at the AFAs. You know how I look forward to your presentations.

He's always felt that the quality of Lily's prose lacks something when compared to the standard of her verse. But, damn, he did forget about the AdForge Awards. Roebuck checks his calendar. She is right of course: it's this coming Thursday. The date completely slipped his mind. Which reminds him that he still needs to work up a presentation. Though that now, too, will have to be rethought.

Roebuck is disturbed that he's forgotten. It's his normal practice to take awards very seriously. All agencies do, although at the same time everyone pretends not to give a crap. Roebuck doesn't play that game. Or, more accurately, he prefers to play it at a higher level. He knows—and this truth he holds absolutely—that if there's one thing his business is about, it's recognition. That's pretty much *all* it's about. An advertiser not interested in receiving recognition is like a carnivore not interested in meat.

His facial muscles twitch while Roebuck gazes at the ceiling.

Potential.

He settles back, taps his fingers on the laptop, still staring at the ceiling, opens up his Axiom File, and for a moment weighs the pros and cons of tacking on a supplementary clause—something like "both are heading for extinction"—but decides to keep it clean and simple.

"Speaking of the AFAs," he writes, returning to his email, "how's this …?"

Over the span of their relationship, Roebuck has entertained Lily with many such sayings—aphorisms? epigrams? adages? squibs?—he's never really certain what to call them, but he's confident that she enjoys their deconstruction as much, or nearly as much, as he enjoys composing them. Often they will serve to stimulate argument, which for the two of them is tantamount to sex, or the next best thing to sex, when sex itself is unobtainable.

He's fairly certain this one will strike a chord, if not for its wit then at least for the memories he knows it will arouse. They'd talked about exactly this subject at last year's AFAs. Or rather, some hours after, in a room at the Four Seasons; one of the few nights they have ever spent together. There are strict rules: chief among them that, although Roebuck is entitled to cheat on his wife, he is not permitted to steal time from his family. With rare exceptions, he and Lily see each other during daylight hours only when they both can slip away from work. Weekends, holidays, even the hours between school and his children's bedtimes are, for him at least, the exclusive property of domestic hearth and home.

So special events like the AdForge Awards are cherished all the more for how rarely they come along. Roebuck was a panelist last year, provided with a room at the hotel where the other judges were put up. Some of Lily's work was nominated so she was in attendance that night too. He'd told Anne that it was sure to be a late night of drinking, catching up, shoptalk, and so on. There was the expectation he would crash at the hotel.

Anne used to go with him to events like these—and still enjoys the trips to Cannes or London when those ones come along—but years ago decided that sitting in a ballroom stuffed with hyperventilating advertisers was worse than riding with a busload of alcoholics midway through a pub crawl.

"Better you than me," she said.

Roebuck repeated his wife's observation that very same night as he and Lily lay together in their rumpled sheets, overlooking the display of hardware lined up on the dressing table. Quite a haul, despite his having withdrawn from competition in the categories he was tapped to judge. Officially, top prize each year is The Golden Anvil Award, presented to whichever agency has made the biggest impact, overall. Winning The Golden Anvil guarantees a glowing feature in *AdForge*—the year he got it for the Ripreeler campaign, they published a cover of Roebuck with his chin pressed against the anvil and a No. Six Spinner clenched between his teeth—but there are dozens of lesser prizes, including his own hands-down favourite: Best Art Direction in a Radio Spot (one Roebuck covets, but has never achieved). Another that has always tickled him was sitting on the table, not six feet from his toes—The P. D. Harper Award for Most Imaginative Use of White Space—part of Lily's catch that night.

It was this award that had put them in the mood for disputation.

Lily took the position that a category like that was flat-out ridiculous and that her march to the podium to receive the prize for it was plain embarrassing. Roebuck's bias was more nuanced (he admits a higher tolerance for inanity), and Lily didn't really mean it; at least not in that articulation.

Truthfully, there's just no denying the practical value of awards: they inform the world its winner does good work, which in turn attracts business, which in turn pays the rent. Clients attend these events and, more importantly, other people's clients comparing them unfavourably to you. Lily knows all that. But recognition was never really her complaint. Her true objection, and something of a delicate one owing to the circumstances, was—and still is—that she honestly believes the entire industry is run by crooks and shitheads.

Although it's true that Roebuck and his ego have developed a healthy working relationship, the same cannot be said for many of his associates—the very ones he was supposed to be carousing with that night. Lily, with a shade more smugness than he thought was fair, hadn't hesitated in pointing out that there he was with her instead of them.

"Well you can hardly fault me for that. Plus, that argument is beside the point. It's not people I'm defending. It's the awards."

The difficulty, with so many of his peers, is their willingness to interpret success in advertising as a measure of success itself. Roebuck is amazed at how repeatedly he sees this. Advertising itself is void of meaning. Or rather, it has meaning only as an aid toward a far more fundamental chase. As an occupation, it's extremely verbal and tends to generate a lot of money, a combination which—to a greater degree than any other profession he considered in his youth—attracts the attention of women like Lily (and Anne, of course, and Yasmin possibly, and certainly Zhanna). But this line of reasoning would have been an unproductive one to have pursued in that particular context.

"You're right," he'd said, following up. "The business is a showcase for misguided self-esteem ... all those egos strolling to the podium in ragged jeans and ripped T-shirts, making the exact same speeches as the ones jumped-up in their Armanis. I totally agree. It's all so obvious ..."

But, on the other hand, wasn't that the *nature* of the business: segmentation of the obvious? He might also have mentioned his own special loathing for creative directors who sit smugly at their tables, pretending to ignore the applause while sending up some blushing junior to accept the prize on their behalf. Roebuck really does despise that brand of arrogance. But this, too, was not germane, nor was his reply to Lily, though he went ahead with it anyway, because he really wasn't able to resist. "But if you want to talk about posing, you have to admit it's not restricted to the advertising business. You'll agree the literary community, for instance, has its share. What about that guy who won that big prize a few years back for an entire book made up of only vowels? Or was it consonants, I forget?"

"I wasn't talking about posing," replied Lily after considering her response for maybe a quarter of a second. "You were. I was talking about assholes. And for the record, it was one vowel per chapter, asshole, not the whole book. And none of that changes the fact that the only reason I'm here tonight is to be with you."

Sic probo. Or so Roebuck believed at the time.

His computer pings again, and he draws it to him eagerly. Lily is not a postponer.

Considering this as a line in your address? It's definitely your voice, though you know how much I disapprove of

what it is saying. But it has a kind of cadence, and I'm
sure you'll make it work. Though I think you might want to
add a preface, something like: "Awards are the proteins of
our business: an advertiser not interested in recognition is
like a carnivore not interested in meat ... (bletch)." Curious
to hear where you go with it. Looking forward to debrief-
ing. See you Thursday!

Amazing.

It had never crossed his mind to use this phrase as a line in his
speech. He was weighing it only as a possible addition to his epi-
gram collection. But she's completely right. It *would* have been a
perfect fit. In fact, he could easily have worked it up into a theme
for the entire talk. Roebuck has to stop himself, even now, from
shifting to a blank page and fleshing out the concept.

He activates his client file instead. The other thing he's going to
have to deal with is the organizers, who are going to be extremely
pissed. One complication at a time.

It takes a bit of browsing, but eventually he finds it. Roebuck
double-checks the dates and confirms they do indeed conflict. It's
Helsinki—so he'll have to spend a lot of hours getting there and
back—but that's no hardship. The longer Roebuck studies the invitation, the more he's convinced that this is what he's looking for.
In fact, now that he considers it, he has to wonder why he didn't
give this one more serious consideration when it first arrived. It's
undoubtedly the kind of thing he *should* be attending. And such a
golden opportunity to reaffirm relations with what is, unquestion-
ably, his number one client. Roebuck studies the list of attendees.
Some very key players. Funny, sometimes, the twists fate takes; there
are moments when he suspects he might actually have a guardian
angel, working his corner. Really, it *would* have been a serious miscal-
culation to have taken a pass on a conference this high level.

It's always better to face the hard things head-on and get them over with. Roebuck takes a breath, channelling that plough-ahead-until-the-page-is-full technique he taught himself all those years ago in Iowa.

Lil,

I don't know how to tell you this, but I can't make the AFAs. Turns out I have to be in Finland. Honestly, I still haven't figured out how this has happened. Looks like the original invitation got lost somehow.

I only found out about it when someone noticed I hadn't replied and sent a follow-up. Lucky, that, because it would have been a disaster if I'd missed this conference. The Ripreeler Group has purchased a company in the Philippines that claims to have developed a chemical that mimics fish pheromones. If it works, it's an industry-changer. I'm expected to attend a planning session in Helsinki going forward with a global marketing strategy. As you know, I have their N. America business, but this is a foot in the door for a much, much larger possibility. So you see that it's an offer I just can't refuse. I'm so sorry, Lily. I'm broken-hearted over this …

14

The easier the practice, the deeper the conviction.
The Collected Sayings of Julius Roebuck

And it's true. He is broken-hearted.

So much so that he hasn't had the nerve to open Lily's response.

Roebuck has driven to the office early Monday morning. There's a lot of catching up to do, starting with the AFAs. But first he needs to clear his mind and sort through all the mail that's piled up while he's been gone, including a series from Greenwood who seems to be convulsed with issues out at Artemis. Roebuck deletes half a dozen he arbitrarily decides are junk and forwards several more for the suits to follow up on. He replies to the ones he knows he can wrap up in under sixty seconds and says no, regretfully, to an attractive OCAD student looking for a summer internship. There's another invitation from those guys at Omniglobe—eighteen holes at Glen Abbey, this time. Definitely an escalation, but he doesn't want to think about that now. Which leaves only Greenwood's stream. Judging by the subject headings, something's got Daniel definitely riled; the last one's written all in caps and exclamation points. Roebuck reminds himself that Greenwood is a picture guy, not a writer. But even so … He starts at the bottom, slowly working back.

It's obvious soon enough that Daniel is tripping over the usual hurdles of corporate realignment. He has presented three new sets of boards to the senior team at Artemis. They rejected the first, waffled for days over the second, but announced that the last concept they definitely didn't hate. After much debate and many changes, the VP of Sales and Marketing has finally signed off on the new packaging ideas, so the process was officially supposed to be a go. Except that certain other departments seem not to have bought in. Just this morning, some unnamed production manager sent out an art file with the old blush logo rather than the scarlet red now mandated company-wide.

Roebuck is still deciding whether he should intervene—Daniel is right to come down hard on any violations to the brand, but wading into internal debates is also dangerous—when he decides he can't stand the strain any longer. He opens Lily's email.

> Well, fuck you then, Julius.
>
> I'm joking. I guess. Yes, I understand. You have to go. These things in life are what life does. I'm disappointed, no hiding that, but don't worry. We'll make it up. And anyway it's not me you have to think about, it's the AdForge folks who are going to want your balls when they get this news. This could be damaging if not handled delicately. You have to admit it's a little late in the day for them to find a replacement. (I, on the other hand, can substitute you at a moment's notice.) Can you help them find someone else, possibly? Give this some careful thinking is my advice.

God, she's wonderful. He really does not deserve such generosity of spirit. And she's completely right about the AFAs. He must be very careful not to underestimate potential repercussions there. They *are* going to want his balls, shaved or otherwise. Roebuck is known in the industry as a giver of good talks.

But at least, speaking of which, his balls have definitely turned a corner. Hardly any pain today, even when he shifts position in his chair. Roebuck admits that this is one of those mornings that has involved a lot of shifting. He is therefore not surprised when another mail from Greenwood lands smoking in his inbox. This time it's the layout for the latest transit ad. The manager in charge is balking because she thinks the tone is "too affirmative." Greenwood wants to know if Roebuck can shed some light on what the fuck "too affirmative" is supposed to mean.

You would think a guy of Greenwood's seniority could deal with this kind of chatter.

Roebuck sits bolt upright in his chair.

Greenwood!

Why not? He's a decent presenter. Tall, sufficiently attractive. Plus he's got the position, if not the gravitas. No reason Daniel can't adequately represent the agency. Roebuck will prepare the text—it's halfway written in his head already—all Greenwood has to do is move his lips and read it.

Roebuck hits "Reply":

Don't worry, Daniel. I'll call Artemis. Something else we need to talk about. Do you own a tux?

15

Destination murders Journey.
The Collected Sayings of Julius Roebuck

At thirty thousand feet, generally speaking, Roebuck is relaxed. Although most people he knows have come to loathe it, Roebuck still likes flying. Not the taking off and landing part, true. And, certainly, he would happily avoid the parody of public good advanced in Homeland Security's neo-Newspeak. But he loves being up in the air. Especially a flight like today's, with the North Atlantic glinting in pewter furrows down below. Only in times of emergencies does Roebuck permit himself to work while in an aircraft, and today's flight, happily, does not coincide with one of those. Instead he reads and sets his mind deliberately to wandering. He cherishes these periods of disconnection, insulated, for at least those hours in the sky; unwired.

The return flight from Helsinki has been as close to perfect as it gets: cloud this morning over northern Europe with driving sheets of rain, the kind that wraps the cabin in a winding shroud of murk until, suddenly, blindingly, it breaks through into that brilliant, crystalline blue. Roebuck has always gloried in that moment. There's a particular variety of solitude that satisfies him to the core, passing through cloud like loose bales of light. A concentration of focus, a consolation of private thought.

He is a realist. He knows it.

Roebuck understands completely that if the roles were reversed—if Lily was the official spouse and Anne the woman he was seeing on the sly—then Anne would be the sweet one and Lily the reproachful wife. This is in no way a reflection of either of their personalities. Either one. It's just a function of marriage as he sees it in the twenty-first century. Roebuck has lost track of what evolution they're now in—fourth wave? fifth?—but he does know that the early days of feminism foretold a world in which men and women behaved the same, but they don't because they can't, which has pissed off every generation since. He wonders how bad things will be when poor Zach comes of age.

By now the cloud has mostly burned away. A short while back they passed a ship—passenger or freighter, Roebuck couldn't say—just an arrow-tip of darkness disappearing off the starboard wing behind a trailing fletch of wake. Whitecaps scatter on the sea below like grains of melting salt. Sometime in the next hour Labrador will appear and after that the long, narrow ribbons of fields radiating at precise right-angles from the banks of the St. Lawrence. With his cheek against the window, Roebuck will be watching as forest gives way to fields, whose square concession blocks in turn become the grids of cities melding into one another on the shores of the Great Lakes. He'll be struck, as he is each time, by the turquoise ovals of suburban swimming pools, at how reproachfully they mimic the darker, deeper ponds that dot the landscape farther north.

He loves Helsinki.

He loves the herring and the cloudberries and those rumbling blondes with voices like laughing rocks. It's that familial northerliness; so much the same as home, yet so completely not. Helsinki is headquarters to the biggest, most important—and, yes—happiest of his clients: the bedrock of Roebuck's fortune. Today, today in particular, his esteem flows above all from his meetings in that loose-limbed city; his meetings have gone very, very well with the promise of better still to come. At thirty-thousand feet, Roebuck's contentedness planes above the atmosphere. It occurs to him, as the aircraft dips a wing, beginning its descent, that his balls have not twinged even once during the entire flight.

It is not until he's in the limo, heading for the office, that Roebuck's happiness bumps into opposition. His luggage for this trip was strictly carry-on; no wasting time banging elbows at the carousel. Roebuck has breezed through customs, despite the undeclared bottle of Lakka tucked into his flight bag as a thank-you gift for Daniel Greenwood.

He is now studying a photograph of Daniel Greenwood. More precisely, BlackBerry in one hand, chin in the other, Roebuck is rereading the caption:

"Advertisers not interested in recognition are like carnivores not interested in meat," whiz kid Daniel Greenwood tells AdForge audience.

Whiz kid? The pic shows a chiselled and tuxedoed Greenwood, nicely backlit, one hand extended, brow contemplatively furrowed. It's a flattering shot.

According to his custom, Roebuck has waited until he's seated in the cab, briefcase at his hip, seatbelt buckled, driver instructed to take the 401 not the Gardiner, before opening his mobile and reconnecting with everything that's been switched off since they rolled out on the tarmac at Helsinki-Vantaa. Earlier this morning, he was surprised to find no mail from Lily. What with the difference in time zones, Roebuck was in bed last night before the show got underway, but he thought she would have sent him a quick note to tell him how the evening went.

Turns out she did. Later. Much, much later: 3:48 AM, her time, to be exact. Roebuck had never before received an email from a Lily so unmistakably inebriated.

> Like listening to you in a different package. Did you write that speech? Must have. Very, very strange, hearing your words coming out of somebody else's mouth. But the mouth was good. He's a good presenter. Also very nice. You nevr said. You'll also be happy that you had a good night. Eight awards altogether if I counted right which I probbly didn't, including the one accepted by dear little me. Remember that stuff you had me working on for the Donlands account? It won!!!! Daniel asked me to go up to the podium to get it. He said he wasn't even working here when that account was handled so it was ridiculous for him to take the credit. He really is very sweet. I think I'm tipsy. Haven't been out this late in centuries. When are you going to take me out late? What's going down in Finland?

Roebuck opens up the on-line edition of today's *AdForge* and checks the tally. Sure enough, his agency has been awarded prizes in a total of eight categories. Not as good as some years, but nothing to sneeze at, either. And there is the picture of Greenwood. Roebuck thumbs the text.

> Daniel Greenwood, hot new talent at Roebuck and Associates, got the crowd going at last night's AdForge gala with a clear-eyed appraisal of the industry today. A last-minute substitute when creative partner Julius Roebuck was scratched, Greenwood clearly enjoyed the

opportunity to remind his colleagues that award shows like the AdForge are a vital link between advertisers and agencies. "Awards are like the proteins of our business," noted Greenwood ...

Roebuck is pleased.

His shop won eight awards; his speech was clearly a success; Greenwood did everything asked of him and more; the AFA appears delighted with how everything worked out. Even Lily—obviously—isn't mad.

How could anyone not be pleased with that?

Part II

May 2008

These nuptial gifts, which can include captured prey, spermatophores, or various male body parts, are intimately tied to both precopulatory and postcopulatory relations.

Sara M. Lewis and Christopher K. Crastley,
"Flash Signal Evolution, Mate Choice, and Predation in Fireflies,"
The Annual Review of Entomology

16

Angels don't get laugh lines.
The Collected Sayings of Julius Roebuck

Eight weeks.
It's not as if he has been marking each day on the calendar. It's not as if he's been scratching nightly notches on the bedpost. But Julius Roebuck has been yearning for this moment for what seems like a very long time. Two months.

Two long months. Fifty-six sunrises; fifty-six sunsets—ardently dodging the hours between.

Meanwhile he has recovered so completely that Roebuck has forgotten, almost, what it was like to be invalidated. The titanium clips now buried deep in the regenerated tissue of his groin are, by every outward indication, holding true. He will know for certain very soon. All swelling has long since disappeared; the scar beneath his penis is insignificant, and for practical purposes, invisible. Roebuck's pubic hair has returned to re-assertive normalcy. He has completed all twenty ejaculations, as prescribed, plus a few more for good measure, although it has been lonely work. But very soon all that will be behind him, too. Today is not the big day. But the big day is just around the corner.

In Roebuck's pocket is a plastic vial.

This is not the sample jar that Yasmin pressed into his trembling palm. Nor the one he left for Anne those long eight weeks ago, although this one is identical in size and shape—and, indeed, prescription—right down to its orange lid and paper seal. Today that seal is broken. Today the label is inscribed. Today, like Hardy's Tess, Roebuck's sample jar is virgin no more.

Inside it is a quantity of sperm. Or, rather, *not* sperm—no sperm at all if there's a shred of justice in the universe. Ejaculate. A quantity of ejaculate, then, presumptively sperm-free, produced not half an hour ago and transported fresh, according to instructions.

As Roebuck has discovered earlier this morning, it is one thing flushing a wad of sticky Kleenex down the john at 2:00 AM when everybody's sleeping; it's something else again achieving accurate expression into a tiny plastic cylinder while the kids are fighting for the toaster and Anne is pacing past the bathroom door, yelling for him to step it up or everyone's going to be late. And in retrospect, too, it would have been a little weird, driving to school with a jar of jism, jingling alongside the change in his pocket.

In the end he's had to wait until the kids were safely off, and Anne departed for her morning run before sneaking back into the house and finishing the job. He'll definitely be late for his 9:30 conference call, but Greenwood can take care of that.

Gama-Care Laboratories is not what he'd expected.

Roebuck isn't sure what he was imagining. Something somehow more … clinical. This looks more like the kind of place a Baptist outreach group might set up shop—or one of those relax spas specializing in prostate massage. He drove by twice before spotting the tiny sign mounted on the door beside a same-day dry cleaner.

Roebuck has switched off the engine and decided to not to pay for parking. There's a buzzer mounted on the doorframe. He presses and waits, hands in his pockets, until it occurs to him that it must be wired to some other apartment. The door swings opens to his pull. Roebuck climbs the narrow stairs.

The reception is a tiny landing no more than eight feet square. Two women sit behind a counter that has further shrunk the space. They're having a discussion with a third individual who Roebuck almost bumps with the door as he enters. One of the women is wearing a lab coat, which Roebuck interprets as a positive sign. The conversation seems to be in Mandarin and each of them is lobbing comments through a sliding glass window set into the wall behind the chest-high counter, although Roebuck discerns no reply emerging from the other side. He edges in sideways and waits in the corner.

"Know what?" he says after a while. "I'm just going out to go check the car."

Ten minutes later by the dashboard clock, he attempts his next ascent. He is feeling somewhat awkward, not altogether confident, truthfully, about how to handle this. Before leaving home, he has inked his name on the label, very clearly with a new black Sharpie, alongside his work address and his private cellphone number. Tucked into his pocket, neatly folded, is the requisition form provided by the No Fuss Vasectomy Clinic. But he's still uncertain of the protocol for transferring materials of this nature.

When he climbs the stairway this time, the person by the door is gone. The remaining two stare as if they have no idea how Roebuck has materialized in front of them. The woman closer to the sliding window rolls her chair back and sends another stream of diphthongs through the void. Roebuck clears his throat.

"Um," he says, "I should give you this," and hands over his Post Vasectomy Semen Analysis form. The woman takes it, scans the essentials, and extends her other hand. All business, now,

Roebuck briskly removes the sample jar from his breast pocket and places it in the woman's waiting palm. She holds it up to the light like a jeweller examining a lump of zirconium, grunts, and lobs the jar into a wire basket. She has passed his requisition form to her colleague, who drops it in another tray at her end of the counter. Voices now come from behind the window. Both women pause respectfully to listen.

A few moments pass before Roebuck realizes that's it.

"By the way," he says, nonchalantly, "how long before the result comes back?"

The woman nearest to him perceives that Roebuck is still in the room. "Wa?"

"How long until I get the result?"

"Two week."

"Two *more* weeks?" But that's …"

"We tell No Fuss. No Fuss tell you. Two week."

"It can't be two weeks, I have …" he hears his own voice failing. The women behind the counter aren't listening anyway.

Two weeks.

Lily is expecting him Monday. Yasmin, even more so. Roebuck retreats to his car. He has cut this too fine. Way, way too fine. If the thought of Lily getting pregnant is beyond frightening, the idea of actually fathering Yasmin's child is full-spectrum nightmare. Roebuck understands that there is absolutely no safe way of dispensing any of his body fluids until he is categorically, unambiguously, 100 percent certain there is no trace of Roebuckian sperm in the mix.

The past two months have been difficult enough. Two more weeks is going to totally screw everything up. He doesn't even see the traffic cop slipping the ticket beneath the blade of his wiper.

All things considered, keeping Yasmin contained has been the biggest challenge. Lily only slightly less so. As far as Anne is concerned, the time has passed without incident of any kind.

Throughout this phase, he and Lily have kept in frequent touch by phone or email as usual, but Roebuck has succeeded, for the entire eight weeks, in steering clear of her reproductive tract. He has missed her. They have shared a couple of innocent lunches, a few drinks together after work, and now—this afternoon, when he has foolishly agreed to drive her home from work—some dangerous moments alone in his car. But he caught a lucky break with the timing of a cruise that her parents thoughtfully provided: sixteen whole days on a boat with an ocean between them. Since she's been back, though, tensions have escalated sharply. Lily has never been one to let things fester.

"Has it run its course? Just tell me. We both know this was never meant to be permanent."

"Oh jeez, Lil, no. No!"

Roebuck takes at least a little moral solace from the honesty of his distress. The hand-wringing is no act. "Honestly. It's just … circumstances. Awkward timing. I had the flu, remember? And then that meeting in Helsinki …"

"That was *months* ago."

"Two months. Barely two months. Then it was Dallas, then that snag in New York I told you about. I told you about that, didn't I? Then that thing in Halifax. And you were off in the Caribbean with your folks, don't forget. It's just … unlucky timing."

"But you'd tell me, wouldn't you? You *are* the kind of man who'd tell me. Tell me you are." Lily is wild-eyed in the passenger seat. Roebuck with his motor running is parked against the curb outside her house.

"There's nothing to tell! Seriously, Lily. It's just …"

"All right. All right! It's been so long, that's all. I'm not convent material; you're the one who's supposed to appreciate that. I know you can't right now, but you *are* coming Monday? Better say you are."

"Absolutely. Monday. Of course. I blocked off the entire after-noon. Definitely."

Yasmin, in her own way, has been more problematic still. Though not at first.

For several weeks following that inspirational visit to his sickbed—memories of which have played a central role in the functionality of Roebuck's spermatozoa cleanse—not a peep. Nearly a month in ab-solute silence. Of course he heard *about* her, daily: Anne and Yasmin were off to see some Moore Park speculator envisaging a pop-top; Yasmin has patched things up with that inspector who's been jerk-ing them around over the variance on Heath; Yasmin has gone and booked a test drive with a new yoga instructor, though Anne doesn't see what's wrong with Willow. But not a word, all the while, to him directly. By this time Anne was convinced their troubles were behind them; Roebuck more than half believed his wife was right.

Then Yasmin staged her intervention.

"That's a very dedicated decorator you got there," said Carol, his receptionist. Roebuck had just stepped off the elevator. "Owe her money?"

"Excuse me?"

"Sorry. My bad. It's just that she sat there waiting half the mor-ning. I told her you weren't likely back for a while. But she kept staying."

At one level, Roebuck's brain was at that very moment con-sciously reminding itself that he and Carol still needed to touch bases about the functions of Reception Desk, but pretty much every other circuit was lit up to the single throbbing question: "*She's here?*" He caught himself, for just a second, lifting his heels for a better view across the cubicles.

"Nah. She left."

"Right," said Roebuck, grounding. What was he expecting, Yasmin on his sofa in red satin sheets?

"But she said she'd be back in an hour."

"Anything else?"

"There's a package from Ripreeler. It's on your desk. Also your BlackBerry. You left it in the boardroom again."

Roebuck walked in measured paces to his office and instantly checked messages.

The usual: a cluster from Artemis, one from Anne reminding him about a charity dinner they've promised to co-chair next month, a new gripe from his client in Framingham, two from his accountant, followed by another of those disconcerting probes from Omniglobe.

And four more flagged URGENT from Yasmin. That day was the turning point.

It was the day that Roebuck committed.

Stepping back into the lobby, he told Carol in his sternest straw-boss voice that he had several important calls to make so could she please do her job effectively for once and be certain he wasn't interrupted? Then he closed his door and locked it—something that hardly ever happened—and commenced his preparations.

Throughout that afternoon—throughout the ninety-odd minutes between Yasmin's first and second appearance that pivotal day—Roebuck's hands kept returning to the fascinating parcel on his desk.

One of the nice things about a client in the fishing business was the steady stream of tackle. As a valued partner in Ripreeler's North American retail operations, Roebuck received samples of every new product his client released. Most of it was overkill; last summer they sent a marlin rig that was bigger than the rock bass he and Zach fished for off the dock. But the supply of spinners, jigs, and plugs, to say nothing of all those glossy crankbaits, had made their tackle box the envy of all the other fathers on the lake.

This package was different. First of all, it hadn't come from Ripreeler directly. This one had been delivered by courier from a location in Manila, the Philippines. Roebuck removed a pair of scissors from his drawer and cut the wrap. Inside he found a flat polyethylene bottle, like the nasal spray dispensers he and Anne used when the kids were still in diapers, the kind you squeeze to make the medicine gush straight up the nostril.

It was, he realized, the new pheromone product poised to revolutionize sport fishing. Attached was a handwritten note from the marketing manager, an American he'd met briefly in Helsinki. Roebuck unscrewed the cap and tentatively sniffed. He jammed the lid back on. It smelled exactly the way you'd expect a fish extract to smell; worse. But that was good. They were selling to the fisherman, after all, not the fish, and that stink would certainly leave an impression. Roebuck put on his reading glasses to make out the tiny print. Not good. Anglers fall mainly into older demographics. The font size would definitely need to be increased, though the instructions, once in focus, seemed straightforward enough: "Spray a small quantity on your lure and watch the fish jump into your boat! This amazing product mimics key pheromones that send fish into a feeding frenzy."

And there, at that moment, Roebuck found the crisis he was hoping for.

Pheromones, as everybody knows, stimulate the desire to mate, not eat.

Or at least that was the argument he intended to put into play the moment he heard Yasmin coming through his door. The note from Manila had thoughtfully included the sender's home phone number. Roebuck programmed it into his speed dial, made sure the door was closed but unlocked, and waited.

❀

An hour later, he was waiting still.

In the meantime, he'd consulted his time-zone converter and determined that in the Philippines it was very, very early in the morning. In fact, it was tomorrow. With any luck at all, marketing manager Frank O'Neil would be a light sleeper. But at least at that hour he was almost certain to be home. Roebuck was never entirely comfortable conversing with speakers on the far side of the dateline. He enjoyed a good paradox, but that one had always unsettled him: today and tomorrow being one and the same. This conversation was certain to be awkward whenever it was situated in the time-space continuum.

Though that, too, could prove beneficial.

When the line from the reception desk buzzed, he only just stopped himself from answering. Roebuck sprang to his feet. The buzzing stopped. Silence. Then another, longer burst. By this time, his earlobe was applied directly to the inside panel of his door.

Voices, raised voices; a confusion of footsteps …

Leaping back to his desk, he hit the call button and hovered— still on tiptoes—while the connections clicked through. A phone in a bedroom somewhere in a residential district of Manila commenced to ring. Roebuck almost feared no one would pick up when at last he heard a female voice, groggy, in a language he took to be Tagalog. "Hello!" he said loudly, cutting over it. "I'm calling for Frank O'Neil, please."

More Tagalog. An alarming silence. Then, finally, a different, hoarser voice. "Hello? Hello?"

"Is that Frank O'Neil?"

Cough. "What time is it?"

"Frank! This is Julius Roebuck."

Roebuck pressed the button to increase the volume as he spoke. "Who?"

"Julius Roebuck! From Roebuck and Associates. We met in Helsinki. I've just opened your sample bait."

From out in the hall beyond the door to his office came the sound of a struggle. One of the voices he recognized as Carol's.

"Oh, Julius, of course. Hello. Nice to hear from you. You know it's …"

The other voice was definitely Yasmin's.

"I'm very sorry for disturbing you, Frank. But I'm afraid we have a problem."

A covert knock; more scuffle.

"It's four o'clock in the morning!"

Carol—he will have to do something to make up for this, later—was bravely mounting a last-ditch resistance. But Yasmin had leverage and far more capable hips.

"A problem, Frank. A very big problem."

Roebuck had ensured his back was turned, precisely at that moment: the better to spin dramatically in shock and consternation. Right on cue, his door burst open.

"I'm *so* sorry Julius!" Carol was flushed and possibly bleeding from an ankle. "She just wouldn't …"

He made a point of staring, mouth agape, as if not quite believing the effrontery of this, then whirled and cupped his hand over his ear, furiously deadening the interruption.

"What do you mean, a problem?"

"Julius, I …"

Roebuck rounded for a second time, eyes ablaze, throwing up one hand like a Columbian traffic cop, still concentrating mightily on the telephone pressed against his ear. "I mean we have a problem, Frank. The messaging is wrong."

"Messaging? What messaging?"

Yasmin took a step forward.

"The messaging, Frank! The central messaging. It's totally wrong!" Then another step.

Mashing the phone against his chest, glaring ferociously, Roebuck snapped his fingers. He'd been practising his snap the past half-hour: its percussion echoed off the walls like gunfire. Yasmin and the receptionist froze like rabbits. Roebuck jabbed a furious finger Yasmin's way and aimed it at a chair, then glared some more at Carol and jerked his wrathful thumb toward the door.

"Could you maybe be more specific?"

Carol backed out of the room. Yasmin crept softly to her chair.

"I'll explain when I get there."

"Here?"

"This is critical, Frank. I'll be landing," Roebuck furrowed his brows and studied his watch but gave up on the time-change calculations, "in a matter of hours!"

"Here? You're coming *here*?"

"See you shortly."

"But …"

Roebuck slammed down the receiver.

He took a moment to allow his stare to linger in the space between them: a man only just containing his wrath.

"Julius, I …"

Roebuck clenched his teeth until he felt his molars squeak, then stabbed the button on his phone. "Book me a flight to Manila. Today! This afternoon!"

"Yes, sir."

She had never—or anyone else, for that matter—called him *sir*. It wasn't even the receptionist's responsibility to look after travel arrangements. He would definitely have to find some way of making up for this. Still staring into nothing, Roebuck brought his fist to his chin and studied the wall a measured heartbeat longer.

After a time, exhaling loudly, he moved his hands to the armrests of his chair. At last he eased himself back and slowly, consciously, relaxed his body. "Yasmin …" he said, tasting the syllables.

For a while no other word was spoken. Her eyes were on the floor, and Roebuck used the opportunity to take her in. She too was out of breath: adrenaline—and a cocktail of other, more arresting hormones—spiking through her system. Roebuck absorbed the lambent rise and fall of breast.

"It's today …" she whispered in a voice that rustled like the fabric of her skirt.

Roebuck kept his tone as hieratical as he could make it. "What's today?" He wanted to hear her say it.

Yasmin's tongue emerged, slid across her teeth. Her lips parted then opened then parted again. "I … I tried calling. You, you didn't get back."

"Yasmin, I have a company to run. I've been tied up the entire day."

"I'm ovulating. Right *now!* Today … maybe tomorrow."

"Tomorrow I'm gone. Tomorrow I'm on the far side of the dateline. Which makes it the day after tomorrow as far as you are concerned."

"What …? I mean … Can't you just …?"

Already he could feel the vascular shift, the blood rushing from his brain, rerouting. He was very glad he'd had the sense to stay behind his desk. The phone startled them both. Roebuck picked it up.

"I found a flight."

"A flight?"

"Direct to Manila."

"Yes. Excellent … When?"

"It leaves this afternoon. Not much time to pack, but I can get you a seat."

"Book it," he said. And then, "Well done."

"Yasmin …" Roebuck quietly replaced the phone. "This has gotten out of hand."

Several seconds more elapsed in silence. An interesting transformation: Yasmin meek; Yasmin suffused like this in blush. She
was looking at him, and he tried to hold her gaze. "I have a lot to
do ..." he said. "I'm at the airport in an hour ..."

"Couldn't you just ..."

"Just what?"

"No. You're right. You're always right."

The phone went off again.

"I forgot to tell you. Daniel wants to see you. I had the feeling
this might not be a good time ..."

"What would give you that impression? Two minutes. Then
send him in."

Yasmin had risen, smoothing her skirt in that way of hers, fingers in the dimples of her hips.

"I should go."

He needed to be careful. "I'm sorry it didn't work out this time."

She stopped and caught her breath. He could almost feel the
heat from where he sat behind his desk. "This time ...?" Yasmin
was standing, poised beside his door.

"In future, if you could provide me with some warning ...?"

He still can't decide if it was deliberate, but Yasmin's fingers ca-
ressed the doorknob as she spoke, turning and unturning the latch.
"Twenty-eight days," she whispered. "Just count."

"I'll make a note in my calendar."

"You're such a lovely man!" Yasmin swept toward him for a
lingering embrace. "I brought this ..." she said, unfastening her
purse. She had misread his expression. "Oh. But of course you
can't right now. Anyway, you can keep it for next month." She
placed a plastic sample bottle with its now-familiar orange lid on
the corner of his desk.

On the way out, she blew a kiss.

"Who was that?"

Greenwood was stopped outside the door watching Yasmin, weaving down the corridor. Roebuck swept the sample jar into a drawer.

"Can I help you, Daniel?"

"What? Yes. Just wondering if there's any development on that drag and clop concept?"

"Still holding tight on that one. But since you're here, look at this." Roebuck held up the pheromone dispenser and, once Greenwood stepped into range, allowed himself a purging squeeze ...

He doesn't see the ticket until he's pulled out into traffic. Roebuck unbuckles at the next light, hops out to yank it off the windshield, and almost doors a cyclist; he is not as apologetic as the circumstances warrant. More bad Karma. It has now been twenty-three days, exactly, since Roebuck staged his show with Yasmin in his office. He has indeed been counting. According to his calculations, Yasmin will be in the sweet spot of her cycle this coming Monday. Again his plans are in ruins. And what was he thinking, not feeding the meter?

As expected, he has missed his teleconference.

"Sleep in?"

Greenwood is wearing that look he gets whenever he senses the moral advantage has tilted in his favour.

"Nose to the grindstone, Daniel." Roebuck heads for his office, yellow parking ticked crumpled in one fist. "No rest for the weary."

Greenwood looks as if he's not quite certain whether the remark was meant for him. "You know," he calls out, "I had to throw that shirt away. Did I mention that? Two times to the cleaners and it *still* stinks!" But Roebuck has already passed out of hearing.

Almost always, now, there's some new treat waiting in his private inbox.

It's been an interesting tutorial, these last weeks, on the finer points of human oogenesis. He is glad he had no need for all this earlier in life. With Anne there was no science. It took a little longer than expected the first time, with Katie, and for a while there they started to worry. But after that, all the mechanics just fell into place. They had sex, they had kids; they had sex, they had kids. In retrospect, so elegantly simple. Yasmin monitors her ova like FedEx tracks its waybills. She set up Hushmail accounts, early on, to facilitate the flow of information. Roebuck has only to log in, now, to receive his daily update. "I've begun the Luteal Phase," she informed him back at the start of things, which to his ear sounded like the title of a Michael Crichton novel.

Though the Luteal, as it turned out, was by and large a friendly interval, at least at the onset. A week or so later, when a message headed "The Ischemic!" blazed in (he had to Google that one, too), things turned decidedly hostile. This was when Yasmin coldly informed him of her preference for freezing his sperm in order to accomplish their objective with a minimum of personal contact. Subsequent investigation, luckily, revealed that the process called for liquid nitrogen and a range of technical abilities well beyond the scope of home enthusiasts. As the cycle advanced, her interest in cryogenics quietly ebbed.

Menstruation itself, by comparison, was a fairly calm and quiet time. But things took a radical turn once the Follicular Phase commenced in all its fearsome splendour.

The Follicular, as Roebuck has now amatively grasped, is where the rubber truly hits the reproductive highway. Throughout this past week, Yasmin's estrogen levels have been twitching skyward. A newly bathed and scented ovum now quivers at the gates, straining for release. In one of the most bizarrely erotic texts ever to have shivered down the length of Roebuck's spine, she has described for him in detail how the mucus in her cervix has changed from thick and clumpy to slippery and thin.

Roebuck is barely able to withstand the strain.

The Follicular Phase, as he knows, is not the big day. But the big day is just around the corner.

And once again he is going to have to take a pass.

⊚⊚

Though almost not. Roebuck very nearly convinces himself to go ahead and damn the consequences. He has, after all, completed all twenty ejaculations, plus. It *has* been a full two months, plus. The considered sum of Roebuck's intuition is advising that he must by now be safely shooting blanks.

Except that, from the start of this, he has set rules in place.

Roebuck's respect for his own standards has bound him to the sovereignty of reason. And it isn't just Yasmin. It's Lily, too, who is expecting him for more than lunch, come Monday. He gets up to close the door, then contritely opens it again. This sort of thing has been happening too much lately. There's a recession, after all; revenues are down. His people have reason to be nervous. That sudden, emergency flight to Manila didn't help, though Roebuck has a strong sensation that one, at least, is going to work out in the long run; a very strong feeling that that piece of theatre may have achieved much more than was intended. Wheels are in motion. He makes a mental note to stand a round or two this Friday night at Matrix Three and hint that something big is in the works, which calms and reminds him, too, that it's time to bring Daniel in on this.

But first, a far more noxious piece of business. Roebuck won't commit himself. Not yet. But he has been turning this over and over and still hasn't come up with anything better. He is running out of thinking room and clearly—this time—it will have to be spectacular.

He opens up Google and asks: "What can I eat to make myself throw up?"

Seconds later, Roebuck receives an astonishing sixteen million hits. For a few moments, even Yasmin fades from mind as he contemplates the scope of what this says about his species.

The good news, though, is that he finds what he requires right away.

Later he will learn that it's derived from the roots and rhizome of the ipecacuanha plant, a native of Brazil. He will also discover, subsequently, that many people in the non-bulimic world are legitimately familiar with this substance, too. He will be even more surprised to learn—months on and inadvertently—that once upon a time it was stocked in his own house, before the ban, by his judicious wife as precaution against accidental poisoning. But for the moment, syrup of ipecac is something Roebuck has never heard of, never once encountered.

Owing to the power of the Internet, he is rapidly caught up. It soon becomes apparent that the people who weigh in on this topic—the mind-boggling number of people who post on the subject of self-induced vomiting—self-sort into cohorts. The first group Roebuck would characterize as information-seekers: folks requesting practical advice on the how-to's of regurgitation. A second, and significantly larger, category seems to be comprised of answer-givers: good Samaritans offering a wide assortment of useful tips. The third and final segmentation—which Roebuck deliberately ignores—is a loose collection of observers posting comments on the intellectual qualities of the previous two.

He refines his search, concentrating on utility. Mustard and milk mixed together seems to be a popular suggestion. Another one that turns up often is a litre of warm salty water, guzzled down in one big slurp. In Roebuck's case neither of these are likely to be feasible, but it doesn't matter because syrup of ipecac—by far the most frequent recommendation and obtainable at most pharmacies—is tailor-made to his requirements.

He clicks back to Google and drills a little deeper.

Wikipedia lays out its botanic origins and history as an herbal emetic. Roebuck skips through the account of its more recent popularity with hasty bulimics and begins to browse the dozens—hundreds—of homemade videos featuring boys with acne chugging ipecac so they can be filmed by hooting friends while throwing up. There's a dismal sameness to these postings, and he worries for a while that he's inclined to hurl himself, watching. But his time is well spent. Mostly, what he wants to know is how long the substance takes to work. Several of the videos have thoughtfully provided count-down clocks. In half an hour's viewing, Roebuck has determined that the interval between ingestion and emesis averages out to roughly fifteen minutes, give or take.

Closing down his browser, he returns to the world of sane people and taps out a quick note to Greenwood, asking him to drop by when he has a minute. Not a formal meeting, just a friendly chat.

Then he gives himself a little healing-time and composes a message for Lily. After his past half-hour, the exercise is comfortingly therapeutic.

> What Is Man?
> The Sun's Light when he unfolds it
> Depends on the Organ that beholds it
> Still on for Monday? I've booked us a table.

He has barely thumbed "Send" before Greenwood fills his doorway.

"Daniel! Aren't you prompt."

"I'm heading out to Artemis so it's now or never."

"What is it this time?" It occurs to Roebuck that he should probably know. Greenwood's thoughts, evidently, are running along similar lines; he rolls his eyes. "What is it you want to talk about?"

"Ripreeler. But if you have to go, you have to go. We can pick it up again next week."

"Ripreeler? That's always been your baby. I've never worked on Ripreeler!"

"Only because there has been nothing, since you started here, that has required art direction on that particular account. Now there is."

"Is that what that flash trip to the Philippines was all about? People were making it out as some kind of crisis."

Roebuck smiles. "It's an opportunity, Dan. A very big one."

Greenwood has been lusting for some hands-on time with their biggest account since the day he joined the agency. "All right, tell?"

"Later, Dan. We'll set aside a block of time next week. We have a lot of ground to cover."

"Then it'll have to be Monday." Greenwood is scowling at his mobile's calendar. "Monday. 11:00 AM. And my name is Daniel. Not Dan. Daniel."

That better be Blake, not you, or I'm never letting you see my stuff again. Table, what table?

It's late afternoon; she must have been out. He is only now accessing her reply. Despite what he intends to engineer tomorrow, Roebuck's pleasure is restoratively real. He smiles as he composes his reply.

For the Sexes: The Gates of Paradise. Frontispiece. (Yup, Wm. Blake.)

Think I'm capable of something so subliminal? There's a new seafood restaurant over in Corktown I'd like to try. Thought we'd have a bite then mosey back to your place if that is still on offer ...

An interval, longer than expected, before her reply.

What a relief! I'd hate to think you'd moved up to that guy's level of delusion. Sure you want to waste time eating out? I cook, you know.

He is strongly tempted, but that would be going too far. That would stretch morality beyond the point where even Roebuck is willing to escort it. And besides, he has promised himself not to set foot in her house until the issue of his fertility is conclusively resolved.

No worries, I've booked off the whole afternoon. I'm in the mood for oysters. As it happens, I can stay out late ...

Untrue. Roebuck is scheduled to deliver Morgan to her Monday soccer practice, 4:45 PM, sharp. But by that time he is fairly certain circumstances will radically have altered. Lily's answer arrives with the rhythm of an Attic chant.

Noon, then.
Pick me up at noon.

Roebuck books a table at *Crème de la Mer* for 12:30 PM. He has just logged out of the restaurant's website when a fresh email pings in from Anne, who prefers to use caps when corresponding with her husband.

JULIUS, TWO REMINDERS. PLEASE NOTE:
ONE: YOU NEED TO PICK UP KATIE FOR BALLET AT
5:00 PM <u>TODAY.</u>
TWO: YOU NEED TO GET MORGAN TO HER SOCCER
GAME AT 4:45 <u>MONDAY</u>.

He was certainly aware of his responsibilities Monday with regard to Morgan, but it's true that Katie's ballet this afternoon had temporarily escaped him. Roebuck's plan was to stop in at the pharmacy on the way home. No matter; plenty of time Monday morning.

It's late evening. Roebuck has washed his face, brushed his teeth, and put on the soft flannel pyjamas he has preferred for several years and which Anne has disliked for almost as long. His new reading glasses are positioned on his nose and an advance copy of Malcolm Gladwell's latest, opened to page one, rests on his chest. Roebuck's intention is to read a chapter then slip as quickly as possible into sleep. Anne is speaking.

"Don't forget, Monday I have that session with our new yogini. So it's you taking Morgan to soccer."

Her recent email had spelled out his responsibilities quite clearly, but saying so would sound like bickering. He yawns and, when his jaw rehinges, says, "So you've given up on Willow?"

He is completely wiped. All through this afternoon Roebuck has been trying not to think about tomorrow's lunch and concentrate instead on how solidly he hopes to sleep tonight. He is not normally troubled by jet lag, but that whirlwind back-and-forth to Asia is still messing with his system. He hasn't slept well since Manila.

Anne's reaction warns him that he's touched a sore spot.

"Honestly, that woman!" Whether this refers to Yasmin or the new yoga instructor, Roebuck isn't certain. "Once she gets something into her head, there's no stopping her."

So it's Yasmin. Amen to that. He takes off his glasses and aligns them on the spine of his book. Anne circles the room, lowering blinds, and drawing curtains. "This one spent six months at some ashram in Rishikesh, so she's all the rage ..."

Roebuck gives some thought to asking if a female yoga master can be properly called a yoga mistress, but has the good sense to set that one aside. He's too tired anyway ...

"All this kundalinic energy," Anne says, "and the Shakti goddess and serpent power ... and don't forget the sacred sacrum bone."

He feels the mattress tilt beside him and opens his eyes.

"Really, whatever happened to just working up an honest sweat?"

He has registered an anomaly here, though not as fully as he knows he should. His wife is lying on her side beside him, head resting on her hand, watching his face. It has been a long while since she has been on his bed like this with both feet off the floor.

"I bought you new pyjamas."

"I like these ones." Anne has often bought him new pyjamas. There's a drawer full.

"You've had them forever. Time for a change."

"That's why I like them." Roebuck yawns; his eyes have settled shut. "The longer you've had something, the stronger your attachment." He is aware that this too, has perilous implications as a marketing platform, but never mind. "I'm attached" is the best he can manage.

Anne lays a finger on his cheek. "What a nice thing to say."

He feels the touch, but distantly. He does not hear his wife get up and return to her own room.

17

Smart is to stupid what thought is to belief.
The Collected Sayings of Julius Roebuck

By now he has begun to panic. No, not panic. Roebuck checks the dashboard clock. It's 10:22 AM. He's lost track of how many pharmacies he has stopped at already. Half a dozen, at least. More.

By this time he is well out into the suburbs, or what he considers suburbs; parts of the city there's no reason for anyone to go; endless tracts of endless strip malls. Roebuck marvels that all these people could live so far away. He is waiting at a stoplight, deciding which way to turn. Every direction is more of the same.

He spots a faded billboard straight ahead and rolls across another intersection.

It's one of those vast, wind-swept plazas that must have been at one time anchored by a megastore, now departed. A flat-roofed hulk squats in the centre of a fissured parking lot, boarded up where glass has been replaced with sheets of greying plywood. Remnants of enterprise cling to the perimeter. Roebuck coasts past a dimly lit barber shop, an Afghan family restaurant, and a pay-day loan establishment before he spots the drugstore. This—or at the very latest, the one after this—will be his last chance. He is forty-five minutes, at least, from his office and his 11:00 AM with Daniel Greenwood.

But this place holds out hope. A bell on a string chimes as he opens the door. Roebuck is encouraged by the air of gauntness; an auspicious blare of vacant white: pale dropped ceiling, bleached tile floor, stark fluorescent light casting shadows over empty shelves. A red-faced, bulb-shaped pharmacist sits on a wooden chair behind his counter leafing through a tabloid of the kind that still puts topless women on page two. No one else is on the premises. Roebuck feels his pulse begin to race. He keeps his voice pleasant, modulated, unconcerned.

"I'm looking for syrup of ipecac," he says.

Roebuck smiles and places his hands on the counter, bracing. He is growing used to the reaction. The first one looked at him as if him he'd ordered a dose of Rohypnol with a lollypop to go. This was just around the corner from his house, a big-box drug mart a few blocks from Zach's school. Roebuck had walked serenely past the rows of exfoliating creams and oral hygiene products to the prescription desk where—innocently—he'd made his request. The woman behind the counter took a full step back. "That product has been taken off the shelves! You can't buy that here!"

Roebuck now knows he is an idiot for not having seen to this sooner.

The next place was the same again. Little by little, stop by stop—as he wound his way further and further into the suburban hinterlands—he has pieced the facts together. Sale of ipecac has been restricted or banned outright. On this point he is not completely certain, and therein lies his hope. "That's what killed Karen Carpenter!" one of them informed him, lip curling. Roebuck had forgotten Karen Carpenter.

He has no Plan B.

His one ambition, fading fast, has been to find a pharmacy that still keeps some in stock. This sad little shop is the likeliest he's seen so far.

It has been difficult, maintaining poise. Reaction to his request has been so uniformly negative, so wholly guilt-inducing, that Roebuck has begun to feel a smear of criminality. He reminds himself to straighten his shoulders and not to lick his lips. The pharmacist removes his eyes from his paper and ogles.

"Syrup of ipecac, please," Roebuck says again, dry-mouthed.

This one's smock is striped, alternating blue and white. A large tear-drop stain rises and falls above the belly; its shape is reminiscent of Sri Lanka. Serendip.

"Aren't supposed to sell that."

Hope explodes in Roebuck's chest like summer lightning. He does lick his lips; he can't help it.

"I know," he says, his voice like sandpaper.

The pharmacist does not blink, seems incapable of blinking. A carotene anemone of hair fans softly from his nostrils as the air flows in and out. Sri Lanka bobs and settles on a swell of gut.

"Wait here."

Roebuck battles down the sudden fear that someone out of sight is calling the police. He stands firmly by the counter, hands in his pockets, alone in the deserted shop.

Serendip emerges from a room in the back with a dusty cardboard carton. He sets it on the counter and swipes a rag across the lid; orange bristles curling at the joints of each knuckle, poor man.

The lid comes off, scattering dust. Inside Roebuck counts a half a dozen plastic bottles. The pharmacist picks one out in silence and passes it across the counter. The label is the same as in all the videos. A thought comes and goes—Roebuck pushes it away—that he's been spending too much time in the company of small plastic containers.

"How much?"

A price is named.

"How much for the box?"

A larger sum. Roebuck pays with cash and leaves with his cache of ipecac cradled in his arms, saved.

It's 10:44 AM.

"Epigamic?" Greenwood squints and interrupts himself. "You look all out of breath. Are you okay?"

"It's Greek," Roebuck says. "From the root *epi-*, meaning 'close in space, and time', and *gamos*, meaning 'marriage.' It's used to describe attractiveness to the opposite sex, as in the colours of certain birds ..."

"And there you go again. You're obsessed." Greenwood is now peering at him closely. "You sure you're okay? You look bagged."

"I'm fine, Daniel. Thanks for asking. Just that I'm still a little tired from that run to the Philippines, is all."

"Are we going to talk about that?"

"Yes. Well, no. We *were* going to talk about it. But now we're out of time."

"What do you mean, out of time? You're the one who showed up late!"

"Sorry. My morning got completely screwed. But we do need to discuss the epigamic angle. That's the important thing. Did I ever tell you that I gave some serious thought to using it as a name for the agency, back when I started?" Roebuck allows himself a shade of reminiscence. "Too esoteric." He sighs.

Greenwood isn't interested in history or esotery either. "I'm trying to wrap my head around what you're saying. You want to use *sexual* attractiveness to sell fish goo?"

"Not to put too fine a point on it, Daniel, but sex is what's been driving this campaign since its inception. And anyway, it was you who got us here."

Now it's Greenwood's turn to sigh.

"When I accidentally spilled some on you. Was it last month already? Time does fly."

"That was no accident. And you didn't spill. You *squirted*!"

"I think the better verb is *spray* or *mist*. Anyway, that's what got me thinking of cologne. That began the process."

"Where are you going with this?"

Roebuck has returned to his feet. He'd collapsed in Greenwood's chair, but now his wind is back. "What I'd like you to explore, Daniel, is the epigamic possibilities in Ripreeler's new pheromone bait."

"But it's supposed to make fish want to *feed*, not fuck! Isn't that what they told you at that place in Manila?"

"More or less. And that, my friend, is why they hire people like you and me to see beyond what they do. And by the way, I don't think fish actually fuck. Not in the same sense we do."

"Then how do they make baby fish?"

Roebuck is angling toward the door. "Let's leave that ponderable aside for the moment. It's people we're selling to, not fish. And people—I promise—are interested in sexual attraction. That's what we want to play with in this campaign ..."

"And *that's* what I'm not getting."

"Now, now, Daniel. I'm sure there are certain people who under certain circumstances might conceivably find you attractive."

"Funny. You're so funny. Please explain the epigamic qualities of fish goo."

Roebuck checks his watch. It's a twenty-minute drive to Lily's. "Are you aware that cat urine is used as a key component of perfumes? Beaver oils and deer musk too. They farm civet cats in China, strictly for their musk. Perfumers use it as a base note."

"You're telling me you want to market this stuff as a perfume for fish?"

"Not fish. Fish are not our customers. *People* are our customers. Why do I have to keep telling you that? Not as a perfume for fish. As a perfume for people."

"Are you insane? It reeks! I told you. I had to throw that shirt away."

"So presumably, does civet musk. Reek, I mean. They're closely related to skunks, you know."

"Sometimes I don't believe what comes out of you."

"Neither did the Ripreelers when I told them they should put their fishing lures in the ears of fashion models. It's the same campaign, Daniel. One is a continuation of the other. Think *epigamic*."

"You can't make *everything* conform to that."

"Yes, you can. And yes we do. That's *our* base line. Go back and watch the reels. There's flow to this campaign that has everything to do with that. You've watched the reels, haven't you?"

"Of course I've watched the reels! The Ripreeler campaign is why I'm here!"

"And here I thought it was my mentorship."

Greenwood has no reply, which is just as well because Roebuck is already out the door. "Use your creativity, Daniel-not-Dan," he says over his shoulder. "That's why *you* are here."

"You know I cancelled my other appointments for this!"

But Roebuck is too far gone to answer.

"You're late."

Roebuck has checked his watch as he pressed the bell and is aware of his delinquency. He notes too that Lily has opened the door with a mostly empty glass of wine in hand.

"Yes. But only fourteen minutes."

He has driven through three amber lights and nearly clocked another cyclist. Lily stands aside and gestures him in, but Roebuck holds his ground. He has left his motor running. "We don't want to lose our table," he says, eyeing the pack of boys in low-slung pants and hoodies cruising past his car. Verisimilitude demands its risk.

"You're hot to trot for this seafood place."

"Like I said, I'm in the mood for oysters."

They have discussed, over other lunches, the aphrodisiac possibilities of bivalves; the likelihood that such qualities exist. Lily dislikes the taste, even more the texture, and disbelieves; Roebuck loves a plate of oysters and consequently doesn't care. He is wholly truthful when he tells her that the aphrodisiac is Lily herself, not whatever dish he eats beforehand. But he does enjoy a plate of Malpeques with a side of coarsely grated horseradish and a shot of oily jalapeño.

"You and your oysters," she says.

"Me and my oysters."

He takes a sip of Lily's wine and sets the glass on the table by the door, holding the screen while she turns the lock. On the drive downtown he asks, as always, what she's working on.

"Today I am depressed," she tells him.

It turns out she has received a rejection notice in this morning's mail. "You wait for months. Then you get a little yellow slip of paper saying sorry, try again. On-line submissions are worse. Sometimes you don't hear back from those at all."

"Which one?"

"Which journal or which poem?"

"Which poem?"

"Ha! Serves you right! It was the one about you."

"Well, there you go."

He could quote those verses back to her, verbatim, but won't say that. That too would be cheating. He can't decide what he feels about this: that poem in particular. Not her best work. And probably, he thinks, he has put his finger on why. He also wants to tell her that rejection is inevitable. Clients routinely turn him down; it's part of what they do. What they all do. But that too would be facile. The goal of Lily's writing is to reveal the truth. His is something else again. In Roebuck's trade, sometimes rejection comes as a relief.

"I know what you're thinking."

"*What?*"

Roebuck is shooting through another intersection; he can't afford to turn his head.

"Interesting." Lily in the passenger seat bears no such restriction. "Now why did that startle you? You *like* me knowing what you're thinking."

He has no comeback. What she says is true.

"That's what your aphorisms are for, aren't they? Your collection? Those little squibs you like to have me read. Me. Them. We're what falls *outside* the Roebuck brand, aren't we? We're your *other* self-expression."

It's safe to look now, but Roebuck doesn't. He is giving this his whole consideration. "We can't all be poets," he says gently, wearily. "Regarding truth, I mean. We don't all get poetic licence."

"Ha! Good! You do impress. That may just be the first time I have ever heard that phrase correctly used."

"That's my job, you know. Impressing you."

"Your job is fucking me. That's what you should know."

The restaurant is packed. A young woman at reception informs them tartly that she was just about to give their table to another party.

"Fancy," Lily says, watching the hostess stalk away, hips first.

"Fancy," Roebuck echoes.

"You look tired."

"People keep saying that." He is vain enough to be annoyed. But there couldn't be a better cover. "Just jet lag. I don't usually get it. This time I did."

"It went well, your thing in the Philippines? We haven't talked shop."

Roebuck feels the crinkles of his own smile. "Yes!" He wishes he could lay out for her all the ironies he'd love to share. "*Yes*. It's possible this could turn out even better than I hoped." But now the smile retreats. That trip has brought to mind its predecessor. "I want to say again how so sorry I am, Lily, that I missed the AFAs. I hated doing that."

"Don't worry. Things went ahead without you."

"Ah."

A waiter appears with a wine list. Roebuck picks an Alsatian Gewürztraminer he knows she favours.

"And why don't you bring a plate of oysters," Lily says.

"We have some very nice Bélon."

"Malpeque," Roebuck tells him. "A dozen, please."

"Two." Lily has assumed her impish look. "Two dozen. Maybe I'll swallow some too."

"What?" He's a little sharper than he means to be. "You hate oysters!"

"I am learning to broaden my horizons."

Roebuck scans the list of appetizers and identifies a workable alternative. "Then let's have an order of pâté too, just in case. I'm told they do their own here ..."

The waiter does not contradict him, and Roebuck is reminded that the tip today will need to be excessive. He has a wad of cash, prepared and ready.

"Okay. Pâté too," says Lily.

Roebuck returns the menu to the waiter who obligingly disappears. "We aim to please."

"So," she says. "Catch me up ..."

The appetizers arrive before the wine, which in other circumstances would substantially reduce the tip, though the waiter is profuse in his apology: the bottle they have chosen is not to be found in the cellar; an alternative is offered and accepted. Roebuck is more concerned with making sure the oysters stay on his side of the table.

"Why don't we have a cocktail!" he says.

"A cocktail? You never drink cocktails."

"I am learning to broaden my horizons." He beams at the waiter. "Two Martinis!"

"Are you trying to get me drunk?"

Roebuck begins sliding shellfish down his gullet.

"Vodka or gin?" The waiter is still standing at his elbow.

"Sorry?" Roebuck's mouth is full of mollusc.

"Vodka Martini or gin Martini?"

"Oh. Gin." He looks at Lily to see if gin is all right with her. She smiles to tell him that she doesn't care. "Dry," adds Roebuck, although he doesn't care about that either.

By the time the drinks arrive, his pile of oysters is substantially reduced.

"Are you starving, or fortifying, or both?" Lily is definitely in one of her come-hither modes. "That's good. I have plans."

Roebuck lifts a half-shell in salute and washes it down with another swill of gin. He is relieved to see that so far she has dabbled only with her toast. He is downing the last of the shellfish when the wine arrives.

"You're a machine," Lily says.

Roebuck interprets this as not complimentary, but that's all right now too, because now he can relax. The waiter takes away the stack of empty shells and still unmelted ice. "Any room for real food?" Roebuck's appetite is dead, entirely. But that doesn't matter either.

"Why don't you decide what to order while I visit the men's room?" he says.

Tucked into his pocket, opposite the wad of folded money is a pair of bottles removed this morning from his hidden stash. Roebuck locks himself in a stall and unscrews the first cap. He has told himself there will be no ceremony—no hesitation—and allows himself none.

It tastes like tree sap.

Most years, at the tail of winter, he and Anne drive the kids up to a sugar bush north of the city for the maple syrup festival. Anne enjoys the sweet smell of woodsmoke and the bubbling, ramshackled science of production; the promise of spring. Roebuck and the kids are in it mostly for the pancakes. The taste of ipecac reminds him of raw sap, straight from the tree. Not as bad as he'd expected.

Roebuck waits.

Nothing.

He sets the empty plastic bottle on the toilet tank and deliberates a moment, reviewing. This has to work.

He gulps a breath and holds it, bouncing on his toes.

Nothing. There is no manual for this.

Roebuck opens up the second bottle and knocks it back. He dabs his lips and drops the empties in the waste container, and—having washed his hands and examined himself in the mirror—rejoins Lily at the table. She has decided on a pasta.

The next fifteen minutes are a challenge. Lily is amorous. You could never call her prudish, not in his presence anyway, but she's not usually this forward. At one point she slips off her shoe and props her foot between his legs. Roebuck diligently fondles toes. He does his very best to keep up his end of conversation, but the uncertainty of what is going on inside his gut begins to weigh against his wit. Lily returns her foot to the ground and back into her shoe. It occurs to him that perhaps she too is ovulating. Roebuck is contemplating the uncertain symmetry of this when he feels an odd sensation in what he takes to be his salivary glands.

"I've been worrying about you," Lily says.

And, at that moment, a crackling stream of oysters bursts across the table like a spray of fire from an AK-47.

Roebuck's choice of order has been carefully considered. Oysters, he has calculated, should come up as easily as they go down. And Lily doesn't like them—one of the few flaws in her nature he's aware of, but it's perfect for today because if he's going to put this down to botulism, it has to be from something he ate and she didn't.

"Oh my God!" says Lily, fork pointed to the ceiling.

A froth of gastric juice backfills Roebuck's sinuses and dribbles, bubbling, out his nostrils. He chokes, gags—now he's having trouble breathing—Roebuck is being waterboarded by his own administration.

"I'm okay," he rasps as his lungs backfill with acid flux. He can't stop coughing as the space around his table fills with horrified wait staff, then empties again as all parties back pedal, swinging arms and spilling drinks, avoiding the next gush. Through his tears, Roebuck frames an image of a middle-aged woman in spandex, two tables over, pressing a napkin to her mouth, shoulders beginning to hunch ...

He stumbles to the men's room.

Spasms rack his chest and a gobbet of emerald-green bile dangles from his chin for an oxygen-deprived eternity, then plops into the toilet bowl. When Roebuck's breath returns, he teeters to the sink, tidies what he can with paper towel, and gropes his way back through the door and out into the open room. Lily takes his arm, though it glistens with saliva and much worse. "Hospital?"

Roebuck shakes his head.

Busboys with mops and disinfectant ring the table. Roebuck drops his wad of bills, heaving still.

"Sorry," he croaks to Lily.

"Let's get you out of here."

She has his arm again.

The long-legged hostess has disappeared, but an older man, a manager, hovers by the door, aghast. "Should I call a cab?"

"Fucking oysters!" Lily says.

"I can drive," Roebuck tells them.

And he can, though he keeps to the backstreets where he can stop the car and hang his head out the window when the need arises.

"I'm sorry," he keeps saying. "I'm so sorry."

"It's not your fault." Lily strokes his arm.

When he has pulled up to the curb outside her house, she takes a tissue from her purse and cleans his mouth and kisses it. "Call me, please. Let me know you're okay."

Breathing through his mouth, Roebuck promises to call.

"Fucking oysters," Lily says.

He is able to strip off his clothes and shower, once he's made it home, though the spasms continue on and off until it's time to leave again and pick up Morgan. The deal is that Anne will collect her afterward, but it's Roebuck's job to get Morgan to the soccer pitch in time for warm-up. He would have to be much sicker than he is to leave his daughter in the lurch. Even so, Roebuck is relieved to have experienced no further vomiting since he's left the house.

Morgan crinkles her nose as she climbs into the car. "It smells."

"I'm sorry," he says. "An accident."

She launches into an account of how Ginny Moragani tried to steal her pencil case and how Miss Cram, who hates her, gave her a time out, too. Roebuck manoeuvres his way through the chaos of gridlocks that paralyze this block every weekday at 3:35 PM. A Golden Retriever fogs the window of the car beside him; at the wheelhouse of a monstrous SUV, a Philippina nanny tries and fails to park. Roebuck taps the horn to let her know he's there and gets a fright when she throws up her arms and shrieks.

"Damn!" he says, slamming on the brakes. "I forgot your soccer stuff!"

"I have it." His daughter's tone is a reproduction of her mother's. "Mommy always makes me bring it with me in the morning." All three children take after Anne much more than him, but this one is eerily identical.

"Your cleats too?"

Morgan roots through her knapsack.

"Yes."

"Shin guards?"

"Daddy!"

She opens her lunchbox. Morgan saves a chewy bar for the car ride after school. It's the one thing she can be counted on to eat. When she screws off the top of her drink container, Roebuck realizes he's dehydrated.

"Sweetheart. Can I have a sip?"

"No."

"Please!"

"No."

Roebuck calculates response against motive. His request is selfish. On the other hand, so is her refusal. He puts on his deepest no-argument voice. "Morgan!" It's sufficient. She takes another slurp of orange juice and hands it over. They are good kids, all of them.

He has worked his way clear of the school and the other parents he will have to sit beside next Christmas concert before the juice comes foaming up again. They haven't yet made it as far as the arterial road, so Roebuck is able to stop, fling open the door, and heave most of the liquid outside the car in a lurid splash across the asphalt.

Morgan's still talking about it when Anne and Katie arrive home.

He has parked himself behind the kitchen table, staring blankly at his laptop. Every time he tries to drink, he vomits. He would put this venture down as brilliantly successful, but he's got to be a little worried now about overachievement.

"Daddy threw up three times on the way to soccer!"

His wife's hands move from her gym bag to Roebuck's forehead. "I can't tell if you have a fever." Anne's hands are as accurate as any thermometer. Roebuck knows he has no fever.

"Something I ate …"

"What did you eat?"

"Seafood."

Another thing Anne shares with Lily is distrust for all things piscine—though she does appreciate the fatty acids and affirmative cholesterols. "I keep telling you …"

She turns to the refrigerator and takes out a bottle of ginger ale, shakes it, and carefully unscrews the cap. When she's satisfied the fizz is down, she pours a glass. "Drink," she says. "Slowly." Flat ginger ale has settled many a stomach in this household; he has a pretty good idea what's about to happen, but after all that's the point. Roebuck drains his ginger ale.

Six minutes later he is in the downstairs bathroom transferring soda pop into the toilet by way of his sinuses. In his hurry he has left the door open, but the sound effects would have done the job regardless.

"Wow!" says Morgan. Katie has hung around downstairs too, to witness the show.

"Where's Zach?" Roebuck wheezes, wiping his chin.

"Working on a science project at Niko's house. He'll be home for dinner." Niko has been Zach's best friend since kindergarten. "Speaking of dinner, says Anne, "I'd better call Yasmin."

The plan had been for Yasmin to come over tonight for a barbecue. Anne was going to make a pot of mac and cheese for the kids, while Roebuck grilled some porterhouse.

Today is Day Twenty-eight. On the button.

"I'm sorry," Roebuck says again.

"It was her idea anyway." Anne feels his forehead again, then his cheek. "Will you be able to eat?" He groans. "You *have* to be careful with seafood. I keep warning you. I'll call."

Yasmin has seen to all the details. The plan—refined through a cascade of Hushmails—calls for Roebuck to pop into the bathroom after dinner and perform his special service with the orange-lidded plastic jar, which he will then slip into Yasmin's purse—casually left open—while Yasmin herself maintains a stream of chatter with Anne in the kitchen; possibly offering to help with the cleanup. Soon after—freshness being key—Yasmin will yawn and say, "My goodness, look at the time!" and head home with his semen, where she will see to the next part in the privacy of her downtown loft.

If he wasn't feeling so raked-out hollow, Roebuck could almost enjoy this.

Anne is talking on the kitchen phone. Yasmin's voice is loud enough for him to hear both ends of the conversation.

"What do you mean, he's sick?"

"Food poisoning."

"What?"

"Food poisoning, I said. Seafood."

"What was he doing eating seafood?"

"I guess that's what he had for lunch."

"So tonight is definitely off?"

"I'm afraid so."

"You're sure?"

"I'm sorry Yasmin. It was only a barbecue."

"No, no, it's just … I bought a nice bottle of Barolo."

"Well, keep it, for heaven's sake. We'll reschedule next week."

"Next week's too late!"

"Too late?"

Roebuck puts a napkin to his mouth. He isn't listening.

"I mean, I also got a cream cake from Dufflet's. No way it's going to last until next week."

"You can eat it yourself! Are you dieting again? You've been so edgy."

"I don't even like cream cake!"

"Yasmin!"

"I'm sorry. I was just ... looking forward to seeing you guys. I was hoping ... you know ... good company and all ..."

"What about Friday?" Anne is looking at the calendar attached with happy-face magnets to the fridge.

"Friday?"

"Friday's better anyway."

"But that's ... four days away!"

"Yasmin ..."

"How about tomorrow? Tomorrow might still work."

"Tomorrow's no good. Besides, I doubt Julius will be up for company that soon."

"We could ask?"

"Yasmin!"

"I'll get back to you, okay?"

"Honestly!" Anne says hanging up. "That woman!"

But Roebuck is in transit to the bathroom.

18

Fiction for men is getting the girl;
for women it's getting the fiction.
The Collected Sayings of Julius Roebuck

Yasmin turns up next morning, as Roebuck had hoped and feared, with a crock of chicken soup. "It's vegetarian," she says. Anne blocks her at the doorstep. "Vegetarian chicken soup?"

"It's from Pusateri's! How's Julius?"

"Well, at least the vomiting has stopped."

Roebuck, in bathrobe and pyjamas, is seated in the front room in the sunshine with his morning paper. He *is* feeling better, though still far from up to solids.

"So he's better?"

"I am," he says, folding the business section and joining Anne at the door. "I think whatever it was has passed through my system."

His wife is much less certain. "You were throwing up all night."

This is true. Everything Roebuck put into his stomach has invariably returned by the same route. But he has slept the last few hours and tried a little of Anne's decarbonated ginger ale, which has so far has stayed put.

"Chicken soup!" he says. "That's exactly what the doctor ordered!"

"It can't be chicken soup," Anne says. "It's vegetarian."

Roebuck is worried that Anne will pick up on the undercurrent, but Yasmin's expression leaves no doubt that she honestly believes he's subpar. "So thoughtful!" says Roebuck. "I'm so sorry I ruined everyone's evening."

Yasmin makes appropriately sympathetic murmurs.

"Well," Anne says, "thanks for the soup."

"Let's make toast!"

"*What?*" His wife stares.

"I prefer toast with my soup."

"Now?"

"I'm starving. I have a feeling Yasmin's soup is going to do the trick. Come on!" he says smiling at everyone.

They all troop into the kitchen. Anne is not the happy one. "You have been very sick, Julius. I don't think I've seen you this bad since Sri Lanka."

"God," says Roebuck. "That was a thousand years ago."

"And that was seafood too."

He remembers throwing up for days on that trip; the aftermath of tainted prawns.

"Twelve," Anne corrects. "Twelve years. Katie is turning eleven this summer." According to family history, Kate was conceived in a beach house at Hikkaduwa that same holiday.

"Serendip," says Roebuck admiring how words crop up. "We almost didn't go. Remember? You booked that trip last-minute."

Yasmin is opening and closing cupboards, hunting for a pot; Anne shoos her off. Roebuck begins slicing bread. He is relieved to see that Yasmin is in no way trying to catch his eye, but he's taking no chances.

Anne has got the soup into a pot now warming on the stove. Roebuck keeps his own eyes on his loaf. "Ready yet?"

Anne spoons a taste. When her back is turned, Yasmin slips out the sample jar and waggles it operatically. Roebuck wishes he could snap a photograph of how she looks, just at that moment.

"A few minutes more," Anne says.

The sample jar has vanished back into the hideaway of Yasmin's lap. Roebuck slots bread into the toaster. When he looks up, it's his wife's eyes he seeks. "I'll be right back," he says, heading for the staircase. Anne is pointedly wondering how a chicken is a vegetable. Yasmin tells her it's amazing what they do these days. Roebuck kills some time in his bedroom. He figures he can get away with maybe five minutes. Any longer and they're likely to come looking.

Sure enough, before he's finished, Anne is calling from the second-storey landing,

"Julius? Are you all right?"

"Dish that soup," he shouts back down. "I'll be there in a half a sec."

He has gone this far, invested this much. So now the price has notched a little higher. *"L'chaim,"* says Roebuck, because he has always liked the feeling of that word. From a disguised compartment at the bottom of his briefcase he has removed another bottle from his secret stash. He has considered taking two again, but lost his nerve. Roebuck raises a toast to himself in the mirror—he will allow a little ritual, this time—and drinks more slowly than last go-round. Before he rejoins the women, he tucks the empty bottle safely back into his briefcase. He thinks of everything, does Roebuck.

"Oh," says Anne. "I thought you were getting dressed."

"I couldn't find my slippers," he says, rebelting his bathrobe.

"They're in the drawer with your pyjamas."

Roebuck rubs his palms together like a man with an appetite. "What about that soup?"

Yasmin is at the counter buttering toast. He saunters over, helpfully arranging slices in the rack. Anne is ladling the soup into the bowls. Yasmin rolls her hips and slips the sample jar into his pocket, licking butter from her fingers. Despite what he knows is just about to happen, he feels the pulse straight down into his groin. Roebuck hurries over to the table.

"That aroma! Don't you just love the smell of toast and butter?" He begins spooning his soup the moment it is set before him.

"Well, isn't he the hungry boy." Yasmin is the picture of approval.

"Slow down!" Anne, on the other hand, can barely keep from stamping her foot.

As for Roebuck, he only wants to get this done.

He can feel his stomach even now, sloshing like a half-filled can of motor oil. Yasmin is regarding him more avidly than is prudent. Roebuck keeps his napkin ready. Anne has set her spoon beside her dish too, studying his face. Roebuck feels the sweat begin to bead. He mops his brow. God bless the children: Morgan walks into the room with her geography assignment. "What's the longest river in Canada?"

"The St. Lawrence," he says automatically and burps.

"The Fraser," Anne corrects.

Yasmin surprises everyone. "Isn't it the Mackenzie?"

"You're right!" Morgan beams. "Stupid parents. 'The Mackenzie River,'" she reads, "'is the longest river in Canada at 1,738 kilometres.'"

"Oh, God!" Roebuck says and lurches to the bathroom.

"Daddy's being sick again!"

"Damn, damn, *damn!* I *knew* this was a bad idea." He can also hear—intermittently, though forcefully—Anne leaving no doubt where the blame for this belongs, insofar as she's concerned.

"I only thought it would help build up his strength …"

By the time Roebuck is steady on his feet again, Yasmin has fled the premises.

So all's well that ends well. Except that Roebuck spends the rest of that week flat on his back in a hospital bed.

19

Fuck only those who want to fuck you.
The Collected Sayings of Julius Roebuck

In retrospect, what he feels the worst about was lying to the doctors. Roebuck is seated in a subway car en route to Gama-Care Laboratories. The last time he made this trip, he got a parking ticket. Fate is telling him, on this occasion, that he would be wiser to avail himself of public transportation. Roebuck pays attention to these things: peak oil, greenhouse gases, global warming, and so on. It's hot. Even underground he's sweltering. Today seems to be that day that spring surrenders unconditionally to summer. Every May it's like this. Every year it's a little earlier.

He has told himself that if the results are not positive—negative, rather—this is going to end right here. That's it. Enough. Because he really *has* made a fool of himself. Though no one is aware of the full extent of it, fortunately, but Julius Roebuck himself. And, to be fair, after three days of intravenous tubes and bedpans, he himself was more than half convinced it was cancer. He's still down eight pounds, although—admittedly—mostly because he's decided the lean look is healthy. Roebuck is being very careful, lately, about what goes into his stomach.

Based on his own on-line investigations, his best guess is that it was all some kind of off-the-chart allergic reaction. Nothing else that he can think of could account for the seizures plus the chest pains and the irregular pulse that had them all worrying—on top of all the vomit—that his heart was failing, too. Three days flat on his back with drip lines running in; nearly a week before he could take anything solid; and all the while doctors unable to come up with anything conclusive. Anne was a total mess, and Lily—poor Lily—couldn't even come to see him, knowing that his wife was standing vigil. So she'd drafted Greenwood and made the visit look like a delegation from the office, clever girl. An awkward fifteen minutes, though: the two of them standing by the IV pole not knowing what to say; Roebuck mute and disabled; Anne drumming fingers on the stainless steel sink. It was very kind of Daniel to pass a card around the office for everyone to sign.

Which, apparently, has set the rumours flying: Roebuck has been diagnosed with stomach cancer. Roebuck has undergone an emergency colostomy. The agency is bankrupt. The agency is up for sale. Ripreeler has put them up for review. Ripreeler is about to name them agency of record, globally. The company is in receivership. Omniglobe is offering a buyout. Roebuck wonders how that last part got out. But he's not going to think about it. Not today.

Today, the issue at hand is three stops up the line. It's rush hour. He is lucky to have found a seat, but the car is a steambath. He will be very glad to get out into the air.

He is sincerely resolved about this. Either the light is green or the light is red. Either he goes home an older, wiser, thinner man or he gets to see this through. Again he reminds himself that—whichever way this settles—he'll have to buy some rounds at Matrix

Three and let his people know that everything is hunky-dory. Maybe he should get hold of a colostomy bag and have the barman top it up with Guinness.

The train rasps to a stop and a heavily pregnant young woman boards, puffing and sweating. Roebuck stands and gives her his seat. It's still so early in the season, they haven't got the AC going. He is hanging from a strap, now, perspiring along with everyone else.

Two stops to go and a nearly naked woman occupies the car. She brushes by in an envelope of musk and arranges herself against an upright, radiating sex. Civet cat, thinks Roebuck—instantly—imbibing the scent. Across the aisle a security guard gapes, molars showing, then catches himself and looks away. Every man in the car is acting out some version of the same primordial response. Not naked, on closer inspection; though an awesomely well-crafted facsimile. Roebuck is startled to find himself once again wishing that Greenwood could be made to witness this. *That,* he'd say, is what we mean by *epigamic.* Here's the word incarnate. She's a minor-league version of Yasmin. Younger, cruder—more peroxide than Prada—but packing that same testicular punch. Stretched white crop-top sheared just below the breasts; dangly accessories glistening with the same auric gloss as the gold stud embedded in her navel—and of course those high, high heels propelling her into the world chest-first. Astonishing—truly—the chest. There's a slogan of some kind printed on the fabric stretched across the curvature.

Despite his occupation, Roebuck is at core a literary dweeb. When his eyes behold a string of letters, his brain requires him to spell them out. He tilts a little forward, but he still can't make it out what it says. Several syllables are alarmingly distorted; letters dip and disappeared onto declivities.

Roebuck leans closer. He's got the first part, he's fairly certain—clearly interrogative—but there's a fragment below that he can't make out at all. He is about to give up and get set to detrain when Miss Epigam lifts her shoulders with a fetching little yawn. Suddenly, shockingly, the message pops in perfect, 3-D precision.

WHAT ARE YOU LOOKING AT?
PERVERT!

Exactly at that moment, his eyes meet hers.

The blast of scorn is so intense, so unabridged and unconstrained, that for an instance Roebuck feels as if the force of its percussion has rocked him back into his seat. Such carnal, conquering, all-encompassing contempt! Cortés must have worn that look while gazing at the corpse of Moctezuma. It's another one of those moments he will forever wish could have been archived somehow magically on film. Roebuck would have dearly loved the opportunity to see the look on his own face, just then. Abject humiliation. Total and complete. An image to capture the essence of his age.

He's still laughing when he emerges up onto the street.

A bus nearly nails him—and wouldn't that have been a grand finale—but he makes it across the street with his heart thudding only slightly louder than the rumble of the traffic. Roebuck climbs to the stairs to Gama-Care Laboratories, already out of breath.

The woman in the lab coat nods and grunts from behind her counter. He knows she has no memory of him, but he is encouraged that no one else is present in the tiny waiting room. Roebuck states his business, and she hunts through piles of folders. She can't find his and for several minutes he wonders if she will have to consult the sliding window—but there it is at last. She removes a sheet of paper, scans it briefly, mutters something he doesn't understand then folds it carefully into an envelope.

Roebuck reaches for it, but she slides it back to her side of the counter. There is a bill to settle. Roebuck pays.

He recalls a public bench across the street.

Roebuck keeps both feet on the sidewalk until the traffic clears in all directions. It's afternoon rush hour; several minutes pass before he finds an opening. A hot fist of wind nearly bats the envelope from his hand; Roebuck clamps down hard. He is glad the cardiologist is not present at this moment to monitor his heart rate. When he reaches the bench, he closes his eyes—opens them—and rips the seal. It takes him several moments to decipher the med-speak.

But there it is, toward the bottom, clear in black and white.

Negative.

Negative.

He has, of course, been tracking the calendar. Of course he has been counting days.

There are plans to put in place. Groundwork to be laid. But Fate has rendered its decision: Julius Roebuck is now officially shooting blanks. The light's officially gone green.

Laughing still, Roebuck heads back down into the subway.

20

Heaven is where you have your cake and eat it too.
The Collected Sayings of Julius Roebuck

"Sorry I didn't come to visit you in the hospital."
"Don't be silly. Anne tells me you asked every day."
"I still think you should sue."
"And the flowers. Lovely."
"Yarrow, for health."
"Perfect. Perfectly appropriate."
"Really. I mean it. The loss of productivity alone …"
"They decided it was probably a virus …"
"Anne said. But it started with that poisoned seafood."
"Water under the bridge, Yasmin."
"So you're sure you're in good health?"

Now they've reached the nub. She has been having second thoughts, he is well aware, with regard to his genetic fitness: it's a delicate thing to have to defend. Roebuck has been in business long enough to know when the hard sell is counterproductive. He lets the answer go unspoken because he also knows that Yasmin has already got the goods from Anne.

Anne was worried.

So worried that when the verdict came in that it wasn't cancer, wasn't anything at all in fact beyond a mystery, she raptured like a Baptist climbing back to Jesus. "We played tennis this afternoon and he beat me four sets out of six! Most games it's the other way around! Oh, Yasmin, he's completely recovered. I can't tell you how relieved I am!"

Anne takes her tennis very seriously

Bottom line, in any case, is if there had been a change of mind, he wouldn't be sitting here on Yasmin's safari-inspired couch. Her basal body temperature, recorded just moments ago, is a perfect one degree above its sultry norm.

"I'm fine," says Roebuck.

The loft is exactly how he'd imaged it: Tiger stripes and leopard spots; ebonies and cherry woods; feral reds with blazes of orange and emerald green; rampant nudes stretching tendons on marble pedestals; goddesses in nooks with snakes around their hips and breasts like perfect pumpkins. And of course a wealth of mirrors. Roebuck has never put his finger on exactly what kundalinic energy is supposed to be, but he figures this is it. He permits himself a sip of wine.

"You haven't been drinking, have you? I mean in the last twenty-four hours."

"Are we going to do this?"

Now that he is sitting primly with his back against her sofa, Roebuck finds himself surprisingly relaxed.

If there has been a guiding principle, getting here, it has been his own internal steadiness, Roebuck's rock-ribbed fidelity to his own intentions. When Yasmin suggested she come by his office—whatever time he named—his reply was a firm and confident *no*. "Not the right environment," he returned by Hushmail. "Difficult, in that setting."

"I thought you said you were recovered?"

"This has nothing to do with that, Yasmin. It's a matter of ..." he chose his wording carefully ... "ambience. Privacy."

They'd gone at it back and forth like teenagers passing notes.

"Why can't you do it at home and bring it with you? I'll stop by your office ..."

"Even worse. With the kids screaming and Anne yelling at me to get out of the bathroom. Are you kidding? Plus there's the issue of freshness."

"So how do we do this?"

"Your place."

"You'll bring it to my place? That works for me."

"I'll produce it at your place. Safer."

Nearly an hour of silence before Yasmin's reply. "Julius. I'm not comfortable with that option."

"*You're* not comfortable?" Roebuck had his script prepared well in advance. "What about me? This is awkward for me wherever it happens. Your place is the least awkward option. Plus it's the most efficient. Plus it guarantees freshness. If you want to do this, this is how it has to be."

Yasmin, he knows, likes her logic laid out like sausages in links. But in the end he's fairly certain it was the freshness angle that clinched it.

He sips his Barolo. It's a heady wine for the circumstances. She has unexpected depths, sometimes. Tannins pluck at the root of his tongue.

"Well," he says, standing.

Yasmin stands also.

Eyebrows politely raised, Roebuck glances round the room.

"The bathroom is right this way."

He has wondered how she would be dressed for this. Like a real estate agent, as it turns out, for an upscale showing; careful though observably unbuttoned. He notes that she's in heels as always. Yasmin leads him to the bathroom and halts there by the open door.

Again he is struck by the image of realty and display. She gestures and steps to one side. The room is massive. It must originally have been a bedroom, converted to its present opulence. He can tell, even through the swirl of all these other currents, that Yasmin is proud of her loo: smoked glass and showerheads like enormous sunflowers; a massive tub more reminiscent of a limestone pool; candles here and there in sconces. He smells incense, but can't locate the source. It's the coffee table, though, that draws his eye: elaborate wrought-iron—placed at the foot of a wingback chair. He wonders if this is a permanent feature or arranged just for today.

And there it is: his orange-lidded sample jar, bathed in candlelight, perched tactfully beside an assortment of erotic magazines, fanned for ease of reference.

"It's lovely," he says. "You've thought of everything."

She blushes. "Make yourself comfortable."

The hostess with the mostess, he wants to add, regressing, but disciplines himself.

Yasmin shuts the door, and Roebuck is left to his devices.

He hears her heels receding and settles into the comfortable chair. Roebuck looks over his selection of reading material. He is surprised to see that *Hustler* is still in print. Didn't Larry Flint die eons ago? Or maybe he's thinking of the *Penthouse* guy? Bowing to nostalgia, Roebuck opts for *Playboy.*

He is open-minded on the subject of pornography—as an advertiser, he has to be—but deep down Roebuck has never really understood the appeal. Watching someone else having sex is only a reminder that you yourself are not. Same again with photographs of naked women: they are there; you are somewhere else. Though it's also true that he remembers, back in adolescence, aching at those pictures slipped out from underneath the mattress—and there it is again: cliché. But the moment he was old enough to access the real thing, facsimiles ceased to be of interest. It's been decades since Roebuck cracked the cover of a girly magazine.

The crotch shots are much as he remembers, though come to think of it perhaps more extensively trimmed. And silicone hadn't yet been standardized, back then, so breasts weren't replicated in such spherical precision. But the pouts haven't changed, though the cartoons—which in his memory were daring and often quite witty (is he right in recalling that Heffner himself did the drawings?)—are now depressingly banal.

It was always said that *Playboy* published top-notch writing. Roebuck leafs through pages.

Most of the articles are short and loud. No Norman Mailers, these days; at least not this edition. There's a profile on one of the more recent boy-band castratos, now launched into a career in motion pictures. Morgan would be interested in it, though grossed out by the photographs before and after. Roebuck lingers for a time at the *Advisor* page. A reader wants to know if it's possible to have sex with a ghost. The editor's reply, in italics, is cautiously affirmative, quoting Chaucer. A gentleman from Raleigh, North Carolina, asks if it's all right to have sex with his cousin, and a reader from Georgia wonders what percentage of women shave their pubic hair today as compared to ten years ago? The reply cites a survey conducted at Indiana University which found that 21 percent of women age 18 to 24 are typically hair-free, 38 percent go bare sometimes, while 29 percent trim. With each subsequent age group—and this factoid comes as no surprise—less hair is removed less often. Women who go bare are more likely to receive cunnilingus, to be in a long-term relationship, but not married, and to score higher on measures of genital self-image and sexual function … Roebuck slots this information in with other, complementary data. He briefly considers tearing out the page for Lily's entertainment.

Drag and clop … drag and clop … drag and clop … Back and forth beyond the door, Yasmin is pacing. Shaved, he decides, dollars to doughnuts. He wishes he had topped up his glass while the bottle was still handy.

Halfway in, he finds a short story. Has *Playboy* always published fiction? This too he can't recall. The lead-in is unpromising. Some kind of sci-fi *Star Trek* send-up, by the look of it, but Roebuck perseveres. The plot is not what he would call original. The yeoman is expecting to die; he's the sixth member of a six-man team about to be beamed to the surface of an unexplored planet, and the sixth guy always comes back dead. Wasn't there was a movie on this theme, a few years back with Sigourney Weaver?

Roebuck's glass is now empty.

He gets up, crosses yards of marble to the sink, and refills it from the tap—more a stone lip, really, than tap: water flowing over the edge for the tranquil-mountain-brook-effect. The crystal makes a tinkling sound against the stone.

"Everything all right in there?"

Yasmin is tapping at the door.

"Um …" he says. And not a word more.

Roebuck returns to his fiction. The dialogue is not bad, crisp even; though the Captain Kirk figure is parodied so heavily that Roebuck almost gives up on this writer. The yeoman has a wife, though, who's had enough of her husband's dead-end jobs and threatens to intercede with the chain of command. A nice touch of irony, but he can see where this one's going.

Heels are tracking back and forth again outside.

The away team has beamed down to the planet. The captain immediately goes looking for aliens to have sex with, while the yeoman is sent to explore a dangerous crevice. Roebuck honestly believes that the monologue at the start of the original *Star Trek* captures the true human spirit as accurately as anything he's come across since, though even he would never admit that in public. To boldly go ...

"Julius! What's going on in there?"

"Well ..." he says. "Um ..."

"I beg your pardon? I can't hear you."

He clears his throat, audibly. "Well, I mean ... it just doesn't seem to be ... working."

A pause "Did you find the magazines?"

"I did. Yes. Thank you."

Roebuck gives himself a little breathing room. He coughs a little pointedly. He has decided he wouldn't mind finishing this story.

Yasmin flounces off. Footsteps go stalking in the direction of the living area. She's upending the rest of the bottle, he decides. But in a minute she is back outside the door.

Silence.

He remembers that he should uncap the sample jar.

Roebuck puts his magazine face-down on the armrest so he can free both hands. He untucks his shirt and generally dishevels.

"Any luck?"

"Sorry ... no."

"Oh, for God's sake!"

Now she's really pacing. He imagines her consulting the thermometer again ... escalating anxiety, her window closing ... the clock ticking down ...

Roebuck undoes a little more extensively. He has to look like he's been giving this his all. He stands, loudly buckling, zipping. Sighing, sighing ...

A brooding silence from beyond the door.

"I'm sorry, Yasmin. Maybe this was just a bad idea ..."

It swings open. Roebuck has of course undone the lock.
"What can I do?"
She has, he sees, kicked off her shoes.

Part III

September–November 2008

However, the possibility also exists that male nuptial gifts alternately or additionally serve to manipulate female reproduction in ways that are costly to females.

Sara M. Lewis and Christopher K. Crastley,
"Flash Signal Evolution, Mate Choice, and Predation in Fireflies,"
The Annual Review of Entomology

21

Did you hear the one about the blonde who was so
gullible even she could fool herself?
The Collected Sayings of Julius Roebuck

"*What do women want?*" Freud asks. The answer,
as every marketer knows, is *stuff*. We advertisers need to drill a little deeper. Why does a woman want
stuff? *Because getting stuff affirms the fact that she* deserves
the stuff she's getting. Our job therefore is reinforcement:
Yes you deserve it! And you know what? She does!

People are constantly looking for ways to validate
their sense of self. You—or your product—aim to reward that search. It's just that simple. That's branding in
a nutshell. If you can link your brand to its target's sense
of self, she will need to have it.

The important thing is understanding that it is
not the *stuff* that is of value. It's what the stuff reflects.
Here's a little wisdom, write this down. Your product is

a mirror purchased to provide a reflection of its buyer.

I refer you to Calvin. Sixteenth-century Protestants believed that God identified his Chosen by bestowing them with wealth and status. Accumulating fame and fortune, therefore, was confirmation of God's grace. Calvin's Puritan followers brought that belief with them to America. Your present-day consumer has personalized the doctrine. The more she shops, the more she's confirming that she *deserves* to go shopping. Into that virtuous cycle, we marketers inject our product.

No new insight there, you say: David Ogilvy wrote half a century ago that the consumer is not a moron; she's your wife.

Granted. But the difference between now and then is that Ogilvy was still pitching his assessments *to the man*. Today, our understanding is more finessed. Today's refinement of Ogilvy's message is more intelligently nuanced: The consumer is not a moron.

But her husband is.

Roebuck rubs his jaw. He can feel the heat from the laptop and slips a pillow between himself and it, though he does not allow himself to be distracted by this inward flash of wit. The Calvin reference will have to go. Roebuck highlights the passage. It fits, certainly, but aims a little high. His fingers hover.

"If I asked you to tell me what you know about Calvin, what would you say?"

"Calvin Klein? *Nothing comes between me and my Calvins.* That guy?"

"Good," he says thumbing the delete key. "Excellent."

"What are you writing about?"

"You," he answers then self-corrects. "No, stay." He has looped one hand around her knee. "That was stupid. I've been invited to give a lecture at The Ferrer/Léche School of Business. Something I admit I am looking forward to."

"More of your antlers on the elk crap?"

Roebuck is astonished. "You nailed it."

"So obvious …" Her ankle stays where it is in the nook above his shoulder. "You're just so full of it."

Yasmin is lying on her back with her heels against the headboard, working with gravity rather than against. She will hold the pose for thirty minutes, incorporating yogic principle while Roebuck rests against the headboard, standing by. Their appointment is not finalized, not yet, but in the meantime he will get a little work accomplished. He truly is looking forward to delivering this speech. Although the event itself is far into the future, today he feels especially inspired.

Among the details she's researched—among the *many* details Yasmin has confirmed—is the clear desirability of vaginal upsuck induced through the muscular contraction of orgasm which, appropriately timed, positively enhances sperm retention. Beyond this point, insofar as he understands the literature, opinions diverge. One theory holds that female orgasm should occur immediately *before* male ejaculation. A second and competing hypothesis argues for orgasm at forty-five minutes *following* insemination. With something so critical, Yasmin is taking no chances. It's understood that Roebuck will ensure both bets are covered. He has discovered that for someone so wholly physical, Yasmin can be hard work—though the moment when it comes is massive in its scale. It's what he's always imagined only more so.

She prods his shoulder and squeezes the lobe of his ear with her toes. Yasmin's nails are painted blood-red and decorated with tiny black diamonds applied at regular intervals at a spa somewhere on Yorkville. "Time's a-wasting." She has taken his hand, forceful-ly, and removed it from the keyboard, relocating it to where she believes it can be put to better use. Roebuck types on doggedly, one-handed, but the going is slow. "One sec," he says, returning his hand to its given profession.

"Hey! What are you *thinking!*" Until a few moments ago she has been dozing, possibly meditating, regarding herself in the looking glass attached to the ceiling. Yasmin has just now registered the lap-top. "Don't you know those things cause sterility? *That* explains it!"

For once, Roebuck does not appreciate the incidental humour. "There's a pillow under it, for God's sake!" He looks at his watch; six minutes to go. "Lie still."

Yasmin's research sternly warns against seminal flowback, a wasteful dissipation strictly to be minimized. She will remain flat on her back for thirty minutes with pelvis positioned at an upward tilt so that Roebuck's investment travels on the downhill path of least resistance.

Truth is, he can use the downtime. He's not eighteen anymore. Bounce back isn't what it used to be. Yasmin isn't one for patience in this or any other discipline.

But Julius Roebuck is a master of timely distraction.

"So," he says, "what made you ask about that antlers and the elk stuff? I don't remember us ever talking about that." He touches "Save" and moves his work aside. There is very little they *have* talked about, he and Yasmin, beyond the purely practical. He has been curious to know what age she started shaving there, but de-cided some time ago to forsake that piece of knowledge, too.

"Anne's always on about it."

"Anne?"

He and Anne *do* discuss things—most things, anyway—though at a largely dialectic level. His wife has come to under-stand the marriage contract as a solemn vow on her part to disagree with every word that emerges from her husband's lips. It is painful, frequently: especially on the day-to-day arcana of whether Katie stopped ballet in the winter of Grade Two or the spring of Grade Three, or whether the Maldives are sinking at 2.3 mm per year or by 2.8 mm, or that a penny costs 1.62 cents to mint rather than 1.79 cents, or that orange cats are always male and it's white cats that go deaf—but on the other hand it does have real value when it comes to ideas. Roebuck can be confident in knowing that if a thought survives the battering his wife will surely give it, it's likely to have legs. He trusts Anne absolutely as a peerless perceiver of flaw. But he had no idea that the process transmitted to Yasmin.

"I'm curious, what does Anne say?"

"That you're an idiot and probably impotent."

This he should have expected. On *this* subject—the proper care and maintenance of Roebuck's ego—Anne and Yasmin speak as one.

Yasmin twists his wrist to read his watch. "God you two bore me. If I wasn't there to keep her focused, she'd go on about you all day long. You and her kids." She drops her hands back, palms up, settled on her upturned thighs. "Though she must be right about the impotence. Three cycles now. Still *nothing.*"

Roebuck nearly bites; very nearly articulates the clear distinction between impotence and sterility, ample evidence against the former not a half-hour past; no room for confusion there. But his background saves him.

"I read the same sites you do. You know perfectly well that it's not at all uncommon for couples to spend months trying before achieving a conception. Anne and I did with Katie. In fact, now that I'm remembering, we were worried, too, for a while—I think Anne even booked some kind of appointment. But it turned out all we needed was to relax and let nature takes its course. Katie came along and after that, there was never any issue."

Yasmin is staring off into space, not answering, which is just as well because Roebuck is paralyzed by the sudden beauty of what he is about to say. He's been looking for a workable segue and—suddenly, brilliantly—there it is, dropped like a gift into his lap. He spaces out his words as if the thought has just occurred, which is mostly true—as if this is something he has not before considered.

"It could be that's our problem, you know."

She has sensed his quickened pulse. Yasmin is wary. "What could be the problem?"

Here again he pauses—he really is uncertain how to phrase this. "It could be that we just aren't … properly relaxed."

She misinterprets. "I've barely moved a muscle!" Yasmin waves her hands across her loins to demonstrate how perfectly recumbent they remain. "I've done exactly what it says to do!"

"I don't mean now, I mean … before."

"Before?"

"Listen." If he isn't careful, the opportunity will melt away. "With Anne and me, it was because we enjoyed it, it was nothing special. Maybe that's the insight we're missing here. Maybe we're making this too much of a singular occasion. Maybe it needs to be normalized." In this dim light Yasmin's eyes are all pupil.

"Yasmin," he says, "I want to come again next week."

"I don't need you next week." Her eyes are so dark they are almost black. "If there's any justice, I won't need you at all after today. But if I do, it won't be for another month."

"But I want you next week."

This moment has arrived a little sooner than intended, but he's committed now. No taking this back. "If I can make time for you next month, you can make time for me next week." Roebuck sets his jaw. "I want to see you next week too."

Yasmin is unblinking. He can tell that she's processing, but beyond that he has no read on what is going on inside her head. She is staring at him. Roebuck is very conscious of the rise in thermal pressure, his shortening of breath.

"Well ..." she says at last, "I am interested in *now*." She lifts his pillow from his lap, deliberately, like a cook removing the lid from a pot. Yasmin reaches, then stops.

"What does your watch say?" Her teeth are showing.

"Forty ..." Roebuck clears his throat. "It has been exactly forty-three minutes."

"Almost ..." *Her* fingers curl.

"Yasmin," he says hoarsely. "I want to see you again next week."

Yasmin's black eyes count the heartbeat of his craving. She returns her gaze to Roebuck's face.

"Whatever," she says.

22

When you look at a mirror, you don't see the trees.
The Collected Sayings of Julius Roebuck

And here, my young friends, is where our understanding of *grievance* enters the equation.

It's well known in psychology—and never forget that
advertising is psychology monetized—that any equation
with *grievance* on one side requires a *corresponding* meas-
urement of *compensation* on the other.

A strict but simple formula: The greater the grievance, the greater its need for compensation.

(*Need,* of course, is a word of interest, too—being as
we are in the business of creating and fulfilling it. But
for now let's focus on *stuff.*)

Stuff—getting stuff, accumulating stuff, going shopping—is your consumer's antidote to *grievance.* The
greater the grievance, the greater the need for more *stuff*
to alleviate it. Grievance is our friend. We are negoti-
ators of grievance; grievance brokers.

Against whom, you ask? Grievance against whom? Remember that the biggest force in life is usually the closest.

Roebuck is experiencing a twinge of guilt. He knows he should have checked his messages as soon as he got in, but he wanted to get this part down while it was fresh in his mind and besides— this confession is only for himself—he doesn't like answering emails. He understands this is unwise: the world is transitioning to a digital age and those who don't keep up will fall behind, et cetera, et cetera—and Roebuck *does* keep up, tenaciously— he just can't seem to enjoy it. What puzzles him is how much other people love being so constantly plugged in. Greenwood, for instance. Daniel's devices are like an extension of his body; he could spend all day with them. But Greenwood is a picture guy and maybe that's the difference. For Roebuck, words are too important to fling out like Johnny's apple seeds or Scipio's salt. He prefers to invoice.

Sure enough, he's had to scroll through two full pages before he gets to the bottom, including items from both Anne and Lily. He always reads Anne's first in case of mishap or emergency, but this one is just a reminder, now that the kids are back in school, to log Morgan's fall recital into his calendar. It so happens that Roebuck did not have that one scheduled; he is grateful that Anne has provided him with plenty of lead time. He never misses any of the kids' performances. This year, Morgan will be attempting "Ode to Joy."

After sending Anne a quick confirmation plus fond regards, Roebuck is tempted to open Lily's next, but disciplines himself. Lily he will save for last.

He spends the next hour patrolling business pages and industry blogs looking for some hint that the company he's been watching is about to make a move. So far, nothing. Roebuck returns to his mailbox. Greenwood has forwarded a bunch of junk from Artemis plus odds and ends of several other accounts he wants reviewed. Ripreeler has scheduled its annual meeting two weeks earlier this year, though it's still in Helsinki. That at least is decent news.

He yawns and stretches. He is tired. Unusually tired. Roebuck thumbs his temples, rubs his jaw, and massages the back of his neck. All the emails that needed replies have now been answered; a dozen new ones have come in, meanwhile, and Roebuck has responded to these too. There is just the one outstanding.

"I'm in the office today."

What office? It takes him a second. *This* office?

"Expecting to be finishing up around five. Drink? xo L."

According to the indicator at the bottom of his screen, it's 5:18 PM.

Roebuck sits back down. He had gotten up to check the hall, but has backtracked to his chair. When Lily comes in to do contract work, she sits in a cubicle on the far side of the IT bunker. He had no idea she was even in the building.

It is not at all unusual for him to join the staff downstairs at Matrix Three for an end-of-week unwinder. Roebuck often buys a round, especially if he has an announcement he wants to let slip unofficially. Usually he heads home after that or back up to the office. Most folks stay only for a drink or two. It's Friday; people have weekends to launch.

"You look tired."

He jumps.

Lily never just walks into his office. As a freelancer, she doesn't know him any better than her function would necessitate.

"Stressful day," he says, recovering.

"Maybe you deserve a break." She is leaning on the doorframe, feet still planted in the hall. "Most folks are already there."

"Where did the day go?" Roebuck rubs his eyes.

Lily glances down the corridor. "Everybody's gone."

"I didn't even know you were here." Stupid thing to say.

"Stressful day," echoes Lily, arms folded. She has her knapsack slung across one shoulder, good to go.

Roebuck still sits, bolted to his chair. "What have you been working on?"

"Daniel has me doing mock-ups for some print ads."

"Oh." He didn't know this either. "What account?"

"A bunch of different ones. "

"Oh."

This is silly. Roebuck smiles; he wants her to be certain he is absolutely pleased to see her. He's just surprised.

"Let's go!" he says.

The pub is filling up, but Greenwood and his crew have secured the favoured table by the window. A cluster of account people forms its own detachment opposite. The suits are always overworked and under-thanked—the pit ponies of the ad-world, in Roebuck's opinion—he makes a point of hanging out with them whenever feasible. Lily slips into an empty chair at Greenwood's end, while Roebuck ducks over to the other side. He asks how everyone's day went, and they tell him not too bad. It's just coincidence that he and Lily have arrived together. One of the AEs has a question about today's prepro and they kick that over for a while. The coordinator for Ripreeler mentions that she's noticed a spike in YouTube views of certain second-generation ads. "You mean the ones with the guys on the fishing trip who can't find their favourite spinners because their wives are wearing them at the nightclub?" It's Greenwood talking. "Did I ever tell you that we studied that one in first-year marketing?" All to the good, says the suit—ignoring him—but it's a long time since those spots were aired and she can't help wondering what's behind the up-tick. Roebuck has his own theories, but it's too soon to get into all that. His lager goes down smoothly. He has realized quite suddenly he's famished. What with other priorities, he's missed lunch. The waiter brings a sandwich, and he washes it down with a fresh pint.

It's a beautiful day; a warm September afternoon. The sun is shining through the open windows. Before long the conversation moves on to that casual mix of near and far that burbles over shop talk. A voice down the table wonders if there's any chance the Jays will squeak into the playoffs, which segues to the Leafs, which makes everybody laugh. Carol the receptionist got engaged last week, and everyone who hasn't yet done so admires her ring. Someone's mother has been diagnosed with Type 2 diabetes; the AE who was wondering about this morning's prepro announces that her sister is expecting twins.

He has a long drive tonight and isn't looking forward to it. Three hours at least if he leaves once he's finished this beer; less if he holds off until the traffic eases up. Anne and the kids should have arrived at the landing by now; maybe they're already loading the boat. After all these years of practice, his wife has it down to a science. When the kids emerged from school this afternoon, Anne would have been waiting, motor running, car packed, groceries boxed, the gas tank topped up and ready to go. She'd have asked them each in turn if they needed to pee and, at the slightest hint of doubt, sent them back inside with orders to wash their hands when they were finished and come straight back to the car, no dawdling. Five minutes later they'd be heading north; the kids unpacking snacks and launching into the squabbles that would carry on until they'd either fallen asleep or arrived, with luck, two hours later at the marina.

It used to make him crazy. Anne's family is old Muskoka. She was brought up with the expectation that every weekend from Victoria Day to Thanksgiving would be spent up at the lake. Traffic is much worse now than it was when she was a girl; there's no way Roebuck can get away by 3:30. It caused no end of tension in the early years, but now they have settled on the practice of travelling up in separate cars. Which suits him fine. Roebuck likes night driving. He listens to music or current events or passes the hours in meditative silence, rehearsing. He enjoys pulling in at the landing beneath a ceiling of stars; waiting for the sound of the inboard rumbling out of the darkness, bow light growing brighter through the murk. "Kids asleep?" he'll ask as the fenders bump the dock. "Of course," his wife will say. "Get in."

But right now he isn't looking forward to it. Right at this moment Roebuck is totally wiped.

There's a full glass by his elbow; someone has ordered another round, though the group is already thinning. Roebuck drinks. He is summoning the energy to haul himself up. At the far end of the table, Greenwood is showing off the iPod Touch that he lined up for at the Apple Store this morning. In the short while he's been here, Daniel has upgraded at least twice. People are razzing Roebuck about his antique BlackBerry, which means that now he'll have to organize a newer model. "Excuse me," he says. On the way to the men's room, he dials the cottage.

"Hi."

"Hi."

"Did you make good time?" He can tell already that she's unhappy.

"Morgan forgot her violin. We had to go back. Just got here now."

"I'm sorry."

"We're still unloading."

"Listen," says Roebuck. "I think I'm going to come up in the morning."

"Oh."

"Yeah. I'm still not finished here and for some reason I'm totally bagged. I think it'll be safer to drive up first thing tomorrow."

Silence from the other end. For all her independence, Anne doesn't like to be there without him. Her parents seldom come up anymore; it's just her and the kids tonight.

"They want to sleep in the bunkie."

"All three?

"Yes."

What she's telling him is that she will be by herself in the main cottage with its creaks and groans and branches rasping at the window screens.

"You know what," he says, "I'll ..."

"No. Don't be silly. We're fine."

"Sure?"

"It's not safe to drive when you're tired."

"I'll stop in the morning and pick up Chelsea buns ..."

"Zachary!" Anne says. "You stop that!" He can hear a commotion in the background followed by a splash. "I have to go."

By the time Roebuck is back at the table, the company has dwindled. Greenwood is on his feet. He's heading uptown, he says, if anyone wants a lift. The AE whose sister is pregnant takes him up on it, though Greenwood doesn't look too thrilled. "I should go too," Roebuck says, but it's an effort getting up. His back has been one dull ache all afternoon.

"The busy bee has no time for sorrow," intones Lily, gazing out across the street.

Was that *Blake*? Lily is inscrutable. Of course it was Blake. Roebuck masters his surprise. He makes a show of preoccupation with his retrograde BlackBerry.

Before Roebuck is down to the bottom of his beer, the last of them have moved on. Again Lily is offered a lift. The boss, they know, keeps his wheels in the basement lot. Lily checks her watch and shakes her head. "I'm meeting a friend in fifteen minutes," she says in that way of hers that makes whoever's listening smile back automatically. "But thanks."

Roebuck signals for the bill. The last of his full-time staff have now left the building. He's just waiting for the waiter to bring him back his credit card.

"I just said that," Lily says.

"What?"

"I'm not really meeting anybody."

"Oh."

He is not the sharpest today. Roebuck rubs his eyes. "Did you just quote William Blake?"

"*The Marriage of Heaven and Hell.*" Lily's eyes crinkle. "My corruption progresses."

Here's another way to see it—from the flip side—from the perspective of *forgiveness*. Forgiveness is best defined as the cancellation of debt. What *forgiveness* represents, in other words, is the absolution of grievance. On the surface you would think that this is the last thing we'd want. Imagine the economy if all that debt was written off! But forgiveness is a powerful motivator. We can't afford to ignore it. Instead, what we want to do is leverage.

Who do we want our consumer to forgive? Herself, of course!

Forgiveness, therefore, is our final co-efficient.

Now let's pull it all together.

Our aim is to assure our customer that she has every reason to forgive herself because her grievance is legitimate. It justifies the *compensation* she will award herself by purchasing our product.

That, my young friends, is the virtuous circle of twenty-first-century marketing. Within that cycle, the function of advertising is to provide the spark, the cata-lyst—the push that gets the wheel turning.

Now then, whose shoulder do we put to the wheel?

Roebuck sleeps ten hours.

He has never woken up before in Lily's bed, and it's a shock.

"You conked out."

"What time is it?"

"Early. I've been poking at you." A red sun is coming through the window straight into his eyes.

"How early?"

"Dawn-ish."

"What time?"

"A little before six. You passed out sooner than I hoped."

Roebuck is still half-asleep, but remembers a certain level of activity. "Did I disappoint?" He yawns.

"You never disappoint. On the other hand, you didn't stay awake very long."

She has slipped out of bed and wrapped herself in a blinding white robe. "I'll make coffee," she says handing him his phone.

Roebuck dials the moment she has left the room. No messages. He sinks back into the pillow. Lily reappears with two mugs of coffee and a plate of buttered scones.

"I get you for another hour," she says. "Then you are allowed to go."

There's a new message blinking on the home phone. Anne's voice. "Hello! Hey! Pick up." A few beats of silence. "You must be in the shower. Call before you leave."

Anne assumes—correctly—that because she and the kids are awake before 8:00 AM on a Saturday morning, her husband will also be up. Roebuck dials the cottage number. He knows she has her cellphone, but it's tradition to use the ancient bakelite unit that in former times connected to a party line. She doesn't ask him why he didn't answer earlier.

"I was in the shower," Roebuck says.

"I called half an hour ago."

Anne tells him to pick up a bottle of Ripasso. She forgot to do that and the liquor store in town is useless. Roebuck reminds her that even in the city, most liquor stores don't open until ten.

"Then you'll be here by lunch. That's fine."

After such an earnest sleep, Roebuck isn't tired but parts of him still ache. There was traffic in the city, but now it's moving along. He pulls into a Tim Hortons and treats himself to a vat of double-double and a little stretching walk around the parking lot. It's funny, almost, but Lily and Yasmin have cramped the same muscles. The weather is fine; northbound traffic light. Roebuck switches off the sound and passes the miles in contemplation of *need*, that keenly verbal noun.

He stops in town to buy the promised Chelsea buns and a dozen butter tarts. All the handy parking spots are taken; he has a fair walk down to the landing. He should have called Anne from the bakery.

"I'm here," he says. "So are the bugs."

"Yes."

He contemplates retreating up the hill to wait in the car, but decides to tough it out. By the time he spots them rounding the mouth of the bay, Roebuck is wishing he'd stayed in the car. Zach is standing next to Anne on the passenger seat, gripping the windshield like a maniac.

Roebuck hands his son the bakery boxes and tosses his carry-on into the stern. "Where are the girls?"

"Making pancakes." Anne's tone makes it clear they should be getting back as rapidly as possible.

"I bought Chelsea buns," he says, slapping his hundredth mosquito.

"Get in."

It's a short ride to the island. The bugs are blown away once the boat is up to plane. Anne's cottage is perched on the highest point of land; almost always there's a breeze. Mosquitoes this time of year are not normally much of a concern. Roebuck wonders about global warming.

"Did you get the wine?"

"I did."

The kitchen is a disaster; the stove is cherry-red, though nothing is actually aflame. Katie greets her father passionately. "Morgan broke *all* the eggs!"

"I have Chelsea buns!" says Roebuck.

Anne begins to sweep away the flour he has tracked across the floorboards. "I was going to have you barbecue a rack of lamb," she says, "but I think the bugs are going to be a problem." She considers. "Maybe I'll upgrade the kids' spaghetti into something more Bolognese, and we'll all have that. Yes," she says, deciding. "That still goes with the wine."

"It's just bugs," Roebuck tells her. "The smoke will keep them off."

He will have cause, come evening, to regret this bravado.

Meanwhile, the day passes normally for a weekend at this juncture of the season. The lake is still warm enough for swimming, but the mosquitoes, though fairly mild until the sun goes down, remain a presence. A few chores need seeing to down around the dock, some leaves need raking, but for the most part it's an indoors stay. The kids watch videos until the television is shut off, forbidden, and replaced with board games, after which the acrimony rises sharply. Morgan and her violin are sent off to practice in the sleeping cabin.

Anne and Roebuck monitor their emails. "Yasmin thinks we'll get the Silverstein contract," Anne says, busy at her keyboard. "She ran into Belinda Silverstein yesterday on Cumberland."

"Getting her nails done?"

"What's it to you?"

"You're right. Sorry. Excellent news," he says, "about the Silverstein job."

Sure enough, when the sun begins to sink, the mosquitoes rise in humming waves. Roebuck is committed to the lamb. He bundles up, tucks his pants into his socks, rolls down his shirtsleeves and methodically buttons cuffs. He has doused himself in bug repellent, but they find a way in anyway. Each time he tries escaping back indoors, a cloud of insects follows. Roebuck is told either stay in or stay out, but not to let the bugs into the house.

Notwithstanding, the lamb makes it to the table in a perfect state of doneness. The Ripasso is a flawless match; Roebuck in his wisdom has produced a second bottle. The kids are quietly content with their spaghetti. It's a relief to all of them that Morgan has packed her instrument back into its case.

"I'm glad you're here," Anne says.

"Me too." Roebuck fingers the swelling on his neck.

He endures a new attack at bedtime while lighting the children's way to the bunkie, flashlight in one hand, a jug of drinking water in the other. It's ridiculously uncomfortable having no hands free to swat. They spend the next ten minutes sowing bloody vengeance on every last mosquito trapped inside.

Unlike Anne, Roebuck has never acquired an immunity. As far as he's concerned it's because the bugs target him and leave her be—and maybe there's some truth to that—but even when she does get bitten, Anne never swells or itches. Roebuck does. Fortunately, this time, there's nothing too serious on the visible parts of his face, but his fingers comes away with smears of pink when he probes the back of his neck.

"Don't scratch," Anne says. "I'll get the lotion. Kids okay?"

"I told them they had to have the lights out by nine-thirty or I'd cut the power. The good news, though, is that the bugs will keep them penned in until morning. I'll go check on them later," he says dabbing his neck.

"You're a good dad. Don't scratch."

Anne has put on a bathrobe and got herself ready for bed before administering his ointment. "Take your shirt off."

Roebuck examines himself in the mirror. The parts he can see don't seem so bad.

"Your back looks sore. Lie down."

He stretches out face down as instructed. "A couple of bad ones here," Anne says, tracing a finger down the cleft between his shoulders. "You'll live." He hears the sound of the bottle being shaken, then the coolness of the lotion on his skin. The bed moves as Anne shifts position. "Hold still. I'm getting some Kleenex." The mattress bumps, and then bumps again when she returns. She has climbed on top, her legs on either side of him.

"You did say the kids were asleep?"

It takes him a few seconds to understand that his wife is no longer in her robe.

"Turn over," Anne says.

It has been so long, between them, that it feels for Roebuck almost like being with another woman. On the other hand it is extraordinarily, inherently familiar; that grace that comes with years. "Mmm," she says a little later. "Why did we stop doing that?"

Roebuck has no answer. "Camomile lotion: aphrodisiac."

"Who knew?"

"What's got into you?"

"You, evidently." Anne has slid over to her side of the bed and closed her eyes. "You can go to sleep now."

But first he needs to check the kids. The bunkie is promisingly dark. Dressed in much less than is wise, Roebuck scurries through the undergrowth and cautiously puts his nose against the window. He doesn't want to breach the seal and let the bugs inside, but there is just enough moonlight to see his children through the glass, snugly and safely asleep. Eyes adjusted to the darkness, he now discerns the rhythmic flash of fireflies pulsing in the trees; he has read somewhere that lightning bugs are often active at the same time as mosquitoes. Roebuck stands beneath the moonlight, blinking. In the process he collects a whole new crop of punctures and wonders if he should initiate a second round of treatment, but his wife is snoring gently, too, when he returns.

23

Women are work. Period.
The Collected Sayings of Julius Roebuck

People will tell you that branding is new; that it was invented by marketers at the end of the twentieth century. Bullshit. Branding is ancient. Branding is biology; it's life itself. It is reproduction.

A frog doesn't croak to announce it's a frog; he does it to say he's *the* frog. A peacock grows his tail-feathers to convince the peahen that he's not just *a* mate, he's *the* mate. The one for her.

I know you are all familiar with the concept of brand fidelity: it goes back to this ancient principle. I am not *a* peacock—I am *the* peacock. I am the gift you give yourself. I am your destiny.

That's the meaning we aim to instil. *That's* the value-added in the process of selection—beyond that value of the thing selected: this thing is meant for *you* because you were meant to have it. It is yours by design.

Would you be surprised if I told you that the prime mover in the marketplace is reproduction?

Reproduce is just another way to say *restock*.

For a product to be viable it has to *move*, it has to be selected from the shelf in order to be restocked with one that replaces it, which in turn has to *move*. That's the path of evolution. From time to time it happens that a product is replaced with one that is *not* identical—one that is altered in some way.

If that new product has been chosen in preference to the old one, it's for one reason and one reason only: Because it has found a better way of saying *choose me*.

Now begins a busy phase in Roebuck's life. Professionally, things have heated up. The ethnographic research he's commissioned on Ripreeler's new pheromone bait has been unexpectedly insightful. Teams of anthropologists that fanned out to fishing camps and derbies all across the continent have now returned with their reports. Certain aspects of their findings have taken the marketers by storm.

By far the most frequently reported observation was the subjects' strong reaction to the product's smell. Roebuck had predicted this, of course; also that most respondents were clearly willing to associate the odour with enhanced attractiveness to fish. All to the good.

He picks up his marker and writes:

STINKS

Better still was respondents' willingness to state that they believed the bait was genuinely helpful in catching more fish. The Ripreelers were over the moon about this finding, though Roebuck himself remains cautious; he is forever warning clients not to get too carried away with ethnographics. Even so, a claim like PROVEN RESULTS! is every marketer's wet dream. Roebuck adds a second bullet:

WORKS

But what has really turned his crank is a little gem of startling perception—one the client was not nearly so happy about. And that, says Roebuck, is what separates the sharks from the flounders in this business, the muskies from the perch, the advertisers from the shoals of mere minnow marketers. In one-on-one interviews, several participants—a clear, directional cohort—admitted to a feeling that surprised them, too: a vague reaction variously described as something resembling *guilt*. The bait had worked so well, in fact—had in fact been such a magnet to its quarry—that some reported oddly moral qualms. "It's almost like cheating" was the way one angler phrased it.

Roebuck returns to his whiteboard:

CHEATS

"That's the part that makes the client nervous. But you and I know better." Roebuck erases the board and changes up the order:

STINKS

CHEATS

WORKS

There's something beautiful in there just waiting to break out. He knows it. The problem is that he hasn't yet identified exactly what.

He is frustrated, too, with the lack of progress on his still-too-hypothetical footwear account. There's been a lot of effort sunk into that one by him and Greenwood both, and every bit of it on spec. Roebuck loathes pro bono. And he *will* cash in, eventually; it's just that, so far, something seems to be holding up the process, some kind of delay, according to his sources; some snag in procurement that still needs finalizing before anything can move ahead. Whatever the cause, there's no formal request for proposals and until that happens Roebuck's hands are tied. Greenwood, too, appears discouraged. And of course he's pissed off, still, that he hasn't been informed exactly who this client is supposed to be. What he needs is patience. Roebuck is fairly certain anyway that Daniel's been doing some digging on his own behalf.

But there is no denying Greenwood has been busy. One of the smarter things he's done, in retrospect, was assigning so much of the Artemis account to Daniel's sphere of influence. On the whole, that piece of business has turned out to be the cash cow he had hoped, though a mean-spirited and unconscionably bad-tempered beast inclined to use its horns. As ever in the natural order of things, it's the suits who take worst of it when some sphincter-mouthed product manager fresh out of Wharton decides she hates the colour of that border or the sizing of that font. But in the end, it's Daniel who's responsible for inputting all their endless changes. He's been writing a fair amount of copy, too, in recent weeks. Ah well, he's young.

Roebuck has been fighting back a growing feeling that he himself is not so young. It's painful to admit—physically, some mornings—but sleeping with three women is wearing him down. The question (and Roebuck is honest enough to recognize he will never give himself an honest answer) is whether he would have launched his campaign for Yasmin if he'd still been having sex with Anne. Some days it's yes; others definitely no. Today would be a yes. But that's only because it's beforehand and Roebuck is still riding that tight-chested, hollow-groined ache of expectation rather than the bruised and jaded aftermath he has learned also to anticipate.

"Going somewhere?"

"As a matter of fact, yes." Roebuck is checking his watch. "Sorry, Daniel. Time to wrap this up."

They turn, side by side, and study the whiteboard. Greenwood shrugs. Roebuck, shrugging too, picks up the marker and adds some pronouns and a set of exclamation points.

IT STINKS!

IT CHEATS!

IT WORKS!

"Let me know when you've decided." Greenwood pauses at the door. "Any word on drag and clop? Just asking."

Roebuck is shaking out his jacket. Katie is due at taekwondo in forty minutes. "You'll be in the loop, Daniel, just as soon as there's a loop to be in. Honestly."

"Dad, what's a labia ... plasty?"

"I beg your pardon?"

"La-bi-a-plasty." Zach spells out the syllables, enunciating. "What's a labia-plasty?"

"Um ..."

"I get breast aug-men-tation. That's a boob job. But what's a labiaplasty ...?"

Roebuck has taught his children—from the moment they moved up from picture books—that whenever they're stuck on a word they should look at the surrounding sentence. "Read the words around it," he tells them. "That's where you'll find your clues."

"Um …" He says again.

"*Augmentation* means the same as *enhancement*. Right? That means making something bigger. And buttocks is *bum*. So *buttock enhancement* must mean making a bum bigger. But why would anybody want a bigger bum?"

"Jennifer Lopez," chimes Katie from the back seat.

Zach ignores his sister. "I see why you'd want bigger boobs. But a bigger bum?"

"Booty!" Katie says a little louder.

"Shut up." Zach repeats this phrase so often that no one even listens anymore.

Roebuck has by now figured out that Zach is reading words off a sign on the back of a bus. He steps on the gas and moves the car a little closer. It's a transit ad for an uptown plastic surgeon.

Exceptional Service for Exceptional Clients:
The Dr. Aspara Body-Sculpting Clinic offers the latest
in breast augmentation, tummy-tucks, and buttock
enhancement technology …

Then, below, in bullets: "Labiaplasty … Perineoplasty … Hymenoplasty …" followed by several terms Roebuck himself can't define. The text is superimposed across a very female torso in a purple thong.

So-so in terms of presentation, he decides, though the ratio of waist to hips is definitely arresting.

"Labiaplasty is a plastic surgery procedure for altering the labia minora and the labia majora," Kate intones.

"*Where* did …?"

"I Googled it." His daughter reads on. "A study in the *Journal of Sexual Medicine* reports that 32 percent of patients undergo the surgery for corrective and functional impairment while 37 percent for aesthetic reasons alone."

"Can I have my phone back, please?

"You're driving."

This is true.

The three of them are on the way to taekwondo. Kate has possession of his smartphone. It drives Roebuck crazy seeing people talking on their cellphones while operating motor vehicles—he's been known to yell—so Kate gets his for the duration of the trip. Zach dislikes being forced to come along, but there's nowhere else to leave him at this time of day so in compensation for being here he gets to ride up front. In exchange for accepting the back seat, Kate has full access to Roebuck's BlackBerry, though she's forever telling him he should have got an iPhone. "Piece of crap," she says, navigating back to Brick Breaker.

"What's *labia*?"

"Shut up, Zach!" It's like performance art, the two of them.

"*Labia*," says Roebuck, pedantic from habit where his kids are concerned, "is the Latin word for lips ..."

"*Dad!* Ewww. You're dis*gust*ing!"

"I was just ..." But Roebuck has spotted salvation, straight ahead. "Hey!" he says, a Dairy Queen standard has loomed into view. "Anybody up for a milkshake?"

Understanding *need* requires first advancing it from *want*.
A want is merely something you would like to have.
A need is a thing whose absence causes harm. Our aim
as marketers is the promotion of *want* into *need*.
Remember Maslow? Do people still study Maslow?

Abraham Maslow was a psychologist in the 1950s who described a hierarchy of human needs, starting with the bedrock priorities of food and shelter. Next in order came physical security and, after that, social security: the love and the esteem of fellow humans. Ranked at the very bottom of things we truly need is self-actualization.

Everything below that, Maslow figured, was just *want*.

Our objective as marketers is to elevate our product from something *wanted* to something *needed*. We achieve this transformation by means of advertising. I said a little while ago that branding is not a new thing. But here *is* a new thing:

Since Maslow's time, the order has changed.

Back then, esteem of *others* ranked ahead of self-esteem. That is to say that our need for the good regard of fellow human beings was thought to be greater than our need for the esteem in which we hold *ourselves*. I'm here today to tell you that the single biggest achievement of twentieth-century advertising has been the reversal of these categories. Self-respect now trumps the good regard of others in any measure of consumer aspiration.

From here on in, then, it's just embracing logic.

If self-respect is a fundamental human need, it follows that its absence is a cause of fundamental human harm. It therefore also follows that whatever enhances self-esteem diminishes harm and therefore is *good*.

Your product, for example.

Branding is the process by which your product becomes an agent in the self-actualization of its consumer, and thereby an agent for the greater good.

So how do you establish *good*? Easy. By comparing it to *bad*. How do you do that? You know where this is going ...

24

Stability is the breeding ground of change.
The Collected Sayings of Julius Roebuck

Truth is, Roebuck *does* think about other men. Though only for the purpose of more clearly understanding women. His own value as he sees it—the value of his sex—is mostly as a model for comparative analysis.

The benefit of pleasure is the giving not the getting. This, for Roebuck, is as basic as any bottom-line can go. Which of course gives men the advantage. In all his years of study, he has never once discovered evidence of any woman counting backwards from a hundred by threes, or imagining Donald Trump in a Speedo, or silently reciting "The Cremation of Sam McGee" to prevent herself from coming too quickly. Over the space of this last hour, Roebuck himself has relied on each of these techniques in succession plus several others he keeps in reserve. But it has gone well.

He is now indulging in a little span of self-congratulation.

The advantage to men is that sex therefore becomes an exercise in self-control—that most requisite of human skill—which in turns leads straight ahead to self-improvement. He is fairly certain the same applies to other men, but Roebuck is willing to stand proxy. The problem for women is that men are so easy. God knows, he is.

"I mean it," she says. "Seriously. If it doesn't take this time, it's fucking over."

The last few visits have been structured somewhat differently, but today they have reverted to first principles. Today, officially, is O-Day. Two interpretations of that shorthand come to mind sequentially. Roebuck smiles privately, though perhaps it has shown on his face. Yasmin aims a kick toward his ear. If she were on her feet she'd be dangerous, but since she's flat on her back a lateral strike is the worst she can manage. He pins her foot against his shoulder. Yasmin's adductor muscles are alarmingly reflexive.

"Eighteen minutes," he says. "Hang in."

"I think you're shooting blanks so what's the fucking point?"

Roebuck sighs; they've been through all this before. He notes she isn't moving.

"And definitely no more of those bonus visits in the middle of the month. *That's* over. I mean it this time."

"Okay."

He swings his legs over the side and climbs off the bed. It is an unusually tall structure.

"Stop bouncing!" Yasmin arches and flexes to account for the spring of the mattress. With her feet against the headboard, she can't see where he's going. "Make sure you put the seat down! Last time you left it up. So rude!"

Roebuck's pants are folded on the creases; his shirt hangs neatly on a hanger. Appointments with Yasmin are not occasions for wildly throwing clothes about the room. He is almost fully dressed before she notices.

"Hey!"

"Be still," he says. "Thirteen more minutes."

"Where are you going?" Yasmin twists her head to get a bead, but can't bring him fully into focus without imperilling her pelvic tilt.

"Don't move," he says again.

"We aren't *finished*!"

He considers a witticism on vaginal upsuck, but decides it's inappropriate. Besides, his own reaction to that phrase tends to the Pavlovian, and Roebuck doesn't want to talk himself back into that bed. He really is fatigued.

> And every day that quiet clay seemed to heavy and
>   heavier grow;
> And on I went, though the dogs were spent and the
>   grub was getting low;
> The trail was bad, and I felt half mad, but I swore I
>   would not give in;
> And I'd often sing to the hateful thing, and it heark-
>   ened with a grin.

"What the fuck?" says Yasmin, aiming her voice at the ceiling.

"I'm tired," Roebuck answers, softly reciting while lacing his shoes. Honesty, sometimes, really *is* the better policy.

◎◎

Although he understands the many ways in which he is a fool, Roebuck is not so wholly stupid as to go home drenched in Yasmin's estrus. En route, he stops by at the gym. This is not without its own attendant guilt: his workout schedule has fallen off depressingly these past few months. He does a little shoulder work, a few reps on the bench press, some abs—nothing too stressful, the abs right now are tense enough as it is. The main point today is the shower.

He'd expected to be at Yasmin's for another hour so Roebuck is now well ahead of schedule. The plan, originally, was to stop off at the market for one of their wonderfully authentic precooked dinners. But now he has the option of preparing something of his own from scratch.

Roebuck walks into the kitchen, freighted down with groceries. "I'm cooking tonight!"

"Of course you are."

"Anyway," he says, "I'm making risotto."

What with the demands of his schedule, he is obliged more often than he likes to rely on high-end take-out, though once he has it properly garnished and plated they do all sit and eat together—a family law.

"Need help?"

"Yes!" He is feeling better already. Another thing they do well together, he and Anne, is cook. "Let's open a bottle."

"You go ahead."

Anne is a mystery. She has always been a mystery, but since that weekend at the cottage she has graduated to enigma. He had warned himself that it was almost certainly a one-off; the wine, likely—something in the atmosphere on that occasion in particular; who knows, maybe the mosquitoes?—Roebuck was in no way expecting repetition. Yet there she was, a few nights later, slipping in through the adjoining door. "Kids asleep?"

The phrase has taken on a new and more compelling meaning.

If she were a man, he would think it was Viagra, or Cialis, or one of those blockbusters that have left Big Pharma and its shareholders with such impressive hard-ons. But Roebuck is certain no such product has been as yet devised for women. And even if it was—why now? Carefully, *extremely* carefully—like a sapper approaching a suspected IED—he has sounded out the possibility of early onset menopause or some such evolution in hormonal status-quo. Impossible to broach directly, and anyway it doesn't fit. Or anything else he can think of. On the other hand, when all is said and done, who is he to look a gift horse in the mouth? "Hope you have an appetite," he says chopping his sun-dried tomatoes.

"*Salute!*" Anne is looking arch.

This is eerie. But Roebuck is happy to adapt.

25

When a woman is doing something her husband is not,
he is doing nothing insofar as she's concerned.
The Collected Sayings of Julius Roebuck

"Did I tell you I'm to be a keynote speaker at a Ferrer/Léche
symposium?"

"Really? Interesting."

"Sometimes I worry about how completely cynical I am capable of being."

"Are you going to eat that flatbread?"

"Someone once described me as a romantic who cloaks himself
in cynicism. More and more, I'm wondering if it's true. Maybe I
really am a cynic ..."

"You think?"

"This speech. Somehow it's become ... relevant ... More so
than I thought."

"Where are you speaking?"

"Ferrer/Léche. They're hosting a shindig, kicking off the twenty-first century's second decade. Hundred-proof marketing. You know, the biz school?"

"You said. Right."

"I started out just having fun ..."

"You're always having fun with MBAs."

"Yes! That's how it started. But somehow it got ... I don't know ... significant."

"Will you please pass the bread?"

"Advertising is changing. That's what's emerging. In some ways of course it's the same as always, but in others ..."

"Daniel says the world is going digital."

"Yes. There's that, too, of course. Though that's mostly a matter of platform. But you're right. If the platform changes, what's above shifts too."

"You're not concerned about it?"

"Oh yes. But that's not what I'm talking about."

"What then?"

"That's the problem. I'm not exactly sure."

"When is this lecture?"

"Sometime after New Year. Not this one, the one after."

"But that's months away! Years!" Lily folds her napkin. "What time is your next meeting?"

"Which meeting?"

"Your *next* meeting. Today. This afternoon. What time?"

Roebuck checks his new BlackBerry. "One-thirty. Finance."

"I mean your next *important* meeting."

"Two-thirty. Client."

"Then you have plenty of time to take me home and work on finessing your fireplace technique."

It has been that kind of week.

That kind of month, really. Though quite a lot of it goes by before he hears again from Yasmin. There have been moments—over the span of this relationship, key moments—when Roebuck has surrendered himself to the discretion of fate. As of now, he's reached another one of those watersheds. If Yasmin has decided it's over, then fine. It's over.

Time passes.

Roebuck spends his days in sphinxian silence.

Another week flows by. He bides his time. He is serene. He had by now become accustomed to seeing Yasmin on a semi-regular basis, but that, too, apparently, is finished. So be it. Life will be simpler. Roebuck's life could definitely use a little simplifying.

He taps out a message. "Should I keep the 3rd open? (I have meetings.) J."

November third, according to his spreadsheet, is Yasmin's next *peak*-ovulation. Yasmin and her eggs are like the Capistrano swallows; you could set your clock by them. Her answer pings back immediately. "I expect you on the 3rd. I will advise what time. I am also free this afternoon."

Vaginal upsuck: that deeply comprehensive term. Roebuck reconfigures his itinerary.

He has by now adapted to the quite substantive differences between these unscheduled, off-cycle encounters and their regular O-Day appointments. In terms of contrast, the distinction is mostly positional. When sperm retention is the prime, the singular consideration, Roebuck assumes top missionary spot. For all non-procreative get-togethers—flowback being neither here nor there—Yasmin is the one riding cowboy. Not to say that she doesn't call the shots from either point of view, but Roebuck usually has a better time of it supine. Woe betide him, in either case, if he finishes ahead of schedule. Interestingly, he finds self-mastery distinctly easier with Yasmin orchestrating from above. Roebuck is a maestro of self-regulation.

The other main departure is the conversation.

When Yasmin's ovum is positioned at the centre of the universe, there is seldom much demand for small talk. Both parties understand their roles and responsibilities; things move along succinctly. Yasmin's sole preoccupation is with seizing that tense and fleeting moment when her basal body temperature is that perfect one degree above. Afterward, during hiatus, she concentrates her yogic expertise on maximizing uptake. He is constantly amazed at the contractions she achieves without seemingly moving her legs. As for Roebuck—typically—he spends the downtime with his laptop or, now that that's forbidden, learning applications on his so-called smartphone.

Off-cycle visits, however, have evolved into format all of their own.

These are closer in spirit to, if not to actually a *date,* then at least occasions when some degree of social intercourse is understood to be appropriate. Sometimes she will pour a glass of wine or even brew them up a fragrant pot of herbal tea, depending on the time of day. Once or twice Roebuck has brought flowers or a potted plant and they have talked about her preference for narcissus over, say, daffodils. He has learned by now that it's better to let her introduce the topic rather than throw out something of his own.

Today things have moved along quite nimbly. Roebuck's heart rate is decelerating. Refractory periods tend to be a little less generous than what's allowed for O-Days: three-quarters of an hour, typically, give or take. Yasmin has a question.

"What exactly *is* an art director?"

Roebuck is more than happy to explain that art directors create the images, while copywriters like him provide the words that give them relevance.

"But everyone knows that pictures are more important than words, so why does that make him less important?"

"Why does what make who less important?"

"Daniel."

"*Who?*"

"Daniel. He's the junior, isn't he? He gets paid less?"

"You mean Daniel *Greenwood*?"

"Who else are we talking about? Why does he get paid less?"

"Because he's young! Why are we talking about Daniel Greenwood?"

"But does he make decent money?"

"Of course he makes decent money."

"How decent?"

"A lot. Why are we talking about Daniel?"

"We're remodelling his condo."

Roebuck didn't know that Greenwood even owned a condo.

Yasmin has suspended a pillow at arm's length above her midriff; she's fidgety. "I just want to make sure he can afford us."

"Oh yes, Daniel can afford you. He's very good at what he does. You know, I've actually been considering …"

"I don't care how *good* he is. I only care he has the money. Why are you just lying there?"

26

Same is not the same as equal.
The Collected Sayings of Julius Roebuck

Roebuck has read somewhere that, sometimes, when a woman perceives that *other* women find a given man attractive, she may herself begin to find that man attractive too. It's the best theory he's come up with. Possibly Anne is picking up on some involuntary messaging from Yasmin, chemosensory clues of some kind. Which is worrisome, on its own account. Anne continues to perplex.

Though not half so much as Lily.

Lily—who has always been the picture of discretion—only yesterday strolled into his office and offered him a backrub. It's true that no one else was there and that first she checked the hall. But she'd have never done a thing like that two months ago. The irony, on top of everything, is that he really could have used it. Roebuck's sciatic is definitely compressed. Also, she seems to have lost all interest in discussing art and literature—she hasn't written anything in ages, as far as he can tell—and she never wants to eat at restaurants. "Come to my place," she says. Last week, twice, he didn't even end up getting fed.

At least with Anne there's a blueprint. They were pretty avid in the early years. Though of course back then they didn't camp in separate tents—yet even this, somehow, has upped the present level of engagement. He never knows on any given night when his door will be opened and his sheets stripped away; Anne has no scruples if he happens to be sleeping. Though it's always according to *her* timetable. Roebuck has tried a pre-emptive approach, taking the initiative to her. But any time he has attempted getting into *her* bed, he's been sent packing. As ever, he adapts.

"I must say, you still do pretty well for an old guy."

He has the wit this time to think before responding. Roebuck weighs his options. "I'm inspired," he says with honest affection. Anne *does* do astonishingly well.

He has been wondering if maybe it's time to break down and book an appointment with his GP. So far he hasn't needed it, though a few times lately it's been touch and go. It might be prudent, just in case, to stock up on one of those prescriptions. There's no concern with Anne; Anne always leaves after they are finished; refractory time with him and Anne can still be measured in days not minutes. But for Yasmin—and Lily, too, more recently—Roebuck has been giving serious thought to a back-up supply of those little blue pills.

"Want the shower first?"

"You go ahead."

Like him, Anne is a morning person. Before kids it was mornings that were best; finding one another in the dim before dawn then drifting back to sleep again enfolded as first-light slipped down from the ceiling. His wife has re-established ancient practice—though Anne remains a mother first and foremost: before she comes to him she looks into each room to be sure the kids are safely asleep, then carefully locks his bedroom door. The alarm will ring in half an hour anyway; soon the house will up—no point lounging in bed. While Anne is in the shower, Roebuck slips downstairs to get the coffee going. He has her cup waiting when she emerges in a towel.

"Tell Daniel he left his portfolio at the studio."

It takes a moment. Roebuck has been reflecting on the word *crepuscular*, which to his ear has always sounded like it should mean something much less pleasant. Anne's back is to him as she speaks. "I meant to bring it home with me so you could give it to him this morning. But I forgot."

"Daniel?"

"His portfolio."

"Got it."

Anne is brushing her teeth. She returns to the sink, spits, rinses, and dabs her mouth. "Has he given you any idea what he thinks about the laminate?"

Roebuck nearly blurts that the first he heard about any of this was just the other day from Yasmin, but catches himself. "I don't think so," he says.

"He didn't say?"

"I guess we've all been busy."

"We're suggesting a laminate for the kitchen. I think Yasmin has taken a shine to him. Is he single?"

Roebuck isn't sure about this either. "He was dating someone a while back, but she moved on. Come to think of it, I don't know all that much about Daniel's personal life. I didn't even know he'd bought a condo."

"Really?" She studies his reflection in the vanity mirror. "It has potential. Two levels, facing the lake."

"You've seen it?"

"Of course. It's one of the new builds down at Liberty Village."

"Big job?" Roebuck asks because he doesn't know what else to ask.

"Not especially, no. But on the other hand it's walls-out. Which is of course a challenge seeing as the exteriors are floor-to-ceiling glass."

"Right."

He still doesn't know what to say. He wouldn't mind pursuing the conversation, but Anne has vanished back into the bathroom steam and does not reappear.

27

Branding is biology torqued.
The Collected Sayings of Julius Roebuck

*S*ex and advertising.
Toast and butter. Horse and carriage. Love and marriage. Certain words just go together. Just fit.

Sex and advertising is one of those matches made in heaven. Literally, if you believe in Adam and Eve. Or any other foundational myth I'm aware of.

Everything, *everything* begins with sex. It's so obvious we want to disclaim it. Like saying *breathing is fundamental to life.* So evident, it doesn't need repeating. But with breathing we don't take the next step and deny it. We don't suggest we can discount breathing because breathing is so *obvious*—because breathing is cliché.

When I was a boy, people had *sexes.* We were male, and we were female. These days we have *gender.* And gender of course is a more inclusive term. Many languages have more than two genders. Latin, if I'm not mistaken, has three: masculine, feminine, and neuter.

Which I suspect is the point. *Gender* is sterilizing agent; it's an attempt to rope sex up to the fencepost and sterilize it.

This is the second of our era's great accomplishments: our embrace of gender over sex, which you may interpret as a form of social evolution. Language evolves toward greater precision. But here we're moving in the opposite direction. Which, for us advertisers, is an excellent development. I'm put in mind of a friend who likes to point out that branding is what ranchers do to steers with white-hot irons.

I digress. We were talking sex.

Despite our best efforts, sex remains imperative. Without it, we don't reproduce. Without reproduction, we don't exist. Neuroscientists will tell you that if you want to light up every region of the brain, show it dirty pictures. No other form of stimuli effects anywhere near as broad a range of neural receptors. Sex is hard-wired. As long as human beings remain biological organisms, we will remain keenly motivated by sex.

We have this funny way of neutralizing things, don't we, by calling them clichés? I have always thought this one of the stranger characteristics of our culture.

Sex and advertising are a cliché for the simple reason that they represent an ineluctable truth. The message for both is the same. It's always the same.

Choose me.

What the fuck? Roebuck sighs and slowly scrolls back up the page. What is he thinking? They'll laugh him off the stage. Miles off topic. On the other hand it isn't, really; not really at all. And who cares anyway? He highlights the passage, but that's as far as he gets. Roebuck presses "Save" and, with a conscious effort, moves on to matters more pertinent.

He has lined up a series of appointments this week with his bank, his tax attorney, and his accountant. Housekeeping, these consultations; only distantly of interest, but important nonetheless.

Roebuck is conscious that he's taken his eye off the ball in recent months. But he has by no means left the game. This is not his nature.

28

God is too big to be that small.
The Collected Sayings of Julius Roebuck

The morning of November third arrives in bright blue skies. Starlings gabble in the eves and an optimistic cardinal says "chew, chew, chew" somewhere in the hedge out back. Roebuck pauses, hoping for a flash of red against the yellow leaves. He has always had a soft spot for cardinals, though he appreciates them more come February when they're calling out for spring. Not so long ago he came across a survey revealing that the average North American can readily identify a hundred different advertising jingles, but could barely recognize ten birdsongs in their own front yards. "Chew, chew, chew" goes the cardinal out back. Roebuck turns the key and starts the car.

Normally, she gets in touch before mid-afternoon.

For O-days the itinerary is deliberately fluid. If her temperature is bang-on first thing in the morning, she will want him first thing in the morning—after which he's back in the office by noon and able to reschedule whatever appointments he has missed. More often, though, it's closer to lunch. Which makes arrangements even more straightforward. Roebuck absents himself for what for amounts to a normal midday break and returns to his desk fatigued, admittedly, and hungry—always—but with the remainder of his afternoon intact. He will miss it. He knows he will miss it. But miss it or not, it's finished. He has grossly tempted fate. Elemental reasoning suggests that the farther into this he goes, the farther out he sticks his neck, so today—after today—Roebuck is retracting his apparatus to where it decently belongs. He has been lucky, luckier than he deserves. During the hiatus, probably— when Yasmin launches into her usual post-production crank—he intends to break the news. At which point he has every confidence that she will violently reverse position. Roebuck is curious, in fact—anxious even, admittedly—but genuinely curious, too, to see where her reaction will net out. He hopes it won't get dangerous. But whatever, whatever the fallout, he is resolved. There is pleasure in a decision soundly made.

So it's something of an anticlimax when the morning passes without contact. Roebuck checks his calendar, consults his spreadsheet; counts back the days: twenty-eight on the money. Bang on exactly.

Twelve o'clock comes and goes. Roebuck's eye is on his email throughout a meeting with the manager of the digital agency he has hired to upgrade the Artemis web presence. At one o'clock the outmoded cellphone he relies on for his private calls sits discreetly on the corner of his desk while Roebuck entertains a VP of Marketing, who is here today to tell him that, what with the downturn, Finance will longer authorize his agency's retainer. A few minutes past two, and Roebuck is alone again at his desk. Carol the receptionist solemnly enters his office and places before him an imposingly thick, cream-coloured envelope embossed with legal seals that has just arrived by courier and for which Roebuck himself must sign to acknowledge receipt of delivery.

So it *has* happened.

It's true he's been expecting this, sort of; at least with the logical part of his being. But in every other sense Roebuck is completely unprepared. He wonders if retirement is going to be this way, or the kids' graduation, or his first grey hair: you know it is coming, but the shock of it still stuns the day you grasp the fact it's really happened. Time decelerates with every heartbeat as Roebuck breaks the seal and methodically unwinds the strings from their red paper buttons. With each revolution his senses heighten; he is conscious of the rasp of his own lungs, the thrum of his arteries, the quiet brush of thread against paper. How curious that this has come today.

He reads it over carefully and places yet another call to his attorney—Roebuck has observed due diligence, he has—and then absorbs the whole of it again more slowly. Still he is surprised. More than surprised; shocked. Holding his right hand level before his eyes he sees that it is trembling. Better than he thought. Better than he would ever have imagined.

He needs to talk to Anne.

Roebuck punches in the number, but disconnects before his wife picks up. Anne, he knows, will tell him that a thing like this is *his* decision, his alone—then leave him with no doubt at all about her confidence that whichever way he chooses is certain to be wrong. If he says he is thinking of accepting, she will warn him that he's always rushing in. If he admits he is planning to say no, she'll remind him that the economy is in a downturn and an opportunity like this may never come again. It's a useful way of working through a process, but it's not the kind of feedback he wants right now.

His desk phone rings. It's the attorney's office calling for confirmation that Roebuck has received the offer; their preference is for tomorrow morning if he can make himself available. He dials Lily.

"Julius …"

"Short notice, I know, but can you meet me for a drink?"

"Um ..."

"I need to talk."

"Right now ..."

"It's important!"

"Well so is ..."

"Lily. *Please*. Something really big I need to tell you."

"As a matter of ..."

"I'll be there in half an hour."

"Julius!"

He hangs up. On his way out the door, he pauses at reception to let Carol know he'll be out of office for a spell. Carol is appalled.

"You can't! You have your interview with *AdForge*!"

This isn't like him. Roebuck forces himself to stop and reason this through. "Right." he says. "Ask Daniel to take it."

"Daniel isn't in today."

He leans with both hands on the desk to emphasise the seriousness of what he is about to say. "Carol, will you call *AdForge*, please, and tell them I'm very sorry, but a family emergency has come up. I have to cancel."

If Carol were chewing gum she would blow a bubble while she gave herself the time to think this over. "Sure," she says. "Everything okay?"

Roebuck waves a hand. "Absolutely." He stabs the elevator button. "Where's Daniel?"

The doors slide open, Carol shrugs. "Not here."

"Omniglobe wants to buy me out."

He has planned to hold off telling her until he has a drink in hand, but Roebuck just can't wait. Lily has barely got her seatbelt buckled before he blurts his news.

"Sorry?" she says.

She's been like this since she met him at the door. Roebuck is aware that he should have started with how *her* day is going, but the weight of what he has to say is so immense it is impossible to set aside.

"Omniglobe," he says. "Parent to the fucking world."

"Yes. I know Omniglobe."

"Of course you do! They own half the shops you work for. More."

"Yes."

"Now they want mine."

"Why?"

"What do you mean, why?"

Lily's reaction isn't what he was expecting. Roebuck isn't really sure what he expected; only that she'd be more ... moved. "What kind of question is that?" He has to pump the brakes to make way for a Vespa. "All right. If you want me to say I built this business into an award-winning agency, okay; I'll blow my horn." A bus stops dead ahead, and Roebuck cuts into the other lane. "What it *does* say is that those guys think my little agency is worth the ridiculous amount of money they're putting on the table."

He is hoping she will ask.

"Slow down!"

"Sorry." Roebuck eases off the gas. "I admit all this is ... affecting me more than I thought." He puffs his cheeks. "It hasn't come as a complete surprise, you know. They've been sending out feelers for months. But somehow still it's caught me, I don't know ... off guard. I guess I never took it seriously. Or maybe I've just been too busy to do more than go through the motions. This kind of money, though, definitely makes you sit up and take notice."

Still nothing.

"Bottom line," he says, "is that now I have no idea what I should do."

She is staring out the window. For a moment it looks like she's about to speak, but can't find the words.

"I know!" Roebuck thumps the steering wheel. "Exactly! That's why I needed to talk … What do you do with a thing like this?" She has turned to look at him, but he has swerved around a delivery van. "They want me to stay on for an eighteen-month transition. If I accept, I'd have to pretend I'm still interested in running the business—and who knows, maybe I would be?—question is, what would I do with myself? After?"

Lily sighs. "When I first met you, you said you had a novel in a drawer somewhere."

Roebuck looks at her, stunned—enchanted. "My God," he says, "That's perfect! At the dawn of the digital age, as printed word lies dying, Julius Roebuck sets up as a novelist." He reaches out to touch her knee. "And you're right, too. It's a good time for the likes of me to be getting out of the business. Maybe I should do a memoir. That's close enough these days to fiction. But on the other hand …"

"Pull over at that taxi stand."

"What?"

"Just stop."

Roebuck stops. Immediately a cab pulls in behind him, leaning on the horn. "I have to move," he says, but Lily has unbuckled. Before he knows what's happening, she is standing on the curb, staring through the open door. The cab behind nudges his bumper, horn blaring.

"I missed my period," Lily says and disappears down the stairs into the subway.

When Roebuck gets back to the office, Carol is sitting with her back squared and eyebrows arched. She nods furtively toward a woman seated in the waiting area. "I didn't get to her in time," she whispers without moving her lips. Roebuck has no memory of how he has arrived here. He can't remember driving back or parking the car or riding up the elevator. His cellphone is still open in his hand; he knows that he has been dialling Lily and that Lily hasn't answered. Carol clears her throat and bobs her head toward the waiting woman. "Mr. Roebuck will see you now," she says spacing out the syllables. Even in his fog, he registers that she has been practising this line the whole time he has been away. He turns, habit in the driver's seat, smiles his smile, and extends his business hand. "I'm very sorry to have kept you waiting," says Roebuck with all the sincerity in the world. Escorting her toward his office, he has the presence of mind to ask if she would like a coffee or a soft drink? Anything at all?

"I'm good," she tells him.

At another plane of being he is vaguely conscious that under other circumstances he would be setting up to charm this girl. Something like muscle memory—perhaps a little deeper—has him setting one foot in front of the other as they walk together down the hall.

"Thanks for this." She passes him her card.

Roebuck transfers the mobile to his other hand and receives the card politely. *Senior Reporter.* He has now wrapped his head around the fact that this woman is here to interview him. "It's a scheduled feature," she tells him. "Right now we're calling it 'Changes and Challenges.' The industry's evolving. That's the topic."

"I see," says Roebuck. He has always got on well with the press. "Please have a seat."

"Nice office."

"Thank you." He slides into his own chair behind his desk. Normally he would sit side by side with her, but today he feels he needs the distance.

The reporter launches into her preliminary patter designed to put him at ease, and Roebuck, who's been doing interviews like this since before she learned to spell, replies with prepackaged cant of his own. She asks for his permission to activate her tape recorder; he grants it with his most engaging smile.

Part of him is dealing amazingly well. The other part is spinning in a blinding void.

"Social media," she says. "Is it the game-changer everyone's predicting?"

Journalists always want to talk to him about his only-women-count approach to advertising; it's what he's known for in the biz. Roebuck has been lining up the usual palaver. Only now it's dawning on him that this isn't why she is here today. "Social media?"

"You know, Facebook, MySpace, LinkedIn, Flickr, or the new one, Twitter, which people are saying is going to be huge. Are micro blogs of 140 characters about to change the way you do business, Mr. Roebuck?"

"Got you." He has a strong impression this young woman is more comfortable—and very likely more conversant—than he is on this topic; she belongs to that demographic. "Right."

He has paused to focus and is pleased with what comes out. "A short burst of inconsequential information," Roebuck says and smiles. "That, I believe, is more or less the dictionary definition of *twitter*. Any social force with the moxie to give itself a name like that has my vote as a game-changer."

And suddenly, quite suddenly, he realizes it's this he's been writing about—maybe better to say *around*—in the Ferrer/Léche text he's been fooling himself with. Has he spoken this out loud? "Sure, he says, watching his performance from some place of dim but horrified detachment. "Advertising is changing. But the change is only methodology. In all the other ways it is, as it has always been—and will always be—the same."

The reporter shifts to probe a little deeper. "You of all people should be aware of how social media can impact an ad campaign."

She smiles showing how she can be ingratiating too. "Wasn't it the amazing response you got for your fashion models with fishing lures that turned Ripreeler into a household name and launched your own brand too, incidentally? It's still out there on YouTube."

Roebuck recognizes a rhetorical question when one comes whipping at his solar plexus; he nods modestly.

"People study it in business school," she says.

Roebuck affects a bashful laugh. "You make it sound like ancient history."

"*Yes!* Now you've put your finger on exactly what this story's about! How fast everything is getting old. Communication is evolving at lightning speed. How do you keep up?"

The short answer, in all honesty, is that he doesn't. But even in the state he's in today, he is not about to fess up to that. It is a fact—a well-disguised fact, he hopes, but a fact nonetheless—that Roebuck is not the biggest fan of a digitized universe. It has always been the message, for him, not the medium, that's at the heart of everything. He has not the slightest doubt that social media will only increase in significance, but so much of it annoys him. And all the extra back end stuff is just so … tedious. Roebuck has yet to see a banner ad that doesn't make him think it was written by someone squeezing zits.

"Look," he says. "Here's what I'm about to tell you …"

This is good—or at least not bad—being forced like this to think in clear straight lines. "We know already that the television market is fragmenting and that digital platforms are picking up the traffic. True. My agency will spend more this year than it did last year contracting out the digital components of our work to companies who have the expertise we lack. Also true. Next year, our spend is likely to be greater still and, yes, sure, that is damaging my bottom line. Some people go so far as to say there's a revolution underway, that old-fashioned advertising is dying. Bullshit."

Roebuck pauses because stagecraft requires a pause at this nexus; he looks at the reporter who returns the gaze benignly. He clears his throat.

"Absolutely, changes are coming. And yes I'm hearing footsteps. But anyone who tells you advertising is dying is an idiot. Media may change, but the *message* never does and the message is and always will be the same: Choose me. That doesn't change. That never changes. What *has* changed, and what will make my job easier going forward, not harder, is that the chooser is more and more certain to be a woman ..."

Now she reacts. "There you go with your fem-centric thing. Your file is full of articles on that. I read them. But the story today is digital ..."

Roebuck holds up his hand. "Kindly remember that the word *digital*, in primary definition, means fingers. Digits are fingers." He wiggles his own. "In my business, we're all about stimulation, that's *our* medium; yours, too," he says, and then regrets the phrasing. He has no wish at all to make her think he's flirting. "Look, people are still under the impression that The Internet is male. False. The Net—like everything else—has feminized. We describe it as a place for the exchange of information, as if *information* is cold, hard, masculine data. What's mostly trafficked on the Net is *emotion*—precisely what I deal in." Throughout the first part of their conversation, she has been jotting notes. Now the notebook rests open on her lap, pen immobile in the crease. Roebuck has always had good relations with the press. "Go on," she says.

"You mentioned Facebook. Facebook started out as way for frat boys to rate the girls at Harvard, if I'm not mistaken. Then it evolved into a place for adults to reconnect with people they wish they'd had sex with back in high school. But what it's morphing into now—above all else—is a venue for people to emote endlessly about *themselves*. That's information, absolutely. Billions and trillion of bites of it. But it's *internal* information. It's information about *feelings*." Roebuck waggles his digits again. "Which fits it perfectly to *my* field of expertise. The future holds no fear for me."

"This is interesting."

Roebuck nods. He could keep this up all day. A phone goes off.

He snatches up his mobile, but there's no one there. The reporter is embarrassed. "I'm so sorry!" She's blushing. "We must have the same ring tone." She mutters something about editors texting in the middle of interviews and fumbles in her purse. "Excuse me. I have to take this."

And now Roebuck grasps that fortune has forgiven him again. What a terrible mistake, answering if the caller had been Lily— with a tape recorder running and a journalist taking notes. She has opened up her iPhone. Roebuck uses the pause to check his mail. The reporter is scribbling in her notebook with the phone tucked into her shoulder. Her attitude has altered, but Roebuck isn't watching. He scans the queue and there, near the bottom, finds an unread item from Yasmin. It has come through on his normal account, not Hushmail.

Congratulations Big Boy! You rock!
Never too soon to start planning. Call ASAP.

Roebuck can't quite seem to take his eyes off his computer screen. He is aware that the reporter is speaking to him from the far side of his desk. "Mr. Roebuck?"

"Uh huh."

"Sorry about that. This is not the way we usually do things." She looks like she's expecting him to say something, but Roebuck isn't with her. "… Only my editor is telling me to ask if you had any comment about Daniel Greenwood?"

It's not that Roebuck is being cautious. It isn't that he's reacting to a question from left field with well-considered hesitation. It's just that Roebuck hasn't taken in the question. "What?" he says, then corrects himself. "Sorry, I beg your pardon?" Politeness is the habit of a lifetime.

"We've just picked up an item saying Daniel Greenwood has been named creative director of a start-up shop in Sydney." She's squinting again at her phone. "It's a digital agency, apparently. There's a video with moose, or lions, or something, that's getting tons of hits." She has paused again to scroll. "I've never heard of this outfit. But they are announcing that they've landed Drogonie Claude. That would be a sizable account. Daniel Greenwood is quoted as saying they're launching a campaign that focuses on *sound*, whatever that means. He says it's going to revolutionize the business. Do you have any comment? The story is datelined Australia."

Roebuck has no answer.

"Any comment, Mr. Roebuck?"

"Daniel is in Australia," he says. Roebuck's brain has framed this as a question, but a question of such limited significance it arises with the profile of a statement.

"So you knew! I *knew* you had to know. So then, what about the video?"

The same feeling of enhanced detachment informs him that if ever there was time for disconnection, that time was now. "I'm sorry," Roebuck says, eyes still glued to his screen. "I've just received an urgent message. I regret to say we have to wind this up."

"Daniel Greenwood?"

Roebuck has to think. This is what is meant by "information overload." "No, he says. "Daniel's in Australia."

Carol walks the reporter to the elevator. Roebuck, minutes later, departs the office too.

Gama-Care Laboratories has remodelled since the last time he was in. The walls are now a harsh and brilliant white. With that subjacent part of his awareness still functioning below the surface churn of panic, Roebuck records the change as positive. He plunks his sample jar smartly on the countertop. His hands, he sees, are shaking.

"I need this analyzed. Immediately."

"Two week," replies the woman, eyes still focused on whatever she is busy with behind her ledge.

It's the same person from the first time he was here. Roebuck has come prepared for this. "No," he says pushing his jar directly into her line of vision. "I need a fertility test. ASAP." Producing this sample was harrowing and very nearly unsuccessful; even now, with that part of it behind him, Roebuck is appalled at the things he was forced to imagine in a men's room two blocks down the road at Taco Bell.

"Two week," says the woman.

"I can't wait two weeks."

He has seen this done on television. Roebuck takes out his wallet and begins counting out hundred-dollar bills, placing them one by one on the countertop beside his jar of specious semen. At five bills, he stops. The problem is a lack of specificity beyond this point. The woman is looking up now, but has not blinked. Roebuck adds more notes. When he has counted out one thousand dollars, he stops again. This is all the bank machine would let him have. If he had considered this more carefully, he would have used a teller and withdrawn a larger sum, but Roebuck is running on terror and terror alone.

"Okay then," he says, nearly weeping, gathering his cash. The woman places her hand over his. That's also how it happens on TV. She glances over her shoulder at the sliding window, nods, and lowers her voice. "Possible something day after tomorrow." She passes him a slip of paper and a pen. "Please leave telephone number."

Roebuck has a terrible two days.

Still not a word from Lily: no reply to his emails; no answer to his calls. On the way back from Gama-Care, he stops at her house but she isn't home—either that or she's not opening the door. Roebuck considers sneaking around back and peeking through a window, but figures he's exposed enough as is.

For want of a better option, he retreats to the office, closes his door, and Googles "failed vasectomy"—then spends an electrifying hour browsing a series of case histories documenting one post-procedure pregnancy after another. Roebuck quietly digests the significance of *non-clearance* and *recanalization*. He internalizes the conclusions of various experts who argue that two months and twenty ejaculations is sometimes insufficient; that some men require much longer for their sperm to reliably clear. Roebuck is on the brink of howling when he remembers that he *has* been cleared. He leaps from his desk, dives through his files until he tracks down the certificate from Gama-Care.

There it is in black and white: Clear-0-sperm.

But that still leaves the possibility that his severed tubes have reconnected. Roebuck is not exactly certain what *spermatic granuloma* is, but now he knows that the severed ends of his vas deferens, like lost lovers, are capable of finding each other again and that such recanalization is most likely to happen in the months immediately following the procedure. Which in his case would be exactly now. Images appear to him in sequence: the sweating doctor; the problem with that second tube, the left one; the appearance of the no-scalpel scalpel; that nurse's interruption—Oh God, the evil bitch Nurse Helen! What if …?

Roebuck is not aware that he is pacing until he realizes that someone is knocking on his door.

"Who is it?"

"Carol."

"Carol?" Yes, of course, Carol. "Come in."

"Is it true?"

"No! What?"

"About Daniel. Everybody's talking."

"Oh." Roebuck has lost track of Daniel Greenwood. "Daniel is in Australia."

"So it's true! Do the clients know?"

"Yes … the clients." It registers also that his clients definitely do not know and that he has to find some way of spinning this before it's out as common knowledge …

"Artemis especially," Carol says. "Daniel's the face of the franchise as far as Artemis is concerned."

"I'll take care of the clients. Carol, have you seen Lily?"

"Lily? I don't think Lily's in today."

"When is she expected?"

"You'd have to ask Daniel."

When he checks his mail, he finds nothing from Lily, but a new one from Yasmin. "Julius, call. Take this as a friendly warning."

Someone is at the door again. "Sorry," Carol says, "Forgot to give you this." She is holding out a purple post-it note. "Kramarich, Beatty, and Mastropietro called. I'm assuming that's a law firm. They said you should get back to them at your earliest convenience." Roebuck makes no move to take the note so she walks over to his desk and sticks it to his phone. "Everything okay?"

"Totally fine."

There are indeed several unread messages from Kramarich, Beatty, and Mastropietro in Roebuck's inbox. The cellphone in his pocket vibrates; he has it out and open before the second ring.

"Hello! Hello! Lily?"

"Who's Lily?"

"Oh. Yasmin. Hello. How are you today?"

"Who's Lily?"

"Oh, you know, just a freelancer. What can I do for you, Yasmin?"

"Excellent question, Julius. Why aren't you answering my emails?"

"To be honest, it's been a hectic day."

"Are you dodging your responsibilities already?"

"Sorry?"

"Society has zero tolerance for deadbeat dads."

"Yasmin, I'm ... I don't understand ..." He really doesn't. Roebuck's cognitive functions have congealed into a state of barely operational paralysis.

"What's there to understand? The stick turned pink; my gynecologist confirmed. I'm pregnant. *Finally.* I'm having your baby, Julius, and you have obligations ..."

"But ... How ...?"

"You've been fucking me, that's how."

"Well, yes but ..."

"No buts, Julius. Time to get your act together! There's a lot you'll need to tee up: school fees, college fund ..."

"*School fees?*"

"If it's a girl, it's Havergal. For a boy I'm still considering UCC."

"Yasmin, *my* kids don't even go to private school!"

"This *is* your kid. And if your other ones don't, it's only because their mother is an idiot. Speaking of which, if you want, we can leave Anne out of this for the time being. You and I can decide things on our own. Or would you prefer she be brought in at this stage?"

"*No!* I mean ... Yes. I understand what you're saying. But can't this wait until ...?"

"Until what?"

"Yasmin, I'm having a horrible day! If you're telling me that you're ... Even if you are, I mean, it can only be ... There's still months and months ..."

"My lawyer advises me that the sooner we finalize support mechanisms, et cetera, the smoother this will go for all parties concerned. I'm anticipating a difficult pregnancy, Julius. I could be confined to bed."

"Your *lawyer*?"

"You think you were going to fuck me without me speaking to my lawyer?"

"I don't believe this!"

"Julius. Not to put too fine a point on it, it's you who's fucked."

"But I'm only supposed to be the *donor*!"

"A little more than that. But anyway, it doesn't matter. Even if you *were* just a regular donor, it wouldn't matter. You are the father and that's all the courts will care about. The law of the land puts the benefit of the child above all else; everyone knows that. There's no wiggle room, Julius. If I'm confined to bed, I won't be able to work, which means you'll have to start payments immediately—afterward goes without saying. These are details that we need to iron out. I'm willing to be reasonable. But my lawyer can play hardball too, if that's what you want. I've made an appointment for us with her tomorrow, by the way. You can bring Anne. Your call."

"Tomorrow?"

"You want us to talk to her now?"

"*No!* No. It's just that … really, tomorrow is a very bad day. What about next week?"

"Like I said, Julius, if you want to go down that road …"

"No! No, I don't! Yasmin! Please! Just give me a day or two. I'll do whatever is … required. I promise. I just need …" Roebuck feels as if his head is about to burst and pieces of it fly out the window.

"You can have until the day after tomorrow."

"What day is that?"

"It's the day after tomorrow, Julius. Consult your calendar."

"I mean, what time of day, the day after tomorrow?"

"I'll get back to you with that information."

"Can we possibly make it late afternoon?"

"*Julius!*"

"Jesus, Yasmin. I have *meetings*! Give me a break! Honestly. This is all so …"

"I'll get back to you."

"Thank you."

"You'll get used to it, Julius. I know you will. Everything's going to work out. And I want you to know that there are things about you that I … like. Who knows, once we come to an understanding … It all depends on how sensible you are. I've always admired your centrality."

"Goodbye, Yasmin."

"Always a pleasure, Julius. See you soon."

A stretch of time passes. He isn't sure how long. Roebuck, cradling his head in his hands, perceives that Carol is again in his presence with another oversized envelope. "You all right?"

"Carol! How goes it?"

"Fine. Are you okay?"

"Just a little headache."

"You were looking for Lily. Speak of the devil, here she is."

"Lily!"

Carol places the envelope on the corner of his desk. "This seems to be another piece of correspondence from those lawyers. Lily is in the lobby. She says to say she doesn't have an appointment, but she's hoping you can spare a minute."

Before he knows how it has happened, Roebuck's feet have moved him to the lobby where he finds Lily standing primly, heels together, a small purse clutched in both hands pressed against her skirt, dressed like she's interviewing for a position with the revenue department. "Thank you for seeing me."

Carol wanders back toward reception shutting drawers and closing files. "It's quitting time," she says contentedly. "I'm outta here!"

"Hi!" says Roebuck idiotically.

Lily moves a small step closer. "I was hoping we could talk?"

"Absolutely!" Roebuck stares blindly at his watch. "It's quitting time!"

In the elevator, and outside on the sidewalk in the gathering November gloom, he has opened his mouth and spoken in what he hopes are sentences with verbs and nouns, but has no recollection of what he might have said or how or if it has been answered. They walk together through the doors of a restaurant down the street. Drawing Lily's chair, he notes and records that the last time he was in this place was with Anne, three tables over. "Whatever it is you have to tell me," he says before the waiter intervenes, "it does my heart good just seeing you."

"Please, Julius! Don't make me cry."

They listen in respectful silence while a young man in a creased white shirt recites a long and complex list of specials, including several items that were on the board earlier in the day but are now regrettably sold out. "Thank you," they chant together.

"I went to the doctor."

Roebuck nods.

"It's confirmed."

He hopes the nod has somehow carried all the meaning he has intended it to hold.

"Two things you need to know." Lily unfolds two fingers. "No, three. I'm keeping this baby"—this fact is to her so self-evident it does not warrant explanation. "Two. This is my responsibility, not yours." A longer wait while Lily stares at his face, slowly breathing. "Three. You might not even be the father."

He knows immediately, absolutely, that she is lying. To herself or to him is still unclear, but Roebuck is certain that she herself does not believe this last point. It doesn't matter.

"Lily …"

She presses a finger to her lips. "Shh. I need to finish …"

He nods again, or maybe bows. The waiter reappears. Lily asks for just a glass of water. "Scotch," says Roebuck. He doesn't drink Scotch.

"I'm no homewrecker."

"Yes."

"And anyway it might not even be you …"

"Lily …"

"But I want this baby. It's *wanted*."

"Yes …"

"So it's up to me. Just me. Not you."

"You know I …"

"You don't have to! I don't want you to! This is me and me alone."

He understands that she is not being wholly truthful with this statement either. This is Lily being Lily.

"What if I …?"

She laughs, surprising them both. "You're a decent guy for such a prick."

"That's me," says Roebuck. "Don't go. You're always getting up and leaving …"

"I have to." Lily is on her feet.

"Folic acid!" he says, standing too. "Plenty of folic acid! Spinach, if I remember right, is the mainstay of a healthy pregnancy. Stay, and I will feed you spinach."

"I have to go."

"And no more wine!"

"I know that, Julius."

"Then this will be a cinch. I'm here, Lily, in …"

"I have to go."

He watches her leave. Roebuck nurses his Scotch, pays for it unfinished, and, like the salmon swimming blind against the current, lurches homeward to his wife.

He knows Anne knows.

He doesn't know what she knows, or which part. But from the moment he walks through the door, he knows that she knows it.

"Hello!" she says brightly, coming to a full stop. Anne is constantly in motion; when she speaks—at least to him—it happens by and large in passing. "So you've come home."

She is still frozen to her spot, eyes boring.

Roebuck has exhausted the power of speech. He fumbles his keys from his right hand to his left hand and so into the pocket of his coat. "Oh!" he says, clutching a thought. "I'm cooking tonight!" He slaps his various pockets: no dinner there. "I didn't shop," he says, concentrating the sum of his confessions into this singularity.

"It doesn't matter."

She has not altered her position. Roebuck, too, remains rooted to his spot on the drip-mat just inside the door.

"You're sure?"

"What? What do you mean?"

"Dinner! You're sure I shouldn't go out and get dinner?" Normally she would send him out—rain, shine, blizzard; no hesitation—if he'd come home like this empty-handed Roebuck would be made to go back out and complete whatever task he'd been assigned. "You're sure?"

Anne spins on her heels and heads back upstairs though he is fairly certain she has just come down that way. Roebuck imagines himself in the check-out at the grocery store. Like a man ascending the scaffold to his guillotine, he follows his wife to the floor above and then up again. She's being pleasant, kind even. But she can barely stand to look at him. Anne aims her smile at a place above his shoulder; it's a lovely and unbearably horrifying smile. He wonders vaguely where the kids are.

"I sent the kids to a movie with the sitter," she says in the way of married people, "so we could have this talk." They are standing in the third floor hallway; neutral territory. Anne takes him by the hand and leads him into his room. Oh God, he thinks, sitting on the bed.

"Anne …" he says.

"I have something to say to you."

"Anne …?"

"It's a game-changer, Julius."

"Oh Jesus, Anne …"

"There's only one way …"

"Please, Anne. Please …"

"We're going to have another baby."

Of all the shocks today, this one somehow seems the least percussive. Roebuck has moved well beyond bewilderment into a serene and witless state of grace.

"Oh." He says.

"I thought that part of life was done for me. I guess it's not. I'm pregnant, Julius."

"You. Pregnant. *You?*"

"The stick turned pink."

Now he sees it on the bed beside him, a home pregnancy test. He hasn't laid eyes on one of these in years, and now suddenly they're everywhere. "I booked an appointment with the Ob/Gyn," Anne says. "Tomorrow morning. But I'm sure." She touches herself. "I know what this feels like."

"Spinach," Roebuck says because life is a wheel, and he's out at the edge. "We'll have to stock up." In their first prenatal class, all those years ago, Anne was advised to increase her intake of folic acid. Roebuck plagued her—through that and each of their pregnancies to follow—with spinach chopped discreetly into everything he served.

It was the right thing to say. Anne's arms and legs go around him, tears trickle down the back of his neck as his wife hugs his face to her breast.

"I *knew* you'd be happy!" Anne sobs.

29

Everything important is cliché.
The Collected Sayings of Julius Roebuck

To his complete amazement, Roebuck has slept. He is further astonished to find his wife beside him in his bed. Reality begins to coalesce as Roebuck ascends into the layers of his waking nightmare. Anne is pregnant. Lily is pregnant. Yasmin is especially, malevolently pregnant. The No Fuss Vasectomy Clinic has failed him, failed him spectacularly. Tomorrow he will be put to the torch by Yasmin's attorney; thank God, not until tomorrow, which in its turn reminds him of his appointment with Kramarich, Beatty, and Mastropietro at 10:00 AM *today*, and here at last he finds an anchor for his mind to grapple, one decision at least that Roebuck can begin to hold and shape.

"Anne," he says, "I also have news." He senses that her eyes are open. "I would have told you yesterday, but ..."

"Tell." She reaches out to put her hand on his the way she used to do when they were lovers.

"I've decided to sell the agency."

Perhaps it is as simple as a solid night's sleep, or the presence of his wife here beside him, glowing with a tenderness he hasn't felt in years, or just a fierce desire to survive—possibly as straightforward as that—but Roebuck is aware that his brain is beginning to re-boot. "Subject to your approval," he says, "of course." Though the more these pieces come together, the more he's sure that he will get it. "There's a buyer," he adds. "Plus a very solid offer."

Anne is a nester. Her choice of career—this he's known since the beginning—is only the most outward and obvious expression of her quintessential nature; some people are lucky that way. With each successive pregnancy, their house has undergone a transformation—the uber-pink nursery in advance of Kate; that Disneyesque bedroom for Morgan; then the wholesale gutting of the entire second floor in time for Zach's arrival—the scale of each project limited only by the capital available. And *this* time she will have a fortune to apply. Leading with his strong suit, Roebuck states the figure. Anne's eyes widen. "That's a *lot* of money."

"Yes."

"And you want this?"

"You can't argue the timing, with a baby coming."

"Yes," she says. "But what about you?"

"Me? I'll find new challenges." And then, because that irony was not at all intended, he asks, "What time is it?"

Anne—a naked, pregnant Anne in his bed beside him—leans on an elbow to peer at the bedside clock. She glows. "Just after seven."

"I have a 10:00 AM with the firm that's handling the deal." He climbs out of bed and opens his briefcase. No, the envelope is still on the corner of his desk where Carol left it yesterday. "I need to stop in at the office and pick up some papers." He's still worried that she will be angry at how far along all this has moved without her.

Anne giggles "Funny! My gig with the Ob/Gyn is at ten this morning, too!"

"Serendipity."

Again he has chosen well. Anne lays back, smiling, hands on the swell of her pelvis. "You're going to be *a dad* again!"

"That's me."

Roebuck showers, shaves, and when he's back from the bathroom finds that she has a cup of coffee waiting. Anne is still undressed. "Aren't you going in to work?" He is rooting in his sock drawer.

"Fuck that," she tells him happily.

Roebuck selects his darkest blue suit, recalling his father's advice that a man must always wear a suit to church, to the theatre, and to *any* occasion involving the legal professions. As he dresses, Roebuck sketches out the details, trusting Anne to point out anything he's missed, explaining how—in so many ways—the offer has come so opportunely. "These big multinationals are always on the lookout for fresh injections of creative talent. It's like insulin for them; they've grown so huge they don't produce their own. And of course they'll be absorbing a very solid client base; I know they've had their sights on Ripreeler for years. It's recession-proof, especially now with this new pheromone bait. Though I'm not sure how well informed they are on that. And they still don't know about Daniel, though that's just a matter of time."

"Daniel?"

Roebuck pauses, a dark blue tie half-looped around his neck. "Right. I didn't tell you that. Daniel has absconded." He fills her in about this part too: that Greenwood has taken off to Sydney, Australia, that he has stolen at least one client and possibly more, that his departure now complicates *all* relationships. "Funny how you see things so clearly, after the fact. This explains so many little things ..." But for this morning Roebuck is focused solely on the hopeful. "Anyway," he says, "none of that matters. Once this deal is inked, it's all somebody else's issue."

Anne is silent. Then it hits him; Roebuck is a fool. "Of course! The condo! He screwed you too. Was he into you for much, you and Yasmin?"

She turns and walks toward the bathroom.

"Anne!" he calls out, sharply. He's been looking for some way of saying this; now it has to be straight out. "Until we get this signed, I need you not to talk to anyone, please … not even Yasmin."

Anne's back is still turned. "Fuck Yasmin," she says, and then more dimly from the far side of the bathroom door, "and fuck Daniel too."

Roebuck is fairly sure he hears the sound of retching. There is so much he has lost track of. Does morning sickness start this soon?

◉◉

Carol is in a fluster. "Everyone's calling! All the clients! *All* the clients. Have you seen your email?" Roebuck has not seen his email. He's prioritizing.

"Carol, you just got married. Correct?"

Carol pauses in her tumult, blushing. "Engaged," she says. "Just engaged."

"So you'll have a husband to support?" The blush deepens. "I'm promoting you to office manager." He'll have to check this with HR, but he's fairly certain he remembers Carol's compensation package. Roebuck now proposes a figure slightly less than twice her present salary; he doesn't want to overdo this; there are several other adjustments he intends to put on file with payroll before the day is done. "Effective this morning." Roebuck is all business. "Please send out an email to all staff, informing everyone I'm calling a meeting for later this afternoon. Meanwhile, I'll write up a boilerplate we can pump out to the clients, announcing that the agency will be issuing a formal statement later today. That should hold them off for now."

"Thank you."

Roebuck has moved on. "What?"

"For the promotion," Carol says.

The envelope is waiting for him on the corner of his desk. He cracks the seal and spends some quiet time, familiarizing. Everything is as expected; some newly added clauses his own advisors have inserted for the purpose of negotiation. If he wants to get this signed today, he'll have to waive these sweeteners and who knows how much else. By 9:15 AM Roebuck has evolved his strategy, tried and true. Now he wishes he had dressed a little more proactively, this morning.

En route to Kramarich, Beatty, and Mastropietro he stops at a men's wear and changes his sober blue tie for a louder, sillier red one in chiffon silk. Then he buys a pair of ridiculously shiny, ridiculously pointed, psychotically expensive cowboy boots that scatter light like shards of Venetian mirror, and a hand-stitched Stetson. If there's anything his years in the business have taught him, it's that audiences—any audience—will accept the premise of the dickhead male. Inject a little testosteronic self-regard, a brooding blend of louche with macho-dolt and, presto, there you have it: our century's most effective marketing tool. Roebuck has the part down cold.

He lets it out early in the coffee stage, while everyone's still smoothing skirts and crossing legs, that he's made the mistake of telling his wife how much money is on the table here today and now she has it spent already, ha, ha, ha. But seriously, folks, if she pushes him too far, let it be here known he's willing to walk. Period. It's *his* show, right? *He* makes these decisions. And he's still of two minds about this whole frigging thing ... What's he going to do with himself afterwards, still in the prime of his youth, with his company sold out from under him? Just because she's creaming for a house in Palm Springs ...

And so it went.

They pushed. Now that they knew he was an idiot—and negotiating without counsel—they went at him full court. But as things moved along, they also came to understand that if they bulldozed this guy just a shade too far, his brand of ego could rebel. They'd seen the likes of him before. Plus, tomorrow it might dawn on him that his attorney should be present at the next go-round …

Roebuck likes to think that in the end all parties got what they were looking for. A little after noon, he departs the offices of Kramarich, Beatty, and Mastropietro, significantly less wealthy than he might have been, but still stupendously, awesomely in funds.

"Anne," he says, opening his phone as soon as he's out on the street. "We did the deal! It's sold!"

"Does this mean from now on you're going to be home all day? I don't think that's such a hot idea."

Lily doesn't even answer.

Even so, Roebuck has begun to form a vague and forlorn hope that he might—with respect to Anne and Lily, at least—conceivably live through this.

He stops at his broker and ties up substantial sums in trust for Morgan, Katie, and Zach, locked down as tight as common law can bind it, then creates another, more discreetly structured fund for Lily. Anne, of course, holds title already to the bulk of his estate. He'd have liked to sock away a bigger stake, but knows he'll need to stay liquid. Roebuck is gambling that a lump of gleaming cash up front might serve to buy out certain claims against the future. It's a risky strategy; one that could easily backfire. But he doesn't have a lot of options. Yasmin is the one who's going to sink him. Roebuck is determined to save whatever he can.

Checking his mail, he finds a curtly worded message, advising him of tomorrow's time and place. It's one of the big Bay Street firms, top drawer. What else was he expecting? The tone is factual, noting—as per his request—that the meeting has been scheduled for 12:30 PM and reiterating that for the present time his legal spouse has not been notified by either Yasmin or her representatives.

Anne, as he discovers moments after his arrival home, remains primarily concerned about the details of his long-term future. He has barely put down the shopping bags, before the interrogation activates. What with all that has happened—the defection of his creative partner, the sale of his life's work, the sudden acquisition of a minor fortune, to say nothing of a baby underway—he would have thought she'd have a lot to occupy her mind. But no, all she wants to talk about is what *he's* going to do all day, now that he is unemployed. Roebuck explains that he'll be staying on as interim president for the next eighteen months, minimum; it's right there in the contract. He can show her.

Anne is of the view that this interval is ludicrously brief. "Have you given any thought at all to what's going to happen, *after?*"

Roebuck's world view is narrowed down to what is going to happen after half-past twelve tomorrow.

"There's nothing more destructive than a man without a purpose," Anne says.

It slips beneath his guard. "Wow," he says. "That was a good one! Can I add it to my collection? Would that that, technically speaking, be plagiarism?" Despite his best intentions, Roebuck has allowed himself to backtalk.

Foolish, foolish. He's an idiot. Anne pretends to smack herself on the forehead, stunned. She can be quite the drama queen when the mood comes on. "Why didn't I think of that?" She has followed him into the kitchen. He has been hoping that the bags of spinach, set out like bales of fodder, might provide distraction—or at least divert her temper in a new direction—but no such luck. "*That's* what you can do with the rest of your life," she tells him, escalating volume, "polish up you little proverbs!" Once her voice gets up like this, there is really no other option but retreat. "Watch out, Oscar

Wilde," Anne warns the neighbours. "Stand aside Hippocrates. Here comes Julius Roebuck!" Any second now she'll be starting in on Blake. Anne loathes Blake even more than Lily; this is another example of evolutionary convergence Roebuck has grasped, but never fully comprehended.

"Oh look," he says. "I forgot the goat cheese!"

Once he's in the car and safely out of sight, he tries again. He has become so used to no one answering that the sound of her voice almost causes him to drop the phone.

"Hello." It's as if she's sitting right there in the car beside him. "*Hello!*"

"Lily! How *are* you? How are you feeling?" by which he means, "Are you having morning sickness too?"

"There's something I have to tell you," Lily tells him.

"I thought you already did."

A long silence. Roebuck's attempts at levity are not remarkably successful today.

"No," she says. "Something … related."

"What?"

"I don't want to have this conversation on the phone."

He has learned from experience that a woman in the initial stages of pregnancy is like a woman with PMS 24/7. "Tell me what you want me to do," Roebuck says, "and I'll do that."

"Can you come over?"

"Sure. Absolutely!"

"Now?"

His heart sinks. "It's dinnertime …" He hears himself falter. "I'm expected …"

"Of course."

The absence of bitterness, even now, stops his breath. "What about tomorrow? Would tomorrow work?"

"Tomorrow, yes. Come at lunch."

"Good. No! Dammit! That's the one time I can't. I have an appointment. It's … impossible to miss." The thought of seeing Lily is like a shipwreck's sudden glimpse of land. "After?" he asks. "What if I come right over afterward, after my appointment?"

"Too long. Before?"

"Okay, before."

"I have a project due at 10:00 AM. Come right after that."

"10:15?"

"That's good. Be here at 10:15."

Mood swings. Another chapter straight out of the manual. Anne is a different person when he ventures back into the kitchen, elbows on her teakwood table, chin cradled in her hands, eyes smeary-red. "You got *spinach*," she says, pushing the fat green bags around the polished wood.

To be honest, he'd expected the spinach to achieve the opposite effect. Last time around, while she was carrying Zach, even catching sight of leafy greens, let alone detecting them in what she ate, was enough to set Anne spitting like a rabid cat. She puts her arms around him from behind and hugs. Roebuck drops his tub of chèvre, pivots from the hip, and hugs her back. "I'm *sorry*," she says.

He says he's sorry too.

Anne is still clinging. "Remember when I took you to Alison's?"

"We had sex in the bathroom!" Roebuck smiles and shifts his feet to embrace his wife more properly. "I've never been more surprised."

"Seems like a thousand years ago." The memory has made her wistful.

"We can go again if you want. It's still in business—at least it was a few months back."

"And how would you know that?"

"Ha! Funny. Greenwood, of all people. He went there with his girlfriend."

"Girlfriend?"

"A former client, as a matter of fact. I was a bit worried for a while there that things would get awkward. Professionally, I mean. But she left the company a while back. Funny," he says, recollecting. "She always reminded me of you."

He would gladly have gone on longer with this neutral train of thought, but Anne has lost interest and exited the kitchen. Mood swings.

Roebuck chops his spinach. The kids straggle in for dinner. Katie first, rubbing eyes from too much Facebook; Morgan, who's had to be called twice, clumping down the stairs blaming Katie for her missing calculator; and Zach, with his jeans ripped out at the knees for the second time this week; one cliché after another. And it washes over him again, how good this is, domestic normalcy, how calming to the heart and soothing to the soul. He has done everything he can, until tomorrow. They eat and bicker and bicker and debate at length whose turn it is to do the dishes and eventually—much later than it should have been, as ever, the kids are packed off to their beds. Roebuck, expecting a long night, settles in to read. Sometime later he is startled by his wife. Anne puts her head on his chest and a long bare leg across his hips and in minutes falls asleep. Roebuck breathes from his stomach listening to his heartbeat and drifts off, too, subsiding pulse by drowsy pulse.

30

The future never lasts.
The Collected Sayings of Julius Roebuck

Lily is on the phone when he arrives, waving him in with that
look that people put on to show how embarrassing it is to be
caught at the door while talking to somebody else. Her deadline, he
guesses. Either late or sent with missing pieces; he catches a reference
to a file not uploading, possibly corrupt. Roebuck knows his way
around. He lays a finger to his lips and squeezes by, kissing her cheek
as he passes. Lily's brows are furrowed to almost comic depths; she
smiles and scowls simultaneously. Roebuck makes himself scarce in
the kitchen. She was preparing coffee by the looks of it: water poured
into the pot; filter in its basket; beans ground but not yet spooned.
Roebuck finishes the job and pours himself a cup, his eighth or tenth
this morning. He's been up since dawn, measuring time. "The font
you sent *was* Times New Roman," he hears her growling through the
wall. "What would make me think they wanted sans serif?"

He has always loved this kitchen, so bright and self-contained.

For him it is a sensory amalgam of good things caramelizing while soup pots simmer at the back of the stove, of stews and baking, of citruses and cloves: of Lily. "You said *Photoshop*," she says heatedly. "*Now* you tell me Illustrator!"

There's an avocado plant growing the in window, up from its divided pit. The stem has bent toward the sun. Roebuck shifts the pot a quarter turn and wipes the counter, then turns the pothos cuttings she's been rooting. Philodendron they are called in his house. Lily pronounces it *pathos*. She stalks into the room, head still crooked to the phone, sketches an indignant wave, turns, and marches out again. Roebuck wishes he had something he could say. It comes unbidden, out of nowhere: Choose me.

And she has.

Whatever happens this afternoon, whatever the fallout, he will defend this. Anne, too. Anne's choice, too. What does he deserve, in all of this? Pointless asking.

Lily is pacing. He can hear her in the other room, back and forth, her voice rising and falling. Roebuck is not aware his cellphone has been ringing until he feels the ticking whirr against his chest.

"Hello" he says. "*Hello?*" The coffeemaker rattles. Lily's voice grows louder; she isn't given to anger, but he can tell she's very angry now. Somewhere outside an ambulance wails by. Roebuck puts his finger to his ear. He doesn't recognize this number. "Who's calling?"

"Ophelia …"

"Ophelia?"—at least that's what it sounds like—then something else he can't make out. Roebuck doesn't know any Ophelias. "I think you have the wrong number."

"Mistalowbak?"

"Sorry, I can't hear you. Who is calling?"

A crackle; traffic noise beyond the house, then a little clearer. "MistaLoebuck, this …"

"Holy crap, what a bunch of pricks!" Lily is standing in front of him. Roebuck has been head down, concentrating. "Sorry about that," she says stepping close.

He holds up a finger for her to hang on just one sec. "We have a bad connection. What did you say ...?"

Lily wraps her arms around him. "Sorry." She's waiting for him to hug her back. "The phone I mean. Julius, I just have to get this said ..."

"Mista Roebuck. This is Opheliafromgamacrackle ..."

"Ophelia *who?*"

"Opheliafromgamacrackle ..."

"Cama what?"

"I've been practising. Actually practising how I'm going say this. Rehearsing. And then the phone rang just as you were coming up the walk ..."

"Gama-Care ... test results ... You ..."

"It's been a nightmare, Julius, keeping this inside ..."

"*Test* results?"

"You know those, Julius. I'm pregnant, that's established. But what you don't know ..."

"*Who* did you say was calling?"

"Gama-Care Laboratories ..." He hears it this time, clearly: "Semen analysis ... MistaLowbak ... results ... maybe ... happy."

For Roebuck it is like that liquid pop inside the ear that happens sometimes when he steps out of the shower, an instantaneous transition to hearing from not-hearing. It stuns him, shocks his balance as he wrestles with the incredible, the unbelievable discovery that he's forgotten this, that in the tsunami of these last hours, Gama-Care and what it represents has been completely swept from mind. Lily is saying something, but Roebuck is now absorbing the harder blow that follows. That it doesn't matter. That they are only calling to tell him what he knows already. Except for that one word ...

"Did you say *happy?*"

"No. I said Danny."

"What? What does that mean?"

"Not permitted to say."

"It means I slept with Daniel. That's what it means. How hard do you have to make this?"

Roebuck is holding the phone like child with a disconnected walky-talky.

"Did you just say …?"

"Cannot provide that information on telephone …"

"Not *you!*"

"Yes, *me*, Julius. *I* have to live with this too!"

"I wasn't …" Roebuck, like a carnival automaton, slowly cants the phone back toward his ear. He is aware that Lily's mouth is moving, but now other sounds are coming through. "Shift ends … come … noon."

"Julius! Hang up the phone and talk to me!"

"Say that again …"

Lily snatches the phone and hurls it across the room. "Listen to me! *Listen to me!*"

Roebuck watches, slow-mo, as his phone goes spinning end-over-end along a shallow arc clear across the kitchen. His same finger, dumbly tracking, follows its trajectory. It strikes the corner of the stove and breaks into balletic fragments. Roebuck's eyes tack from piece to spinning piece and come to rest on one that's skidded to a stop just opposite his foot, a modem by the look of it, possibly a piece of motherboard.

"Lily …" he says.

"I think it's you. But you have to know it could be Daniel."

But Roebuck is thinking: Could it be? Could it really be? Is that *possible*?

"I have to go," he says.

"Oh, Julius! Please don't do this."

He stares at his watch. "It's not …" But of course it partly is. "I mean …" But he has to know.

"Please, Julius. *Please!*"

"It's …" His finger drifts moronically toward the scattered bits of circuitry.

"You're leaving me because I broke your phone!"

"I have just received a very important …"

"Oh, my God! Your call means more to you than *this?*"

He doesn't know how to answer that one either. "I'll be back … I promise. It's not … I'll be back."

For the rest of his life, the name will lose all connection to Hamlet or to Shakespeare, to willows grown aslant the brook or the properties of rue—and relate only to this small and oddly hostile Chinese woman in a lab coat frowning from behind the breastwork of her tall white counter. He can make out only the top half of her face.

"Ophelia!"

"MistaLoebuck."

"Ophelia!" Roebuck's heart is beating so spasmodically his hand is pressing at his chest. He gulps down gouts of air. "I'm here!"

"Ejaculate analysis complete, MistaLoebuck."

"Oh please, what does it say?"

Ophelia lifts a sheet of printed paper from a stack of documents and arranges it neatly beside her, squaring its edge to the rim of her desk. She selects another page and sets it down precisely alongside the first, edge to edge in perfect symmetry. "I ordered *two* tests," she tells him primly. "Make sure." Roebuck cranes his neck and jacks upward from his toes to see over the counter. "What do they say?" He's still clutching his chest with the hand he's not using to hold himself up. Ophelia extracts from her drawer a pair of bright red reading glasses, raises the first page, and studies it narrowly. "First test, azoospermic."

"Azoowhat? What the fuck does that means?"

Ophelia looks reproachfully away.

"Please, Ophelia. Just tell me what that means. *Please!*"

Roebuck wonders if he's panting audibly. The blood in his ear is pounding so hard he can't really tell. She lets him wait another, sterner interval, then says, "Negative sperm count. No sperm."

Relief floods over him in a tide of oxygen, the whole of him is trembling, then a second choke of panic. "The other one! What about the other one?"

Ophelia locates the second sheet and reads it thoughtfully, looks Roebuck up, and down, returns her eyes to the page, coughs, removes her glasses. "Second test also azoospermic."

He needs to spend the next few seconds with both hands on the counter, gasping at his shoes. "Thank God! Thank God." When his heartbeat has reduced to something near the hundred-beats-per-minute mark, a whole new terror strikes. "You didn't fake the results?"

Ophelia—who up until this moment has been carved in stone—shoots backward in her chair and bounces to her feet, hissing. "You pay to go first, not *cheat!*" The chair careens off a metal filing cabinet and clangs into the wall. Two bodies freeze, two sets of eyes dart fearfully toward the sliding window. Roebuck and Ophelia share a long and agonizing silence. When at last it's certain no one's overheard, she sets into him in a grim and glottal gush. He doesn't follow word for word, but Roebuck grasps enough of it to comprehend.

What she has done, she tells him, is divided his ejaculate into *two* batches, each analyzed independently. The double-testing was *her* initiative, because *she* guessed it would be useful to *him*. She also wishes him to understand, to clearly understand, that there's a backlog at this clinic, that she broke the rules to help. What she did *not* do is tamper with the data. What she did not do was *cheat*. Only accelerate the process.

Roebuck lets the waves of wrath wash over him. Now that he's sure he's not having a coronary, he wants to vault across the counter and kiss her on the lips.

"Bless you," he says, reaching for his papers.

Ophelia snatches them away. "You pay for one, you get one." She passes him a single sheet. The other she has put behind her back. Roebuck checks his wallet: two twenties, only. "Would you accept a cheque?

"Cash!" This Ophelia is more practical than her literary her namesake. "ATM across the street." Roebuck skips out. She affects not to notice his return a few minutes later, or the lather he's worked up racing to and from the bank machine. Roebuck places five $100 bills reverently on the counter; his hands are damp and shaking. Ophelia removes a single note and pushes the rest away with the tips of her fingers. Roebuck takes possession of his second certificate.

"You ..." he says, quoting blindly before bounding down the stairs, "are of the angels."

◎◎

It is exactly 12:00 PM.

Roebuck has made a snap decision. He is making them small and snappy now, one-at-a-timers; no scope for grander vistas; no panoramas, no wide-angle lenses. When did people start *taking* decisions and stop making them? *Making* is constructive; *taking* more in line with common theft. Around the time the biz-heads took over. Yes, almost certainly then. Stop that. His brain is skittering all around the back seat of the cab. Give it a break; it's had a tough week. Roebuck will devote every available neuron to Anne and Lily,

294

later. Later. Right now every time his thinking tries to sneak away in that direction, he's going to put a bag over it, tie it in a knot, and lock it in the trunk. Right at this moment, Roebuck is aiming squarely up the road with Yasmin. Yasmin and her lawyer. Right now that's all that matters. He is aware he's in a hurry. He has left his car parked on the street outside Gama-Care and hailed a taxi. That was his decision. Roebuck doesn't trust himself to drive.

It's 12:05 PM.

He can afford to be a little late. But not *too* late. So he takes out his crisp, new hundred-dollar bills, making sure they're visible, waves them like the high roller he is and asks the cabbie kindly to speed it up. Roebuck is on a roll. Oh what a roll he's on. Should he stop first at a bank?

No.

Another key decision firmly made.

He has his credit cards, in case of emergency, his cheque-book. Ophelia the Blessed. Like those bits of broken cellphone. Motherboard he thinks. Oh, ha ha. One funny thing after another this morning.

But it isn't morning any longer. It is 12:37 when the cab drops him at the curb. Roebuck is certifiably late.

It's an eighty-story glass cathedral, and he takes the wrong elevator. This wasn't a decision; this was an honest mistake. He has boarded the one that goes only as far as the fortieth floor; he has to get off, go back to ground, and change over. The elevator's walls are mirrored on all sides. Roebuck's image is reflected back upon itself into eternity. It's confusing.

It is nearly 12:45 when Yasmin's lawyer finally shakes his hand, utterly unsmiling. At four hundred an hour, she's already a C-note ahead so why not crack a grin? Roebuck has been imagining some kind of troll-like creature with a hump and sharp teeth; something like a cross between a fire hydrant and an English bull terrier. Instead, Yasmin's lawyer is elegant; beautiful, even. In fact, she reminds him of Yasmin.

"I am truly, very sorry I am late," he tells her as she leads him down the plush and silent carpet to her office, walking like Yasmin, too. Roebuck is aware that he's aware of the comparison.

Yasmin has arranged herself like a puma on a couch beside the lawyer's desk. "You're fucking late!"

"I am truly, very sorry."

He is offered perfunctory refreshment and humbly declines. There's a cup and saucer on a low table beside Yasmin's couch; quality china. A nice bowl of biscotti. Roebuck is directed to a chair that has been situated so as to face his accusers in the manner of a plaintiff set before his judge and jury. He meekly takes his seat.

Because he is late, because he has, by his lateness, more than sufficiently demonstrated his contempt for these proceedings, his contempt for her client, and her client's condition—which assuredly entails meaningful and incontestable obligation on his part—in light of Mr. Roebuck's clear and thoughtless disregard for the situation in which he has placed himself and her client, Yasmin's lawyer will waste no further time today in preamble. A net of legal jargon descends upon his head, statutes quoted, disclosures demanded, contracts proffered, interlocutory remedies particularized and figures—a welter of figures past, present, and most significantly future—bind him to his chair. Anne's name crops up parenthetically.

Roebuck nods, tries to look worried, and thinks about Tchaikovsky. Although he has tried his best, his very best, he really cannot bring himself to like ballet. Every year around Christmas, he takes the girls to see *The Nutcracker*. But Roebuck is a plot man. He prefers the subtleties of dialogue, the real and human tensions of script without the clutter of costume and the crutch of orchestration. Tchaikovsky is an improvement on most of those Italians, sure—and then of course there's Wagner—but always, always, by the middle of Act II he finds himself addressing the question of which of the Marzipan Shepherdesses likely has the largest breasts. It's like that now with Yasmin and her attorney. He ponders what these women would say if they could read his thoughts. Perhaps they can. Probably they can. Of course they can, and that's why he is here. Roebuck enjoys a sudden, spontaneous image of Yasmin's leopard-spotted bra. They'll be even larger, what with pregnancy; rounder. Enough. He removes the neatly folded sheets of paper from the inside pocket of his dark-blue suit—the same one he wore yesterday, for luck—smoothes them on his leg, and slips them silently across the gleaming surface of the lawyer's desk.

"What the fuck is that?" asks Yasmin, stroking her prehensile hips.

The attorney, having a better feel for the relationship of time to money, accepts the documents and silently reads. Roebuck watches her eyes move from top to bottom, pause, blink—lovely eyes, also—and blink again before shifting the page.

"These of course could be forgeries."

"And I, of course, am willing to verify them in person at any medical facility of your choosing." He practised bouncing that one off his multiple reflections on the way up in the elevator.

The lawyer sighs. She is a real professional. "If so, this alters … the circumstances."

"*What* alters the circumstances?" Yasmin is sitting up a little straighter.

Her lawyer gives her a lawyerly look; some would swear it was almost a motherly look. "It would appear that Mr. Roebuck is … infertile."

"*What!*"

"Shooting blanks," he offers sweetly.

"But …"

Roebuck has no desire to be cruel. He has no wish to see his former procreative partner flounder upward through the necessary stages of cognition. Besides which, this is Yasmin. "I had a vasectomy," he says cutting to the chase.

Years of legal education pounce on that one. *"When?"* Roebuck has to admire the tenacity. "When do you purport this procedure took place?"

"Before. *Well* before. Which means," he says, returning to Yasmin and her nascent expectations, "the father can't be me."

"You ... *asshole!*"

The lawyer clears her throat, a warning her client chooses to ignore.

"Do you mean to tell me, you fucking asshole, after all this ...?"

Roebuck nods. "I'm definitely not your guy."

"I would like us to return to this presumed vasectomy ..." The attorney isn't willing to let up. He can see the wheels turning: perhaps there is some new action possible, some parallel line of attack. False representation? "The timing of this procedure is suspiciously ..."

"So if it's not me ..." Roebuck is still eye-to-eye with Yasmin. "That means ...?" He wants to hear it said out loud, that she can have no claim on him.

"Fucking Daniel!"

"Sorry. What?"

But Yasmin is now deep in the thickets of her own considerations.

"Did you say *Daniel?*"

"I should say the *alleged* vasectomy, because this *presumed* procedure has in no way been established ..."

"Daniel *Greenwood?*" Roebuck massages his scalp. His head feels itchy. "Daniel Greenwood's in Australia."

"I know that, Dipshit."

"And, even in the event it *is* established, notwithstanding ..."

Roebuck's fertile mind, which has until moments ago been relaxing with pleasant images of sugar plum fairies and leopard-spotted breasts, of habeas corpus and the etymology of *tort*, now presents him with a brand new sequence of connected thoughts at the end of which arrives a seismic, though achingly practical, conclusion. He understands. He does understand. At last. Roebuck smiles; he actually smiles, a real smile—it all makes so much sense now—and withdraws his chequebook. One thing at a time. He asks politely if it might be possible to borrow a pen. The lawyer courteously hands him hers.

"You and I have wronged each other," he says addressing Yasmin. He has always had a talent for the talk, has Roebuck. "That is clear to me now. Perhaps in some small way this will ... ameliorate." He turns again toward the attorney. "Is that the proper word?"

"Prick!" shouts Yasmin. "*That's* the proper word!"

Roebuck clicks the lawyer's pen and writes a cheque for fifty thousand dollars. Then another in the same amount—*so* much nicer being rich—payable to Yasmin's lawyer. He hesitates. "Should this be made out to you or to your firm?"

"That would depend on what service it is intended to retain."

Roebuck nods and smiles. It's a serene smile, he can tell. He has floated to another plane, hovering in a spot just below the ceiling, watching himself and these two women in this glass-walled office like a fish tank high, high above the city. Is this what closure turns out to be? He truly does admire this attorney. "As a start," he says, "with your permission, let me enquire: do we have reciprocal enforcement agreements with Australia, do you know?"

"That is not my area of expertise. But yes, I believe so. Yes."

"So it would be possible then to launch, hmm, similar ... proceedings there ... with respect to Mr. Daniel Greenwood, in Australia?"

"Presupposing Mr. Greenwood has indeed ..." The lawyer interrupts herself. "Yes," she says simply. "Definitely."

"Then please accept this"—Roebuck slides the cheque across the desk—"as a retainer intended to further your client's pursuit of justice in that jurisdiction. I assume your firm has correspondents on the ground there? Good. I will also require you to provide assistance in winding up your client's business connections here in this country as rapidly as possible. Before the end of next week, shall we say?" He places the other cheque on the fabric next to Yasmin's twitching thigh. She doesn't touch it, but he knows she's counting zeros.

"Yasmin," he says. "You'll want to get yourself to Sydney right away. I would advise next week. Why don't we say next week at the latest?"

"Shut up. I'm thinking."

"It's never too soon to start planning."

"I said shut up …"

"The sooner you finalize your support mechanisms, the smoother things will go. You could have a difficult pregnancy, Yasmin. What if you're confined to bed?"

"You are one incredible prick."

"That's me. Additionally, I will arrange with your attorney to provide you with a living allowance of, say, five thousand dollars per month for a period of …"

"Ten thousand," corrects the lawyer.

Roebuck nods. "I will arrange with your attorney to provide you with a living allowance of seventy-five hundred dollars monthly, for a period of nine calendar months. After which point I believe we can assume you will have achieved full financial independence."

Yasmin has taken on a posture he hasn't seen before. She looks … thoughtful.

Even now he knows he'd like to … "Listen," he says, "Daniel's the Creative *Director*. That's almost top of the heap. It may well be a partnership arrangement. He'll be pulling down a very substantial salary."

Yasmin strokes her thighs and consults her counsel. "Can you garnishee wages there, too?"

"That would be a start," Roebuck says.

That odd, unsettling gaze shifts back now to him. Yasmin's eyes are probing, studying. The nagging doubt that he has all this while been fending off comes back and settles like a cooing bird on Roebuck's shoulder. "... Daniel *Greenwood?*" he mutters, shaking his head. "I always pegged him for the quiet type." Could there have been a shade of admiration, there, he let creep into his voice?

Yasmin's hands have come to rest. He notices in passing the shadowed, dimpled skin around each fingertip, the unctuous swelter of thigh. Otherwise she's silent, breasts rising and falling in a cadence that feels almost like music. "I take it back," she says. "You're not a prick. You're an idiot."

And suddenly, Yasmin has dropped into the couch, throwing out her arms, splaying her legs, kicking her feet.

She is laughing.

Roebuck ducks as a shoe sails past his head.

"You didn't know!" The second shoe clatters against the bottom of the desk. Yasmin is banging her heels on the floor. He has never seen her like this. "You really didn't *know?*"

Roebuck's tongue comes to rest at the bottom of his throat. The lawyer is studying him with a look he can't bring himself to interpret. Yasmin is by now so caught up in the moment she's physically shaking the couch, bouncing—hands on her belly, heaving. This he *has* seen. The lawyer is staring.

"Your Daniel had his fingers in all kinds of pies," Yasmin says, gasping. "And you didn't *know?*"

Roebuck sits quietly in his chair in the centre of the room.

"But it wasn't just Daniel! That's the best part! She wasn't joking!"

"*Who* wasn't joking?" It's the lawyer who has put the question, but Roebuck is grateful.

"*Anne.*" Yasmin is smacking her thighs; he can see the outline of her palms against both legs.

"Anne?"

"Anne! Oh Anne, I always thought *Anne* was the idiot ..."

"Yasmin, what are you *talking* about?" Again it's the lawyer. Roebuck is incapable.

"But she really *wasn't* joking. I always thought she was joking. His wife outsmarted all of us."

"What? Joking about *what?*"

"Don't you get it? He really *is* shooting blanks. That's what Anne knows, and we didn't. *Always was.* Always. It wasn't just Daniel. It was before! All those little hints. I never put them all together. *That's* why she let it happen. It didn't matter anyway!"

Yasmin sighs and slowly rises to her feet, rebuttoning her blouse, smoothing her skirt, collecting herself. "And then you ... then me ... Oh, Julius! It's all so perfect!" Yasmin is glistening, giggling. "The joke's on us!"

She straightens her shoulders and draws a long, slow breath, the kind they teach at yoga. Yasmin teeters unsteadily, groggily collecting shoes. When she has found them both, she puts a hand on Roebuck's shoulder, steadying herself. "Don't worry," she tells the lawyer, sighing. "He'll honour them. The cheques I mean. He's reliable that way." Yasmin touches Roebuck's face.

"All's well that ends well," she says, fingers hot against his cheek.

Epilogue

December, 2010

It's snowing, and Roebuck is tired. It has been coming down like this for days. Cursing drivers rock their chassis deeper into drifts; spinning tires drone like brumal cicadas even through the walls of this café. There seems to be a business meeting underway two tables over—young men in goatees and horn-rims who rammed to the door a few minutes ago in a tangerine Hummer. The management has strung up decorations, strings of winking bulbs, which only reinforce that jolly, festive atmosphere that happens every time the snow dumps down like this. The guys with the show truck might as well have swapped their lattés for shots of tequila. One of them looks vaguely like a junior copywriter he interviewed back when. They could be quieter.

Roebuck is not festive. His feet are soaked and frozen. He should have worn boots. He is an idiot for not having worn boots. But standing at the podium in snow boots would have looked even more ridiculous, apparently, than he sounded.

Though no fault of his, half the audience stayed home. He should be grateful, realistically, that as many as did showed up. Even baby biz-heads love a snow day.

He's wondering if he should have hailed a cab. But of course the taxis today are buried like everyone else. Roebuck wipes the condensation from his watch; he has plenty of time to relax and get himself another cup with double sugar. The subways are still running; he'll make it in under an hour.

Lily doesn't qualify for mat leave. Roebuck has persuaded her to let him help, but she says she wants to keep working. She says she needs to get out. The truth is, though, that when she gets tired, she gets a bit bad-tempered. Roebuck double-checks the time. He is happy for this little break, however numb his toes. He will put his shoes against the radiator once he gets to her place.

On the way back from the counter, one of the young bucks leans back in his chair, the better to display whatever's dancing on his tablet, and nearly upends Roebuck's cup. They have not even registered his passing.

It's always a pleasure spending time with Maya, but her mother is definitely a challenge. He was expecting this. Fully.

It happened with Anne. It happens universally, as far as he can tell. They should teach this in grade school, load it into the curriculum—that when a baby comes, the man involved should expect to go from being someone important to someone not at all important, except in his capacity to render aid, which in itself is a minefield of misplaced best intentions. But even so the change has rocked him. Mostly Lily naps now, when he comes over; hands him Maya and shuts the bedroom door.

Maybe she's in there composing. He really wouldn't know.

Of course he wonders if there's someone else.

But it's absolutely to her credit that Maya is such a lovely child; content to ride in the carrier strapped to his chest while he tidies up.

He has discovered that the sound of the vacuum puts her straight to sleep. Her mother, too, evidently. Roebuck stirs his coffee.

Gabriella, regrettably, is not so placid. They haven't come out and admitted it, not yet, that it's colic, but she is definitely a fussy child. On the plus side, Anne has racked up quite a lot of motherhood experience by this stage—him, too, naturally—so the two of them are well equipped to deal with it. It was tough there for a while, right after Yasmin's decampment when the workload so abruptly spiked, but now that Anne has wound down the business, all the stress has wonderfully diminished. She and the baby have moved into his room. When Gabby cries, they're both at hand to answer.

Roebuck yawns and mainlines his caffeine. Monday night he nodded off again. No. Tuesday. Tuesday is Katie's taekwondo, so it had to be Tuesday. Story time, that much he remembers. Diapers needed changing. Thus the reprimands. But by and large, they each know their roles and responsibilities and execute them according to a system laid down years ago, tried and true.

He still lives in dread of calling one of the babies by the other's name, but so far that hasn't happened.

Lily, he is certain, is convinced that he is Maya's father. It's as if Greenwood had never been. Anne's a little harder to interpret. They haven't talked about it, naturally—any of it—and in the way of married people he is fairly sure they never will. It works. It works for him and it works for them and with a little luck it all will keep on working: babies get older, workloads grow lighter. Snow falls and smoothes away irregularities.

Everything balances out.

There's a fresh commotion two tables over. Much snorting and chortling. Something big, apparently, is in the offing. All of them with their tablets and iPhones. Roebuck glances at his laptop, still asleep inside its case. In the subway he thought of something that might work okay for Chapter Two, but right at this moment his feet are too wet. When he looks up, he sees Goatee is staring back. Roebuck begins a noncommittal wave, but the guy has turned away, now, laughing.

He opens his phone and checks for messages.

Management was happy, delighted, to have him out this morning, elevating their profile at a prestigious institution like The Ferrer/Léche School of Business. Doubtless the webmaster will post his lecture on the site; at the very least an item on the newsboard. Possibly a podcast. The new president is all of thirty-three. Roebuck wouldn't be the least surprised to see her posing with these barely whiskered tech-heads and their tricked-out orange tank. She wants him out the door, of course. New broom.

Two items in his inbox: a reminder from Anne to pick up overripe bananas and a formal notice from HR regarding the handover of files prior to the expiration of his contract. That one he's been trying not to think about.

He has no idea what he's going to say to Anne.

Roebuck's feet are still numb, but his coffee is down to the dregs. He is thinking about buttoning his coat, winding his scarf, and gearing up to face the elements, when he becomes aware of a compression in the atmosphere. The room has gone silent. The bucks two tables over are staring, bodies stiffened, tendons straining. And now he hears it too, the sound.

It's the boots that take him first. Knee-high leather with tall, tall heels that strike that rhythm on the tiles. Snow swirls into the room as the door sighs closed behind her. Her long black coat has brushed the drifts and trails a fringe of ice. It falls open in the heat like gift wrap yielding up the skirt beneath, short and sultry, and a tanned and golden span of thigh. She's been somewhere in the sun, this girl. The men at the table stamp and paw.

"Julius Roebuck!" she says kicking off the snow. "Fuck me a mountain, is that really you?"

He can hear her heels against the floor, the drag and then the clop as Zhanna Lamb approaches like forgotten fate. Roebuck feels a wave of strength, his nostrils flare, then a tide of fatigue—he gropes the table and steadies himself—then a new gush of vitality. Tiny lights sparkle and dance in the room.

Zhanna flutters a wave and blows him a kiss as she passes. Two tables over they've pull out her chair. "Gentlemen" she says arching her back as she peels off her coat. "You know how I've been counting on you …"

Acknowledgements

I must first thank my wonderful agent, Hilary McMahon, for her infinite patience and boundless support. The transformation from manuscript to printed book would not have been possible without her. The same goes for its editor, Diane Young, whose firm opinions and firmer defence of them made for many interesting discussions and a much better novel.

Many thanks also to Jim McElgunn and Stan Sutter, for their acumen and insight into the world of advertising. Any instances of hyperbole impute to me, not them.

It's lonely work, novel writing; readers of early, ugly drafts provide not only sound advice but a form of companionship whose solace to the writer is impossible to overstate. To Nancy Kramarich, Lance McDayter, Eva-Lynn Jagoe, Liz Beatty, Christopher Mastropietro, and of course my old, old friend Paul Harper: immense gratitude.

Finally, thanks to my wife Rennie Renelt and my children Dayton and William Gardiner; my family and the point of everything.

About the Author

SCOTT GARDINER began his career in journalism at *Maclean's* and has written for a variety of publications including *Toronto Life*, *Canadian Geographic*, and the *Globe and Mail*. His first novel, *The Dominion of Wyley McFadden*, was shortlisted for the Commonwealth Writers' Prize, Best First Book from Canada and the Caribbean. It was also shortlisted for the Amazon Books in Canada First Novel Award and made the *Globe and Mail* list of 100 Best Books. *King John of Canada*, his second novel, was shortlisted for the Stephen Leacock Medal for Humour. Gardiner lives in Toronto with his wife and two children.

Also published by TAP Books

One Night in Mississippi
by Craig Shreve

One Night in Mississippi is the story of a young activist named Graden Williams, who was brutally murdered in Civil Rights–era Mississippi. After the perpetrators were charged but quickly released, Graden's brother, Warren, drifted aimlessly for decades, estranged from the rest of his family and struggling with guilt over his brother's death. But when the U.S. Justice Department begins re-opening cases like Graden's more than forty years later, Warren is determined to avenge his brother and bring his killers to justice.

A phoned-in tip after a television appearance leads Warren to a remote town in northern Ontario, where he comes face-to-face with Earl Olsen, the only murderer still at large, who turns out to be very different than what Warren had expected.

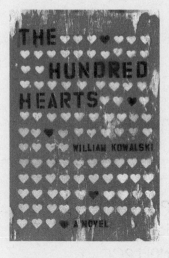

The Hundred Hearts
by William Kowalski

Returning home after an explosion in Afghanistan, in which he was injured and his best friend killed, Jeremy Merkin is dismayed to find that nothing has changed, and yet everything is different. Living in the basement of a house he shares with his grandparents, mother, and mentally challenged cousin, Henry, Jeremy struggles with constant pain and the lingering psychological effects of the war. A death in the family prompts Jeremy to seek out his institutionalised father, which leads to the discovery of a family secret that will alter his life forever.

When, amidst all the chaos, Henry runs away to New York in search of his mother, Jeremy fears for his safety and races across the country in a desperate search to find him. While in New York, Jeremy's world is altered yet again as more family secrets are uncovered, this time with dreadful consequences.

Bruce County Public Library
1243 Mackenzie Rd.
Port Elgin ON N0H 2C6